SPRING
THAW

SPRING THAW

A NOVEL

S.L. STEBEL
With an Afterword by
RAY BRADBURY

Walker and Company
New York

First published in the United States of America in 1989
by Walker Publishing Company, Inc.

Published simultaneously in Canada by Thomas Allen & Son
Canada, Limited, Markham, Ontario.

Library of Congress Cataloging-in-Publication Data

Stebel, S. L.
Spring thaw.

I. Title.
PS3569.T33815S6   1989   813'.54   88-28014
ISBN 0-8027-1068-9

Printed in the United States of America

10 9 8 7 6 5 4 3 2 1

This story is for Jan

Acknowledgments

MY HEARTFELT GRATITUDE to Ray Bradbury, for his limitless generosity, and to Bonnie L. Barrett, for looking into the heart of my darkness and opening a door; Ted Pedersen, for teaching me how to co-exist with computers; Leinie Schilling, for her patience and talent; Harry Zelenko, for his unflagging artistry; Patricia Ann and April, for bringing renewed joy into my life; and my editor, Peter Rubie, for his unerring insights into the material.

SPRING THAW

Captain's Log

1

IT IS FRIDAY, just before midnight of March thirteenth, the air heavy with salt and cold as sin. I am Jason Melman, American-born captain of a sealer out of Boston, the *Seljegeren*. A two-hundred-ton merchantman, converted the year of my birth, twenty-nine years ago, at Stavingen, Norway, into a seagoing hunter, the ship is outfitted for this latest journey with every piece of modern equipment I could find, including a scout helicopter lashed with eight-strand cable to double steel-bolted hatches.

We are heading for the main sealing ground between Labrador and Greenland. Until now our voyage has been uneventful, the ship following the course my father laid out for us as precisely as if the prow cleaved the ruled line on his chart. With the engines going all out at flank speed, dawn should bring us within view of the sealing fleet, which has left the harbor twenty-four hours ahead of the *Seljegeren*.

But suddenly, as we enter the seas between Newfoundland and Nova Scotia, leaving the shelter of the mountainous headlands, giving wide berth to Sable Island, site of more shipwrecks than any spot on earth, crosscurrents at the spot where the Gulf of St. Lawrence meets the Atlantic churn the water into froth, the waves seeming to run in every direction simultaneously, while an arctic wind howling down from the pole whips the surface into icy spumes that look very like the deformed dwarfs my father once told me dance before every storm. In a moment, before I have a chance to get my bearings, we are in the midst of a ten-force gale that comes shrieking out of nowhere like a chorus of lost souls.

"Hard Port Rudder!" I shout to the young helmsman, who is wide-eyed and bewildered by the sudden storm. "Hold her there till we're stern to the blow!"

But before we can get turned about, the radio mast snaps in two as if made of wood instead of spring steel, and the helicopter's rotor blades twist into a knot like the most pliable rope. The ship shudders as heavy water pounds us on either side, and it is only after I leap to the wheel to help the struggling helmsman bring us about that the *Seljegeren* lunges forward and we are running before the storm.

Below decks all is chaos. The crew are thrown from their bunks, and it will be some time before the officers can get them topside to repair the damage. Communication, other than by hand signals, is almost impossible, and until storm lines can be tied from stanchion to rail to ladders no one on deck can survive the gale-force wind and water.

Eventually, hours or perhaps days later, with the hellish storm continuing unabated, I can no longer do without rest. I help the weary helmsman lash the wheel to our present course, trying to reassure him, and myself, that the *Seljegeren* is seaworthy enough to survive the storm. Then ordering him to get what rest he can on the slanting deck and instructing the anxious second mate, Knut, to call me the minute the wind changes, somehow I manage to stagger down the interior ladder that leads to the master cabin. I fall into my bunk fully clothed.

I don't know whether I sleep one hour or six. Then my

salt-caked eyes snap open. I lie still, listening, not realizing what it is that disturbs my rest.

At last I hear it—a hissing silence, profound as eternity. The ship seems to float serenely, as if on an ocean of foam. The storm lantern on a nearby hook hangs straight, as if the earth's epicenter is directly underneath.

Then the ship's plankings groan once more, and under my incredulous gaze the tilting deck seems to squeeze together like an accordian's folds before stretching back out so far I think every timber and joist in her is going to spring apart. The hull rivets scream as they are forced out of their seatings by a power greater than any I have ever seen before.

The posts of my bunk twist, one splintering. The lantern is plucked off the hook as if by a ghostly hand and smashed against the bulkhead. The faucets of my washbasin spin as the water gushes full on. The locked drawers of my desk chatter, furious as banshees. The doors to my wardrobe fling themselves open—and the footlocker, boots, clothing, books, and personal whatnots fly across the cabin every which way.

I struggle off my bunk, trying to keep my footing on the bouncing deck. The paneled wall directly before my startled eyes is bulging—and then the joints in the wood give way and a drawer jumps out.

A scroll of parchment, bound by cord so old it rends with the release of half a century's compression, unwinds, spilling to the deck with a sound dreadful as the cracking of a polar icecap, prelude to the shattering of continents.

As I reluctantly bend for the scroll I hear a pounding at the door. At the same time the whistling from the speaking tube connected to the bridge shrills its way into my consciousness. I can feel the renewed force of the gale in the *Seljegeren's* rigging, and I wonder if we have been in the eye of the storm for a moment—or an eternity.

I have barely time to make out that the scroll in my hands is a nautical chart, somehow understanding, with that part of my mind I cannot control, that these tracings of another's past will become my future, before the door is flung open by my first mate, Tor.

"It looks bad, Captain!" he shouts above the noise of the storm. "We'd better get everyone to the boats in case the ship goes under!"

Then Tor sees what I hold. His face, as lined as the parchment, matches its color. He reaches out, as if intending to pull it from me, as if desperately wanting to race above and hurl it over the rail into the howling wind.

Without thought, though something in me warns against it, I thrust the scroll under my sweater. Then shouldering Tor aside, I fight my way against the tidal pulls down the stressed corridor, struggle up the plunging ladder to the deck, and finally haul myself up the wind-whipped lifeline to the wave-battered bridge—Tor only a half step behind.

Inside, the young helmsman and an equally frightened, battle-scarred Portuguese aged beyond his years by a life at sea wrestle the wheel, lifting bodily off the deck as the ship's screw and rudder rise completely out of the raging waters. The compass needle jumps crazily about the dial.

Outside it is black as nightmare, even the riding lights obscured by the fury of dark wind and sea. It's impossible to tell what is up or down, which blackness is ocean, which sky.

Knotted veins stand out on Tor's neck as he attempts to make himself heard above the gale. "We must abandon ship!" he shouts.

"It'll soon blow itself out," I say, though I don't know why I believe that.

4

"Our lives will be on your head!" Tor cries, his face darkening.

"That is my responsibility," I agree, and we are at a standoff.

Tor looks to the burly figure of Knut, the second mate, and to the sparsely bearded young radio officer, Nils, who has started the automatic distress signals. I guess that they have already discussed what to do should I prove obstinate.

But they hesitate. And pulling the parchment out from under my drenched sweater, I brush the water off. Holding on to the bulkhead for dear life with one hand, I shake open the scroll with the other.

And suddenly the wind abates. The sky lightens. The morning sun can now be seen, if dimly, through a haze. Though the seas continue strong, the storm seems to have passed us and gone, quick as that.

While the men groan with relief, I hardly pause for breath. "Knut, take whatever men are available, and give me a report on the damage," I order. "Nils, see if you can pick up any kind of signal from the fleet."

Ignoring Tor, who seems struck dumb by the sudden weather change, I stretch the scroll's brittle fabric as carefully as possible over the lighted chart table.

Illuminated by the yellowish glow, the faded inks begin to take on a new intensity. The faint lines grow plainer by the minute. I puzzle over the unfamiliar markings. Finally it occurs to me that this aged parchment may be detailing the very area we are in.

And then I see, scribbled in the cracked margins, in the familiar sprawling hand of my father, notes on seal migrations. The course indicated would lead us to nesting grounds not on our regular charts. Excited, I motion for Tor to come look.

"We may be in luck!" I say.

"Bad luck," Tor responds, his feet planted as if nailed to the deck.

"Why would you think that?" I demand. "If this chart is right, we've stumbled on enough fur to fill our holds ten times over!"

"You were still in your mother's belly when that chart was drawn," Tor says, refusing to budge. "It's anybody's guess if it's accurate!"

"My guess is that it is," I say, wondering at the sudden attack of nerves that seems to have overcome this normally rock-solid man. "But I don't see that we have much choice. God only knows how far we've been blown off course—"

The hopeless shrug from Nils confirms that we're out of radio range of the fleet, at least without our mast, meaning that we are days behind.

"By the time we catch up to the others," I continue, "they'll have taken all the quotas and then some. Our only chance at a successful hunt is to set course for these islands now!"

Placing an acetate overlay on the chart, I plot a directional line from where I estimate our position to be toward a group of small, dark areas, drawn by some ancient mariner in a way that resembles a sea monster's spine and accentuated, as if to underscore their ominous nature, by my father's more recent pen.

"The sea changes," Tor warns. "Shoals drop out of sight, channels silt up—"

"We'll keep sharp watch," I say, "and take soundings as we go."

"Your father spoke his instructions plain," Tor reminds me, his face taking on the color of clotted blood with an anger he now makes little effort to conceal. "You swore to keep to the course he charted!"

"Well it looks like he charted this one too," I reply, trying to keep my own anger in check. "And even if he meant this to remain hidden, we don't know that, do we? And we can hardly be blamed for the storm. But if it'll make you feel any better, I'll radio him as soon as we get the mast repaired. I'm sure if he were here he'd make the same decision," I finish, hoping to reassure him, remembering that Tor and my father started out as whaling ship cabin boys out of Spitsbergen together.

"And I'm equally sure that he would not!" Tor snaps, in his fury showing teeth stained almost black.

"He's probably forgotten that this old chart even exists," I say finally, shaken by Tor's intensity, trying to hold down the anxiety which seems to rise in me as inevitably as the tides whenever the subject of what my father would do comes up. "He probably stuck it in a drawer and put it out of his memory, not realizing that when he had the master cabin refitted—"

"It's not his memory that's crippled!" Tor cries. "If that chart was hidden it was for good reason!"

"That may be," I say tightly, finding it increasingly difficult to master my feelings. "But since he didn't see fit to confide what the reason might be, and I'm unable to question him about it, my decision will have to stand!"

We glare at each other. When Tor seems unable to say anything more, I turn to the Portuguese, who is listening with frowning curiosity, and give him the new coordinates.

"Captain," Tor says hoarsely then, putting his gnarled hand on the wheel to keep it steady on the old course, "think again. Those are the Mirabelles. Even if the seals are still there, the islanders will never let us hunt them. Outsiders aren't welcome!"

I stare at him, surprised, wondering why it has taken him until now to reveal that this chart is familiar to him. "We'll make sure to keep our distance then," I say harshly, to remind him that only one of us can be in command here. "It's tempting fate to repeat old journeys," Tor warns, persisting in the face of my increasing irritation, gripping the wheel so hard his knuckles whiten. He holds my determined gaze with his own, his eyes gray and normally unfathomable as these seas—except what is flickering in them now is fear, something I have never seen in this hard old man before.

I am tempted to give in, to cover that ancient chart with one that is comfortingly familiar, to order a course change that will send us after the rest of the fleet, a decision I can justify till the end of time based on what Tor is telling me now.

But if I do that I may never again be given so heaven-sent an opportunity to match my father's giant footsteps. I want to stand in my father's place in this battered old wheelhouse without feeling that I have been less than he was. I have to prove that I can shoulder the burden of command without buckling under the strain.

"We'll make our own fate," I say at last. "Now see to the ship!"

Much as I respect Tor and especially admire his loyalty to my father, I can't let this argument continue without jeopardizing the authority I hold over the crew—a scruffy, down-at-the-heels, dregs-of-all-nations bunch, all that are left on the Boston docks after the other ships have taken an earlier pick.

"At six bells," I go on before Tor can protest further, "I want every man on deck—I'll tell them what the alternatives are myself!" And removing Tor's hand from the wheel, I spin it to the new course, lock the compass heading in place, and turn it back over to the Portuguese.

Tor's mouth works. No words come out. A moment later he spins on his heel and stalks off. From below, I hear his whistle shrilling the men to their tasks.

Avoiding the apprehensive glances of the men in the wheelhouse, I take the chart off the table, tie it with a fresh cord, and take it below, suddenly aware that I am shivering in my storm-drenched clothing.

2

UNTIL DAYS AGO in Boston, I'd had no contact with my father before or since that childhood summer spent sailing the icy waters of the awesome Norwegian *fjords*. I had asked—actually begged—my mother to let him show me how to read the portents of weather and train me in the use of harpoon, net, oar, and gaff. My mother had agreed only after the urging of my dying grandmother.

She needn't have worried. I had been raised by women, kept from my father for over thirteen years, and no matter how hard I was to try, there was a secret, unspoken barrier between us that prevented us from making a solid emotional connection.

My father had returned to Norway alone the year I was born, for reasons I have yet to discover. My grandmother's family had commissioned the *Seljegeren* as a wedding gift, but my mother never referred to the *Seljegeren* or my father in my presence until the day she died. It was my grandmother who told me I had been given permission to visit Norway.

And then my father, whom I'd never seen even in a photograph, suddenly stood before me at the Spitsbergen airport. He was huge as the Vikings in my picture books, his beard golden in the setting sun, eyes blue as the northern sea, with a blunt nose and square jaw I recognized as having been reproduced in a smaller way on me.

"You are Jason?" he boomed, and I nodded, grinning excitedly, expecting I don't know what—to be picked up, swallowed in an enormous hug, his beard prickling my own tender face, or at the least a handshake and an arm round the shoulders while he escorted me to his car.

Instead, he swung on his heel and strode off without another word. I gaped in astonishment, then grabbed my bag, heavy with too many sweaters and scarves, and struggled to catch up.

He spoke not at all in the car; and except to tell me where my bunk was when we stepped aboard his sloop at the fishing docks, he said nothing more until he cast off and maneuvered us through the incoming boats to the open sea.

"You take her," he told me then, and stood me at the wheel, disappearing below before I could protest.

I had never sailed anything larger than a sixteen-foot sea scout day sailer before—on one of the few excursions outside our house my mother permitted me in the company of males. This forty-two-foot craft seemed enormous, its sails stretching so tall I thought they would scrape the sky. Under my sweating hands the mahogany wheel quivered and thrummed.

"What course?" I shouted, though I doubted he could hear, and I watched, my heart in my sobbing throat, as the wind spilled from the foresails first, then out of the main spinnaker, causing the boat to wallow like some wounded animal.

I twisted the wheel first one way then another, squinting to gauge wind direction, desperate to get under way again before that towering giant who had identified himself as my father discovered that something was very wrong. But the sails continued to hang limp as rags, and as the boat slid and staggered I felt his presence behind me.

He didn't say anything. His large hand encompassed mine and squeezed it three spokes to starboard. Like magic the boat stiffened. I heard a rapid-fire crackling as the sails rippled, and then muffled booms like cannon as the canvas popped and bellied full. Our port rail dipped to the hissing waves, and we went racing toward the emerging moon.

For upward of half an hour we stood thus, the only sounds the shushing of wind and water and an occasional thump as the prow cut through an errant wave, causing spray to sting my flushed face. As his hand continued to grip mine I began to understand, as I never had in the protected family harbor, how closely we were bound to the prevailing wind. Moment by moment we seemed on the verge of slipping off. Each time, the slightest adjustment of the wheel kept us sliding along. It was the most delicate and yet the most solid connection of man to element, at once spiritual and real.

When he finally left me I almost did not notice, so quietly did he go. By then my soul and the boat's were one. I could feel every change in her attitude from keel to topsail, anticipating whatever shift the wind or wave motion made almost before it happened, so that not once during what had become a magical night did we even come close to losing way.

The dawn took me by surprise. We had entered a long, narrow inlet without my knowing it. I had assumed the shadows that played all about us were caused by high clouds. Only when the sun rose and illuminated the cliffs rising like cathedral spires on either side did I become aware that we were sailing up a *fjord*.

Ahead I could make out a number of boats riding at anchor before a rocky beach. Beyond that a dozen or so stone cottages surrounded a small church and some other buildings clustered at a village square.

I stooped to shout a warning below, only to find my father already on deck. He indicated that I should take the boat in. Somehow, in spite of—or perhaps because of—how much I wanted to impress him, the confidence I had acquired during the night evaporated. As I attempted to come about I turned the wheel too far. The sudden slapping from above told me I was once again spilling wind.

This time he didn't wait. He lifted me, none too gently, aside, and adjusted the wheel. The boat heeled the other way. A dreadful sound I hear in my dreams still turned out to be the ripping of the topsail. He had grabbed the wheel too late.

I began to cry silently, the tears raining down my face, manfully trying to swallow my salt-laden frustration and grief over having failed to live up to his expectations. If he noticed he gave no sign as he dropped anchor, pulled in the sails, and tied them down without so much as a glance in my direction. Then he shoved an inflatable raft over the side, got in, and finally looked to where I stood sniveling.

"Come!" he shouted, his voice full of what I believed to be anger and disappointment. I ran to the raft and jumped in, keeping my head down as he rowed us ashore.

Fishermen mending nets on the beach offered him needle and twine, grinning and winking at one another.

"It's not his fault!" I shouted, though it was not likely they would understand English.

My father turned on me with a fierce "Be quiet!"

Inside the pub the smell of malt and hot spiced wine was overwhelming. The only customers were aged or crippled. They looked up as we entered, greeting my father by name and staring at me curiously, as well they might. They were dressed in shapeless and faded garments, while I was got up in the very latest sailing gear—bright yellow slicker jacket and red deck shoes from Abercrombie and Fitch.

Behind a counter scarred with glass rings and tobacco burns a fat-bellied, gray-bearded man greeted my father as the others had. My father held up two fingers. The man opened a spigot and filled two glasses with a foaming dark liquid. My father carried the drinks to a table near the tapestried wall and placed one before me.

I tentatively sipped, determined not to gag on the thick, bitter taste. My father picked up a battered silver container and poured salt into my glass, causing the drink to foam even more. But when I tasted again the bitterness was gone.

A fat woman with hair bound in a tattered, faded blue rag brought us plates of scrambled eggs and thick sausage and small pancakes covered with tiny berries of an amazing purple hue. They popped in my mouth like sugared lemon. I had not realized how hungry I was. The woman watched while I stuffed the food in, then asked my father a question in Norwegian.

"America," my father said, and the woman nodded, looking from me to my father and back as if comparing us, unfavorably I had no doubt, before returning to the kitchen.

My father finished before I did and motioned for his glass to be refilled. He swallowed half, then carried it to a narrow staircase I hadn't noticed before, where he turned, saw me still wiping up the last of the sugared berries, and motioned impatiently for me to follow.

At the top of the stairway was a balcony railing in which grotesque figures of trolls were carved. My father strode along the corridor, past crude wooden doors marked with puzzling symbols, to the room at the end, opening it with a key he pulled from his vest.

I don't know what I expected. Certainly not a dark, stale place that smelled musty as an attic—or a used-book store.

I understood why when he opened the window blinds. Every conceivable space was filled with books: large books, small books, books stacked every which way, on the floor, on the chairs and even the brass bed, its faded quilt comforter almost entirely covered with the cullings of a hundred libraries; new books with pages yet uncut, old books with cracked bindings and places marked with strips of paper on which notes had been scribbled.

On the walls were maps, old maps by their look, with indications of ancient trade routes and drawings of mythical beasts rising from uncharted seas, swamping the fragile vessels sailing perilously near the edge of a very flat world. A huge globe stood next to a chart table on which a bottle of ink and several silver-tipped pens lay at hand—his hand, I assumed—to make notes on a parchment map.

Seeing me glance curiously at the map, my father hastily covered it with a sheet pulled from a nearby chair, spilling books on the floor in the process. He swept the rest off the seat with a massive hand, shoved the chair near me, and sat on a stool with his back to the window. What light there was created an aura about his head that kept his face in shadow.

"Sit," he ordered. When I complied he asked, "You like the sea, don't you?"

"Sir?" I wondered, trembling at this sudden interrogation.

"You will make your living from the sea," he announced, like some judgment from on high.

"I don't know," I said hesitantly. "I haven't thought about it . . ."

"You have seafaring blood in you," he said. "That part of you that comes from me won't be able to stay away. The other part I have my doubts about—your mother's family makes their living from the sea, but once removed, preferring to remain on land. They are willing to turn a profit but unwilling to bloody their hands to get it."

I looked at his hands, which were scrubbed clean.

No blood there, at least now. He saw my reaction and following my look flinched as if he saw something invisible to me. Then he leaned very close, his mouth hardening.

"You have fished?" he asked. "Set a hook through a finny jaw, sliced it tail to head, dug your hands in to clean its guts?"

I nodded reluctantly, unwilling to admit that I hadn't been permitted to participate in anything my mother defined as an unclean sport.

"It's nature's way," he boomed, putting his large nose to my smaller one. "We are forced to kill to survive. There should be no shame attached to what we must do to remain alive!"

He stood up then, striding about the room, picking up first one book and then another, examining the strips of paper hanging out of them, finally bringing several over and dumping them into my lap.

"I have read everything I could find on the subject," he said. "Every philosopher, every anthropologist, every naturalist, every historian, every psychologist, and without exception they have pointed out that man only exists today because of his aggressive instincts. If we lose that we are doomed. Our species will be wiped out, either through starvation, or being eaten ourselves by other animals less squeamish about their feeding habits!"

His eyes were glowing like those of someone possessed; with the light flowing in from the window behind him he looked like an Old Testament prophet, bringing the Word to the Infidel—or in this case, me.

But why was he trying so hard to convince me? His word was gospel; I had no reason to disagree. Or was he in fact arguing with himself?

I could not continue to meet his fanatical stare and began examining the books. Did he really expect me to read all these?

"I have marked the appropriate passages," he said. "You need not trouble yourself with anything else."

15

"And do the maps have something to do with this?" I asked, wondering if those drawings on the charts of ancient animals were imaginary, or real species now extinct.

"You are quick," he said, as if grudging me my mind. "I have plotted old voyages and explorations to see if any peace-loving peoples have survived, and have found none."

"None?" I asked, glancing over at the covered chart table.

He followed my look and paled. "You will touch nothing in this room without my express permission," he said. "Is that understood?" I nodded. "Now unpack your belongings, keep them in that chest over there," he continued. "When you've finished, join me at the fisherman's store across from the church."

With that, he left me alone in the room.

I was mightily tempted to walk over to that chart table, lift the sheet, and sneak a quick look at whatever it was he kept hidden. But he'd shown his trust by leaving me alone. I wasn't prepared to challenge him, not then, and not for a long time after.

I hurried to complete my task, then went out through the pub, ducking my head to the proprietor and his wife, and headed across the little square to the shop my father had spoken of.

He was hefting a wicked-looking object, a long-handled steel rod with a barb at one end. "See how this suits you," he said, tossing it to me.

I grabbed the rod, holding it awkwardly.

"It's for gaffing fish," he said. "When a big one's brought up alongside the boat, you'll hook it under the gills with this."

My hands were swallowed by his as he swept the barbed hook around and down, grunting with the effort as we gaffed an imaginary large one.

16

"You see?" he demanded. "Nothing to it!"

I nodded, though I wasn't entirely convinced.

An old man was on the boat when we arrived, putting the last stitches to the ripped sail. He stood, doffing his knit cap while my father examined the job he'd done. When my father dropped coins into his guarded hand, the old man left without a word having been exchanged.

Raising the sails, my father lifted anchor and took the boat back out into the main channel. I watched his every move, determined to measure up to whatever he might ask.

No sooner was the village out of sight than he was calling for me to set out the nets, which he'd pulled out of a locker and slung across the sloping deck. The lead weights made them heavy. After tying the corners to brass hooks screwed into the aft rail, I struggled to get them over the side.

"Don't try to lift the whole thing!" he shouted. "Throw one square in, the rest will follow!"

I did as he said and watched in some amazement as the squares unfolded one after another, until the entire webbing was trailing underwater after the boat.

"Now raise the line!" he shouted, pointing to a winch near where I stood as if hypnotized.

I leaped to obey, cranking the handle and watching as a thin steel line ran over pulleys from the winch to a pole angled aft to the leading edge of the hidden net, lifting it to create a kind of catch basin.

"Enough!" he commanded. "Now keep a sharp lookout for something worthwhile—we don't want minnows!"

A fish darted into the hollowed-out net and could not seem to find its way out again. I debated telling him; it was only a foot or so long, and using the gaff on something so small seemed pointless. I didn't want to settle for anything less than he would. Then another fish, much larger, with fins like knives on a speckled body, suddenly appeared, and opening its mouth, swallowed the smaller silver one whole.

I gasped.

"What is it?" my father demanded from the wheel.

"Nothing," I said.

"Nothing?" he repeated incredulously. His eyes were gleaming, as if focused through binoculars. Even at that distance he could see what was trapped by the net. "Get the gaff!" he shouted.

I moved to obey.

"Don't dawdle!" he cried. "It may find its way out again!"

While I stood at the aft rail with that ugly hook in hand, the creature was sporting about in the curling wake of the boat as if unaware that it was trapped.

"Put the hook to him!" my father yelled.

I leaned over the rail, anxious to prove that I had learned his lesson well. My shadow must have fallen over the fish, for it rolled and looked upward, those bulging eyes staring curiously into mine.

"Hook him!" my father yelled again.

Avoiding those eyes and concentrating only on remembering the stroke my father had shown me, I swung the pole down and then yanked back up. The gaff's upward progress stopped abruptly, and then I was pulled forward so hard against the rail I thought I might break in two.

Somehow I did not let go of the handle. The hook was imbedded deep, just under the fish's mouth. Its head twisted to look up at whatever was impeding its swim. A mucous fluid darker than the water gushed forth, and the fish began thrashing about, gasping for breath.

The pole whipped in my sweaty grasp, bouncing off the rail and thrumming a tattoo on my own head and shoulders that I was too excited to care about. I held on. Though every nerve in me was screaming to let go, I could not release that poor dumb gasping creature while my father was shouting incomprehensible instructions to me from the wheel.

I was dragged from one side to the other as the fish continually whipped about to change directions. Would it never tire? The fluid, what I assumed to be its vital juices, its life's blood, streamed out steadily. Now other fish arrived to suck it up, avoiding the thrashing tail, somehow managing to feed near the gasping head without endangering themselves.

Suddenly the pole was taken out of my hands. "Bring up the net!" my father commanded. He had lashed the wheel in place.

I stumbled to the winch and began turning the crank with both hands, now sore with broken blisters.

Gradually the net lurched up. My father heaved mightily on the pole. The fish seemed to drop out of the sky, thudding onto the deck, where it began flopping about. My father put a heavy foot on its head and stood until the creature lay still.

"You can clean it now," my father said, tossing me a wicked-looking knife before returning to the wheel.

I studied the fish, wondering what it was I had seen shining from its bulging eyes only moments before.

"Set to it, boy!" my father called. "Fix the knife in its anus and slice toward the head."

"What if it's still alive?" I asked.

"Well, if it is," my father said impatiently, "you'll want to put it out of its misery, won't you?"

I knelt on the deck, and cautiously gripping one of the fins, turned the fish enough to spot the tiny hole just forward of its tail. Carefully I inserted the knife point. The flesh seemed to absorb the sharp blade.

"Nothing in there but guts, boy," came my father's voice, as if from a great distance. "Open him up!"

Somehow I willed my muscles to act, and the knife

slid as if through butter down the length of the fish's midsection.

The halves fell apart. I recoiled as out of the steaming guts a slimy thing rose as if propelled by springs, then skittered down the sloping deck to the starboard rail, where it slid over the side right under the astonished gaze of my father.

I looked over at him and smiled. I had forgotten that only minutes earlier the smaller fish had been swallowed whole.

My father stared at me, open-mouthed, shaking as if he'd witnessed a vision. "Did you see that?" he whispered.

"What?" I asked perversely, on the moment deciding to play dumb for reasons still unclear to me.

"She was carrying something live in her," my father said. "She gave birth at the moment of death!"

"Well," I said, thinking it was time to explain—but my father would have none of it.

"Get rid of it!" he suddenly shouted. "Kick it over the side. Do as I say!"

I hurried to obey. I kicked at the eviscerated fish, then using both feet and pole managed to get it, guts and all, off the deck and into the cleansing sea. My father threw me a bucket then, and filling it with water, I washed the deck of any signs that there had been a butchering there.

Without a further word, my father brought the boat about and set sail back to the fishing village, so ashen-faced and deep in thought that I understood he had been shaken to his soul.

That night, after a number of glasses of a clear liquid that a surreptitious taste told me was ten times more potent than the beer, my father began to tell me stories that his own father had told him, slurred tales of seafarers and trolls, strange recountings of superstition and longing. More than once I shivered and combed my hair back with my fingers to keep it from standing on end.

"Do you believe in the spirit world?" I asked him, after a story about an angel in the shape of a fish who had guided a lost ship to safety.

"Only fools disbelieve," he said hoarsely.

"Have you ever seen one?" I asked.

"In my dreams," he said. "I am haunted," he continued, in a voice so full of sorrow and despair that my eyes welled in sympathy.

"By what?" I asked. But he would not answer.

Later, after he staggered up the stairs, accepting my arms about his waist as I guided him onto the bed where he sprawled amidst his books, clutching the near-empty bottle, I ventured another question.

"Did Mother send you away because you are haunted?" I asked.

I thought he might have fallen asleep. Then the bottle in his hand shattered and he moaned as the blood flowed.

I ran to the washbasin for a towel. But he had already wrapped his hand in the bed sheet, and now he turned to the wall, shutting off any further questions.

In the morning I awakened to find him standing by my bed. "Pack your things," he said. "We leave with the tide."

"Where are we going?" I asked, hastening to obey.

"Back to Spitsbergen," he said.

"But I thought I was to stay for the summer!" I protested.

"These waters are bad luck for us," he muttered, and he left me to scramble after him as best I could.

He handled the wheel the journey back, acting as if he had not heard when I asked if I might have another chance at it. When I persisted he suddenly suggested that I choose an occupation away from the sea.

"That rebirthed fish was an omen," he said. "A sign for you to stay away."

"But it wasn't that way at all," I said, struggling to explain. "It was swallowed by the larger fish . . ." But he was not listening.

I walked to the stern and studied our wake for a while. "I'm going to follow the sea," I said when I returned. "I hope to be just like you some day."

He stared as if I were out of my mind. "You're nothing like me," he said finally. "You have your mother's sensitivity—a sailor's life is not for you."

I was angered beyond measure. But to my immense chagrin, I could not speak for the held-back tears that were filling my nose and throat.

All the rest of the journey back to the port I stayed as far away from him as I could get. I climbed the main mast until I could go no further. I shouted my fury into the wind, vowing that if I did nothing else with my life, I would prove him wrong.

At the airport it was I who stood silent and remote, putting my back to him on the pretense that I was watching the planes through the plate glass windows, unwilling to meet his glance, afraid my innermost feelings would come spilling out.

"Tell your mother she's right," he said, when the call came for my flight. "You'll be better off with a life on the land."

He bent down close to me. "You will tell her?"

"No," I managed, and ran for the boarding gate.

3

I WAS NOT to see my father again for sixteen years. He took sick en route to Boston the same year my mother died, and I was forced by his incapacity and the terms of my mother's will to take command of the *Seljegeren* away from him.

It was not something I wanted to do. But the trustees of my mother's estate made it clear that my inheritance would be at risk if my father proved unable to command. As principal owner I could either take the ship over, or the bank would protect its own interests by forcing a sale.

On the day the *Seljegeren* was scheduled to arrive I waited, accompanied by an eminent doctor, a specialist in rheumatic diseases, in the Whaler's Roost, a musty waterfront bar where I spent much of my time after my discharge from the navy. When a dock hanger-on stuck his unkempt head in the door and announced that the ship was at last coming into port, I sent the impatient doctor on ahead, hoping that he could prescribe a treatment that would enable my father to continue his voyage.

But when I boarded the ship myself my worst fears were realized. Tor was on deck, overseeing the short-handed crew; my father, who had always taken a hands-on approach to his ship's maintenance, had been forced to remain below. When I was bidden to enter his cabin, the doctor was giving him an injection. Finishing, the doctor snapped his bag shut and without saying a word left us alone.

My father's appearance was shocking. His large frame was wasted and bent, his eyes hollow with pain, his beard gray and wet with fever. The lines in his brow seemed as deep as if chiseled in stone, and his lips worked as if he were engaged in some interior dialogue.

"You belong in the hospital," I said when I was able.

"Yes," he admitted finally, almost breathless with the effort to speak. "As soon as we pick up more crew, I'll be taken ashore. The *Seljegeren* will sail without me."

"But not without me," I said, wanting to get it over with quickly. "I'm taking command."

He raised himself on one trembling elbow and fixed me with a terrible eye. "You've never hunted seals!"

"One animal's much like another," I shrugged.

"You don't know what you're talking about," he said. "This hunt's not at a distance, with guns. It's close quarters. You have to take care or the pelts will be ruined!"

"I'll run the ship," I replied, trying to be reasonable. "Tor can run the hunt."

"There's a difference between those pampered navy lags you're used to and the riffraff we recruit to hunt seals," he said, anger strengthening his voice. "These men get no pay besides a share in the kill—devil knows what they might do if anyone mucked that up for them!"

"You can't frighten me off," I said, setting my jaw in a manner that mirrored his. "Will you tell Tor, or will I have to?"

"We're already days late," he raged. "If we don't get our quota of skins this year, the *Seljegeren* will have to be sold!"

"You don't understand," I said. "Either I captain the *Seljegeren* or I'm forced to sell it now!" And I showed him the bank documents.

He closed his eyes, as if unable to accept what he was reading. A spasm of pain momentarily overwhelmed the medication the doctor had given him, and a groan forced itself out from between his clenched teeth.

"You would do that?" he asked, so faintly I would not have recognized that hollow voice as his own.

I steeled myself against his anguish and nodded.

"I will chart your course," he said then, finally accepting the inevitable. "But you must swear to stick to it no matter what—otherwise sell the *Seljegeren* and be damned! Swear!" he said, and from his bunk he managed to push an old Bible at me.

"I swear," I said to humor him. I could see no harm in it—he knew those seas, I did not—and if there was to be no handshake, no parental blessing, not so much as a good luck and Godspeed, then perhaps this was the next best thing.

There was no way of knowing, then, as I lay my hand on that holy book, that my oath would be nullified so soon after by a storm that would seem to come out of nowhere, as if from the farthest reaches of the universe itself.

We recruited whoever we could get to fill out the crew—unskilled immigrants without legal status, shifty-eyed dock roustabouts with questionable identities, sailors from foreign ships who had been cast off for reasons best not investigated, every man desperate to take whatever work was available.

This was not the sort of command I'd had experience with. In the navy I'd taken over a troop transport combat landing craft, manned by a disciplined crew. I had enjoyed my times at sea, at long last in the company of men, and when I had put those hundreds of brave, excited, singing young marines ashore to keep the peace in blood-drenched Lebanon, my joy knew no bounds. But I grew bored waiting off the beach for new orders and received permission to visit the marine enclave.

I was within a mile of the encampment when a truck filled with explosives and driven by Arab extremists raced past the casually guarded perimeter into the middle of the crowded camp. At first, neither my driver nor myself understood what that gigantic thunderclap was. The earth shook, the impact blurring our vision and near bursting our eardrums. The driver wrestled the wheel of the jeep to keep us from skidding off the suddenly buckling road.

Then silence, still as the grave. In the distance the black cloud soundlessly mushroomed into the riven sky. Drifting along the desert air came the smell of sulphur and cordite from the funeral pyre, followed by the first faint cries of men hurt beyond repair.

We raced to the inferno. All was chaos. A shoeless foot, a head, a braceleted arm, each had been ripped from living torsos writhing in mindless agony while blood soaked into the parched sands. Flesh stripped from bone fluttered like wet flags against the sandbags, themselves slashed and leaking. Tented barracks had been blown apart, revealing occupants sprawled in charnel heaps. Those still standing plunged about aimlessly, eyes glazed and unseeing as dumbstruck creatures, mouths open, their screams heard neither by themselves nor their rescuers, who, like myself, stood paralyzed at first view, skin almost unbearably overheating while inside a chill starting at the heart spread to freeze every organ. When we were finally able to throw ourselves heedlessly into the midst of the terror, it was only by refusing to acknowledge the awful circumstances under which we were working.

We lifted what was left of once able-bodied men, our hands sticky with substances the mind would not contemplate, murmuring words without meaning intended to comfort, all semblance of feeling thrust below the level of consciousness—as if every bit of emotion once possessed had been drowned in arctic deeps, never to surface again.

The labor seemed never-ending. I don't remember how long it took or how I got back to my ship. My surroundings, once comfortingly familiar, now seemed alien. I found it increasingly difficult to make any decision. I was finally relieved of command and sent home to Boston for psychological evaluation.

When I continued to insist to Dr. Eileen Layton, the naval hospital psychiatrist assigned to my case, that my refusal to discuss my feelings was simply an inability to find words to express the inexpressible, she recommended that I be given a discharge. I was no longer fit, she said, to handle the stress of command. I disagreed, suggesting that time would eventually heal any psychic wound, but the review board denied my appeal.

Afterward, Eileen sought me out, urging me to seek private treatment. I refused but said that I would be willing to meet with her on a casual basis, so that she might satisfy herself that my paralysis of feeling was only temporary.

In spite of what she called my obstinate refusal to plumb my own depths, we became closer than friends. Recently, she agreed she might one day marry me. But she refuses to name a date until such time as she can be sure that I am fully recovered.

Since then I have had no further symptoms of any inner unease, other than a kind of emotional numbness, relieved only by unexplained, infrequent wellings of my eyes at unexpected moments—a random passage in a book, a strain of music, or a particular configuration of sea and sky.

It does not surprise me, therefore, that now I am trembling with more than cold as I towel myself dry, dress, then straighten the storm-tossed mess in the cabin. I am convinced that the decisions I am making are rational and have nothing to do with my past condition or the hallucinatory atmosphere present during that furious blow.

A whistle pipes down through the speaking tube. I pick my way through the debris strewn everywhere and lift the tube off its hook. "Yes?" I ask.

"Crew's assembled on the aft deck, Cap'n," comes Tor's voice, remote and correct but still full of anger.

"I'll be right there," I say.

I place the chart in the drawer and slide it back into its secret compartment.

In choosing to follow in my father's footsteps, I do not feel that I am challenging fate so much as accepting it.

4

THE CREW HUDDLES in a ragged circle for protection against the biting cold, some hunched inside patched greatcoats, others holding faded blankets that occasionally flap like old sails.

As I step out on the captain's bridge overlooking the deck, the chill air immediately tears my eyes and waters my nose, the moisture freezing into tiny icicles against my skin. But I ignore the discomfort and observe the men in silence until the last mutterings die down.

They are of every color and shape, a mixture of young and old, all poor, most illiterate, among them waterfront scavengers who normally work only long enough to buy themselves a night's lodging and a bottle of gin. They are as scaly and rotten as old pilings, and ordinarily Tor would have given them a wide berth. But since the sealing fleet has taken all the experienced men, we've had to make do with this rabble, promising them they'll come back with the equivalent of small fortunes.

Now they realize the storm has blown us far off the main course, and they are edgy and anxious about the ominously hazy steel blue horizon we are sailing toward. They are worrying not about the money promised but whether these unfamiliar waters might hold unspeakable terrors. They've already heard—the old Portuguese helmsman will have seen to that—about my argument with Tor. It does not take much to release the superstitions that lie just under every seaman's surface bravado.

To bolster my authority, I have put on my braided cap

and epauletted jacket. I have to convince them that their young captain has better judgment than their experienced first mate, a task I approach with some unease. If I fail, they will insist that I return to our original course, their right by the agreement under which they signed on.

I cast my eye about for someone who can translate my words into other languages. So many of them, having washed up on the already polluted Boston docks from all over the world, speak only rudimentary English.

I spot a young deckhand, Per, huddling under a blanket with Knut, the melancholy second mate. Per is the youngest man aboard, his white hair, eyebrows, and pale skin making him seem ghostlike. He was hired on the urgent recommendation of the sad-eyed Knut, who, I have been told, "always brings along a bookish companion to cheer the lonely hours at sea."

"Per," I call. He steps out from under his shared blanket, white lashes fringing eyes so pale they are almost colorless. "What languages do you speak, besides English and Norwegian?"

"French, Spanish, German, and Portuguese," Per says. "I majored in languages at university so that I might translate poetry . . ."

"That should cover it," I interrupt, impatient to get on with it, wanting also to keep him from exposing his sensitivity to this dissolute crew. "What I have to tell the men is too important to risk being misunderstood. I'm going to speak in English, a sentence at a time, and then wait for you to translate into however many languages are necessary. Make sure you speak simply, without embellishment, making no interpretation of my words beyond what I say."

"But what if your meaning is not clear, sir?" Per asks.

"Are you suggesting you don't understand me now?" I demand, speaking more harshly than I intend.

The men titter. Per's face flames. Knut turtles out from under his shawled blanket.

It is suddenly so quiet that all that is heard is the groaning of the ship's planks and the roiling wake thrust behind us by the churning screw. The second mate is the strongest man aboard, and no fun is made of Per in Knut's presence.

But I do not apologize. I know that if I am to establish my authority, already weakened by Tor's near insubordinate behavior in the wheelhouse, I can't allow myself to seem intimidated by any of my officers or even to show compassion for any of my men, particularly one despised by the others.

"Are you ready?" I demand of Per, staring at Knut, daring him to protest. He hesitates, then steps back, leaving Per alone in front of the men. But he has left Per with his blanket.

Per is taken aback by my behavior. But he shrugs into the blanket's warmth, nodding his readiness to proceed.

"You will all be pleased to know," I begin, as if speaking to each man personally, "that the *Seljegeren* suffered no major damage." I nod then at Per, waiting until he has repeated what I've said in each of four languages, his voice thin but as penetrating as a bosun's pipe. "The repairs to the radio mast are already under way," I continue, "but I consider it a fortunate circumstance that we are unable to contact the main sealing fleet . . ."—I pause until the looks of surprise appear on their faces, then go on—". . . as we are near a secret breeding ground that has not been harvested for a number of years—so many years that there is more fur there than we will know what to do with!"

It takes a while for Per to make the translation. But finally I have the satisfaction of seeing the crew's avaricious faces light up. "That's right," I say, fueling their greed, "the islands we're heading toward should be swarming with newly born pups. Barring any more bad weather, we should be able to fill our holds and sail for home before the week is out!''

They like that alright, scratching themselves, thinking about the money they can spend on whiskey and women, checking the now radiantly clear sky, so empty of clouds that if it weren't for the wreckage on deck, that storm might have seemed only a bad dream.

"Any questions?" I ask then. Out of the corner of my eye I become aware that Tor has moved, hands clenched to the railing.

A narrow-faced seaman with the eyes of a rodent shuffles forward. "What's the name of these islands?" he asks, touching his oily cap with a tobacco-stained finger in mock deference to my rank. "Why hasn't they been hunted?"

"Too far off the beaten track," I reply. "They've been forgotten. If I hadn't accidentally stumbled across an old chart during the storm, I wouldn't know about them myself!"

"The name?" Per reminds me.

"The Mirabelles," I say.

The men look at one another, puzzled, as Per repeats the name in four languages. Then a grizzled man in a greatcoat stained from a thousand gutters clears his throat and growls something I cannot understand.

"Begging the captain's pardon, but are you sure they exist?" Per translates. "I have sailed these waters for more than twenty years and I have never heard of any Mirabelles."

"The chart is older than that," I reply, "and was drawn by the former captain of this ship on a prior expedition. Isn't that right, Mr. Torgersen?" I demand then, turning to my first mate.

I wonder if Tor is going to reply. His every instinct, I am sure, is to challenge me on the spot, but a deep-seated respect for rank holds him back. Only a full-fledged confrontation will bring what's bothering him into the open. I decide that now is the time to force the issue. Though I risk losing the crew's loyalty, I also stand a chance—perhaps the only one I'll get—of gaining their respect, something I'll need to make this hunt a success.

"Go ahead, Tor," I say. "Spit it out, say whatever you like—either speak now or from here on keep your advice to yourself. I'm damned if I'll let you keep gnawing at my crew's confidence like some rat from the bilges!"

Tor flushes. Not all of the crew can hear me, and of those that can only a few understand the words.

"I suppose it's no secret that Mr. Torgersen and I have had a disagreement over what course to follow," I say to them, barely giving Per time to translate. "I hereby give him permission to tell you exactly what's on his mind. It will be your decision finally what we do, and you can't make the right one without hearing all the arguments for and against. Now where were we?"

"Do the Mirabelles exist?" Per says.

"They exist," Tor growls finally. "And it's true there were seals there once. But how are we to know they'll be there still—or that we can find them if they are? No one can chart an ice pack—anyone who's ever hunted on them knows that—so we'll be sailing into an area that may have changed twenty times over in the years since the master of this ship tried to mark its location. The chart was put away—not forgotten, but hidden, because Captain Melman, Captain *Johann* Melman, thought it best not to leave it where it might cause mischief or worse for those who might try to follow the same course!"

Per looks up at me questioningly. I nod, and he begins the translation. As he changes from one language to another, small groups of the men begin muttering amongst themselves. It's too soon for me to step in. I must let them have their say. When they quiet down, I turn to Tor again.

"What else?" I ask.

Tor stares at me as if there is indeed more. But something keeps him from telling me. "Isn't that enough?" he asks.

"To keep us from going there?" I reply. "No. We're too far behind the main fleet to get anything but their leavings, which will hardly pay the crew's wages, let alone profits to share in. The way I see it the only choice we have is either to continue on to the Mirabelles, where we have an excellent chance to make ourselves more money than we'll know what to do with, or else return home with empty holds."

Per translates. When he finishes, the seaman who spoke first steps forward again, wiping his clotted nose on an already dirty sleeve. "Begging the captain's pardon, sir, but isn't Mr. Torgersen's point well-took? If the terrain ain't the same as it was and the seals is someplace else, how are we going to find 'em?"

"Where's the smithy?" I demand after Per has translated and there is another murmur amongst the men. A bearded giant, whose face looks as hammered and gray as his anvil, steps out of the crowd. "Can you straighten those 'copter blades?" I ask.

The smithy walks to where the helicopter lies snarled in its twisted restraining cables like a huge insect caught in a web. He runs his hand along a blade bent up against the superstructure.

"It'll take time," he says finally. "But it can be done."

"Once the chopper's fixed," I say, "there's no way the seals can hide!"

The men visibly relax. I'd had the 'copter put aboard at the last minute. I thought that with our late start we

34

might need an advantage in tracking those seals—their population already decimated by pollution and disease—that the main fleet might have missed. Now it seems to have been fortunate in ways I hadn't even considered.

"Any other questions?" I ask. The men shuffle about. But no one speaks. "I take it you're all with me then," I say.

I expect at most a mutter of assent. What I get is a cheer.

"Mr. Torgersen?" I ask, turning to him, hiding my pleasure so as not to offend him needlessly.

"I am against it," Tor says.

"Let it be noted that the first mate is against it," I say to Per, "and let it be further noted that he can state no convincing reason to justify his position."

Per translates. When he finishes, all eyes are upon Tor, waiting for him to challenge if he can. But he looks at me and says nothing.

"Mr. Torgersen," I order then, "double the lookouts. The minute we sight land, have soundings taken on the quarter hour. According to the chart, there's a warm water channel that will lead us straight to the Mirabelles. I don't intend to miss it!"

"Aye, sir," Tor mutters at long last, and I release a soundless breath, relieved and elated to have won this confrontation.

5

THE SHIP SLIDES slow and silent as a predatory shark through the icy waters. When night falls with no sign of land, I send word to have the smithy desist from his labors; that clanging of hammer on anvil as he tries to straighten the helicopter blade echoes in my head, making it difficult to think, making it almost impossible to hear the sonar.

According to the chart stretched over the map table—the only place with illumination in the darkening wheelhouse besides the green radarscope—we ought to be very near the channel. But it is as if we are sailing in a kind of limbo, imprisoned in some chill and airless tomb, like a model ship in a gigantic bottle, plaything of a mischievous god.

Then, as I go for the hundredth time to study that glowing parchment, the clanging stops. In the silence I hear the cricket sonar change its tune. There is a deepening of the ocean floor. I signal the engine room to Full Stop, and followed by the other officers, I step outside and strain to see through the blackness.

The air has become suddenly warm. I unbutton my parka. Gradually, to the northeast, the sky is whitening with the rising moon.

No one speaks. We stand for long minutes that turn into hours, scarcely breathing, sensing that the land is there just ahead but unable to make out so much as a shadow to confirm it.

I order Slow Ahead. Again the screw begins its uneven

churn. The lookouts are on extra alert, but after the moon goes down and the stars disappear we are not able to see more than a few yards in any direction. Only the pinging sonar tells us that we are on course.

A fine mist begins to envelop the ship. Beads of moisture form on the rigging but do not freeze because of the balmy air, probably a result of currents heated by springs pouring from deep inside the fiery core of the earth.

When daylight finally comes, we realize that we are sailing into a striated bank of fog that lies stacked on the horizon like layers of fuzzy wool blankets, covering the islands that I am now certain lie directly ahead.

Excitedly, I order Dead Stop. In the ringing silence, I can hear a distant cracking that I identify as warming ice. Then, faintly, there is something else: a chorus of barking, as if a thousand dogs are on the loose and hungry.

"Seal pups," the forward lookout says, as I scramble up the rigging to hang, out of breath, alongside where he stands on the platform. "Sounds like a good crop." His wolf-pale eyes, under brows bleached by salt and sun, glitter with feral delight.

I lift my binoculars, and from this vantage point high above the deck I have a gull's eye view of our surroundings. At first the fog seems impenetrable, with what can be seen of sea and sky blending one into the other until my brain giddies with approaching vertigo.

Then directly ahead something stirs. It is as if some undersea leviathan exhales, and the fog rolls away like thistledown. A corridor opens before us. The channel! I think, terribly excited, as I become aware of the ice pack stretching into the nothingness on either side.

"Ahoy, there, Captain!" Tor hails from the deck below. "We're losing way and drifting. Shall I take the wheel?"

"Signal Slow Ahead," I call down. "Relay my directions to the helmsman."

"You're not thinking to steer the passage from there?" Tor protests.

"Keep the soundings continuous," I go on, ignoring the question. "If that chart's accurate, we're on a direct line to the harbor."

"Slow Ahead!" comes the call finally from below.

As we nose into a channel so narrow we can almost touch the banks on either side, mist continues to steam up from the water. The ice is thicker than I have anticipated, and it is covered with snowdrifts shaped by the wind into patterns like ancient hieroglyphs. Their message, if there is one, is indecipherable.

"Mark, three fathoms," a high, clear voice pipes. It is Per. "Mark," comes his call again, only minutes later. "Three fathoms, but diminishing."

"Two degrees to starboard," I shout below. "Then Very Slow Ahead!"

I hear my correction repeated, however reluctantly, by Tor, and the ship's bow moves precisely down the center of the opening that appears to be parting just for us.

"Two fathoms, five," comes Per's call. "Mark!"

The fog recedes before us as we advance. Vision is limited to our immediate surroundings. Suddenly I smell flowers. Those harsh and oily odors we carry always with us are sweetened as if by perfume. Something is blooming beyond the fog, though it is the dead of winter!

The only sounds, besides Per singing out the slowly diminishing depths and my occasional course corrections repeated by Tor, are the intermittent throb of our engines and the hiss of water along our steel bow. The crew, crowding the rails, remain silent, listening hard for that earlier barking. But that distant herd is hushed, as if in fearful anticipation of what is in store.

Appearing ahead of us now are platforms of ice broken

off from the main pack, which are too small to impede our progress. But the occasional shuddering impact as one bounces off our hull gives notice of how dangerous a larger one could be.

Almost imperceptibly, the channel begins to narrow. The fog no longer retreats but drifts over the forward decks, clammy tendrils flagging the masts. The ship's horn sounds—ordered by Tor, no doubt—and that deep groan, like a beast in agony, rolls into the fog, becoming accentuated and diminished as it is swallowed and then echoed back, alternately muffled and roaring, as if a dozen other beasts, hidden by hill and valley, bellow in sympathy.

The lookout and I hold our ears against the baying chorus. "Shut that damn thing off!" I shout below, making a funnel out of my hands. "You want to frighten the islanders out of their wits?"

In the reverberating silence that follows I feel, rather than hear, a muffled humming, a vibration that makes the ship sing. Focusing my binoculars ahead, I make out that our bow is rolling up a thin crust that now sheets the waters.

As the crust thickens, we begin squeezing it into crystalline patterns. Then a shriek like metal against glass signifies that the ice is shattering.

"Send lookouts forward!" I cry, quickly deciding against signaling Full Stop or Reverse Engines, wanting our momentum to carry the ship forward as far as it will go into the pack, hoping to get as close as possible to where I imagine the herd to be.

Tor himself runs to the bow, squinting over the rail. "Back off!" he yells. "If you wedge in too tight, we'll have the devil's own time getting out!"

"Full Ahead, dammit!" I cry.

Tor looks up, face blazing. But he repeats my command.

We wedge into the ice until it seems the bow must crumple under the strain and the shuddering engines shake the hull apart. The crew grab onto the rails, fearing the worst. The officers gather below, staring up at me entreatingly. When I am certain we can go no further, I give the order for Full Stop.

We are dead in the water. The silence is profound. My ears ringing, I begin descending the mast. I am halfway down when a bell begins tolling faintly in the distance. Hanging onto the rigging with one hand, I shield my eyes with the other, trying to make out from which direction that sound comes.

Somewhere above the fog the sun burns, its blue-cold light diffused throughout the thinning mist. Gradually, the contour of the land locked in by the ice pack shapes itself, craggy snow-shrouded ridges looking like ghostly spines of fossilized dinosaurs frozen in some primeval muck.

A white mountain gradually forms, like a slow developing photo negative shimmering in its bath. Here and there along the snow-covered slopes a ray picks up a glitter, as if some baleful eye regards us.

I shiver, though the day is increasingly warm, uneasy about how fanciful my thoughts have become. My disquiet is not helped by what sounds like distant cries of surprise and . . . something else I can't quite identify. Whatever it is makes my blood run cold.

Looping one arm through the webbing to hold myself, I lift my binoculars and focus on the mountain. Deep in its snowy foothills I make out a few traces of a bluish gray color, which I presently identify as smoke blending into the fog, trailing upward from round chimneys rising above the thatched roofs of crude huts. The smoke is so still the scene resembles a watercolor faded by time. Is anything alive there?

Then, in a clearing that I make out to be a kind of

village square opposite a church steeple, I see a number of figures. As I strain to see, wondering if they are alive, they begin moving, as if the sun has heated frozen limbs, breathing life into cold lungs, enabling them to start walking down the slopes in our direction.

Because of some trick of the diffused light, they seem to walk on air, wavering shadows without substance.

"Prepare to receive visitors," I holler, keeping my glasses on them.

The illusion persists that they are otherworldly. At this distance it is hard to make out individual characteristics. All are dressed somewhat alike in wool knit caps, greatcoats, and a kind of rubber boot laced to the knee. The color of their clothing is gray, as if the raw wool from which their crude garments are knitted has never been dyed. The one exception is a slim youth in the lead, whose knitted cap's tassle, a brilliant red, bobs cheerfully as its owner steps as if dancing along the crusted drifts, reaching back occasionally to take the hand of the person just behind, an older man whose footing is not as secure.

Someone else has climbed the rigging and is now beside me. Tor. He stares into the distance as if he has no need of glasses to know who is there.

"It might be best if I take a party overland to intercept them," Tor says.

"No," I say. "Let them come aboard and see that we mean them no harm."

"I have the opposite concern," Tor says.

"Are you saying we have reason to fear them?" I demand. Tor does not respond. "As far as I can tell, they're unarmed," I go on, looking through the glasses again. "I'd think they'd welcome visitors, being so remote and out of touch." Still Tor says nothing. "In any case," I say, "I want nothing from them but a little cooperation. They shouldn't object to that, especially if I pay them for it."

"Don't be surprised if they do," Tor growls. And he descends, his gnarled hands, unsure of their grip, making his progress painfully slow.

I take one last look at the approaching islanders, then slide down the rigging myself, passing him on the way, jumping the last ten feet to the deck.

"You, there, on the starboard rail," I shout, "put out that cigarette and throw a ladder over the side!" The sailor in the stained greatcoat looks around angrily to see who is talking, then hastily pinches out his smoke, puts the butt behind his ear, and pulls the rope ladder from its locker. "Where's Cook?" I demand of the others.

After a relay of commands an unshaven fellow appears out of the galley hatch. "Throw out that bitter tea you've been serving," I order. "Make fresh—and sweeten it with a ration of rum. Here're the keys." I toss him those that fit the liquor cabinet. The faces of the men brighten; some rub their hands. "Just a minute," I say to the cook before he can go. "The rum's measured, no tricks with it. And the next time I see you I hope you'll be wearing a cleaner apron."

He manages a salute and disappears into the galley. My look suffices to quiet the laughter; I take up my vigil at the rail again.

Our visitors have reached the flat expanse of ice and are moving much more surely. The youth with the tassel cap has dropped back to walk with his older companion, whose step is still uncertain. As they draw nearer, I see that all the men have shaggy, iron gray beards, whether from frost or age I'm not sure.

Some yards from the ship the ragged procession halts. The youth and the older man advance under our bow to where the ice has accordioned into a barrier of broken slabs.

"Ahoy, below!" I shout. "Climb the ladder up—we're preparing hot tea sweetened with rum for you!"

The old man stares up at me, eyes as silvered with age as old coins. The furrows in his face seem to match the rough terrain, and with an untidy beard coarse as steel wool he seems a caricature of an ancient prophet, sculpted by a god with unsteady hands.

"Who are you?" he shouts back in a voice like muted thunder.

"Melman, captain of the *Seljegeren*," I reply.

"Melman?" the old man rumbles, as if deep within him volcanic memory surges. He reaches out with both hands to touch the ship's side. Ungloved hands finger the raised emblem of the ship's name a letter at a time.

Is he blind? I wonder, and have my answer as the slim youth guides him to the ladder.

Once climbing, the old man does not falter. When he reaches the rail, I take his arm and help him down to the deck.

"Melman?" he repeats, as the youth follows him over.

"Captain of the *Seljegeren*," I confirm, "out of Spitsbergen and Boston."

"You dare to return?" he demands, so full of shock and dismay that I take a step back.

I look to Tor, but he seems as suddenly sightless, staring with eyes turned to stone. Then the old man raises his hands. He explores my features—and I can feel his anxiety through his trembling fingers.

"You've remained young, Johann," he says, like an accusation. "You've been cursed with eternal youth. At least I shall die in my allotted span and go to hell, where I belong, to expiate my sins!"

"I'm not Johann," I say. "I'm Jason, Johann's son."

"That can't be," he says after a long moment, breathing so heavily a crystallized vapor comes from his mouth. "Unless he's dead and lives now in you—yes, I feel him in you!"

My skin tightens as if my bones are suddenly too big for my body. "He's alive," I say. "But too sick to make the journey."

"And he sent you here in his place?" the old man asks incredulously. "That will not do—he cannot sacrifice you for his sins—"

"He doesn't intend to," Tor interrupts harshly. "An ill wind blew us here."

The old man turns his head in Tor's direction. "I know that voice," he says. But Tor remains silent.

The cook comes out from the galley then, staggering under the weight of the iron pot. He sets it on a nearby hatch and begins ladling steaming brew into tin mugs. I press the first one into the old man's hand.

"Ah, I can smell tropic palms, cocoanuts, and mangoes," he says, passing the mug under his flaring nostrils and inhaling deeply. "How long since I've tasted island rum?"

"More years than I am alive, father," the youth says, and I realize by those uncommonly delicate treble tones that she is female, probably little more than fourteen, young to have been fathered by him.

"Invite your friends aboard," I say, as he savors the first swallow. "There's plenty for all."

"They've recognized this ship," he says, swallowing again. "They'll stay where they are."

"I'll send some down then," I say, determined to do whatever's necessary to win these peculiar islanders over. "You there," I say to several of the crew who have been edging in to hear what the old man is saying, "help Cook get tea to those people on the ice!"

While they hook a rope to the pot's handle and lower it over the side, I turn back to our visitors. "I'll offer shares to any of your people who'll help us hunt," I say.

"There's no hunting here," the old man says. "Weren't you told that?" His anger is sudden and deep.

"Isn't that sealskin?" I demand, pointing to the coat the girl is wearing. Then remembering he can't see, I go on: "The coat your daughter's wearing—it's seal, isn't it?"

"My daughter?" the old man asks. His face clears. "Ah, yes, Nicole," he says. "I suppose she is, in a way."

"The good Father found me wrapped in this coat as a baby," Nicole interrupts sweetly, so free of resentment or self-pity my heart goes out to her. She shrugs deeper into the shiny garment, hugging it to herself. "My mother made sure I'd be warm."

"It's time we went back," the old man says sharply.

"You're welcome to stay for supper, Father," I say, for the moment putting aside my curiosity about this foundling child.

"You'd be well advised to leave before then," he says.

"We've come here for the seals," I say.

"Go someplace else," he says.

"Too late for that," I say. "This is our only chance to fill our holds before the season ends."

"There's no season for hunting here," he says.

"We have a license from the Canadian government," I say.

"You'll need a higher authority," he says. "Come, *ma petite,* show me the way back," he says to Nicole, draining his tea. She takes the mug from him, handing it to the hovering cook with a heartbreakingly innocent smile.

"But they hunted here once," I protest as she leads the old man toward the rail.

"That was before . . ." he begins, and falls silent.

"Before what?" I say, encouraging him to continue.

"Ask your father that," he says, and puts a leg over the side.

"Our radio was damaged in the storm, or I would," I say, increasingly annoyed with this stubborn old man. "Why are you being so closemouthed?"

He stares at something only he can see. "Though I've left the church," he says, "I'm still bound by my vows to remain silent."

He looks up, his eyes reflecting the cold sun. Then he crosses himself, and before I can ask anything more he has descended swiftly, followed by the girl, to join his companions on the ice below.

6

I watch our visitors move out of sight, the revelation of that sightless old priest's abandoned vocation somehow disquieting. A glance around at those of the crew within earshot tells me that they are undergoing a similar unease.

I instruct the cook to serve an early and heavy lunch, hoping to distract them from contemplating the priest's curious words, and hasten below to examine the ship's log. Maybe there I will discover what may have occurred during the *Seljegeren*'s last voyage here.

Eventually, in the cupboards over the master's bunk, I find a bound journal dealing with the year in question. Blowing a quarter century's dust off the cover, I thumb through yellowing pages with growing anticipation—and discover that an entire month is blank!

I send for Tor. I show him the log, opened to the appropriate place. "There are no entries for the last time the *Seljegeren* came to these islands!" I point out.

"Captain Melman was sick for a spell," Tor shrugs.

"What kind of sickness would so incapacitate him that he couldn't fill in his logs?" I ask skeptically. "A drunken fit? A bad fall?"

"He ran a fever," Tor says, as if I've dragged the words from him.

"Why didn't you make the entries then?" I ask.

"He never let anyone touch the logs but himself," Tor reminds me.

"Surely he would have wanted to bring the log up-to-date after he got well?" I ask.

Tor considers this for so long I wonder if I have to ask the question again. Then: "Perhaps he suffered a memory lapse," Tor says. "After the fever broke and he started making entries again he just skipped the days he didn't remember."

"But you remember them?" I ask.

Tor does not reply, and I can see his eyes darkening, as if shades are being lowered inside. I am pressing him too hard to tell me what my father wouldn't. His unwillingness to cooperate, however, whether from loyalty to my father or not, makes me irritable. "Get a small hunting party together," I suddenly say. "I'll be up in a few minutes to take them out on the ice."

Tor has not expected this. "You told your father I was to be in charge of the hunt!" he protests.

"You will be," I say. "Later. All I intend to do now is reconnoiter the terrain."

"But you haven't been out on the ice before," Tor points out. "You don't know the dangers. With all this snow covering the pack only a trained eye can guess where it might be thin enough to break—I've seen men pulled out after only a few minutes in this water with their blood frozen solid!"

"I appreciate your concern," I say, repressing a shiver. "I'd take you, but I can't trust anyone else with the ship. Of the other officers, would you say Knut has the best eye?"

Tor stares as if confused by my expressing confidence in him while simultaneously continuing to ignore his advice. For a moment I think he is about to break down and tell me what I am so anxious to know. But the moment passes, and with an indistinct mutter he goes above to do my bidding.

As for me, I can barely contain my excitement at the

prospect of finally locating the seal herd. I hurriedly dress and arrive on deck to find Knut and two crewmen already gathered by the ladder, waiting. I am surprised that one of the men is the pale, rabbit-eyed Per.

"He's got to learn sometime," Knut says, bending to make sure the younger man's leggings are laced tight enough to keep the snow out. "If we wait for the hunt, everyone's too busy to show him, and a clumsy hand can cause everyone trouble."

Per tries to smile, and I have to turn away from his look, which is beseeching me to forbid him to go. Though I sympathize, I don't want to lessen Knut's enthusiasm.

The third man, a dour sort with a frost-reddened face peeling under a week's growth of beard, is carrying the sealer's instrument of death: a short-poled gaff called a *hakapik,* with a leaded weight on one end and a hook on the other.

"Why are you taking that?" I ask.

The man looks surprised.

"Helmut's our best gaffer," Knut beams. "I've asked him to show Per how—and you too, Captain, if you like."

"If we have time," I agree. "But I'm more interested in seeing how difficult it's going to be to flush the seals out where we can get at them."

Helmut nods, but he watches me with the intensity of some scavenger bird. There's something unpleasant about his eagerness. But I understand how necessary his expertise is, and I turn, leading the way over the rail and down the swaying rope ladder to the ice pack below.

Above, the crew pauses to watch us disembark. Tor scathes us with a sidelong glance, then shouts at the men to get on with their tasks. Once on the ice pack, I stand aside to give Knut the lead, followed by Per and then Helmut, allowing me to bring up the rear.

As soon as we leave the area of the ship, our boots

digging into the thick-packed snow, a cloud, drifting seemingly out of nowhere, slowly obscures the sun, bringing a chill to the air that frosts our lungs, reminding us that winter is not yet over.

The fog, which has been steadily retreating all morning, ceases its upward drift, shrouding the mountain peak in veils of mourning. The reflected light pinks the snow, making that icy sheen as transparent as flesh through which blood courses. The landscape is lunar, like some cold planet seen once a generation through telescopes, a setting for nightmares.

Knut sets a rapid pace. Even with nail-studded boots, it is difficult to keep our footing, particularly on the gleaming patches of ice swept bare by wind. Soon our exertions, made even more strenuous by the weight of the survival gear we carry, mists our yellow-tinted goggles. Behind us the sounds of the ship's activities become fainter, even the smithy's clanging sledge reduced to the merest echo.

When we finally stop for breath and look back, the *Seljegeren* seems a toy, and the radio mast, being raised as we watch, looks the size of a matchstick.

Overhead the cloud cover is becoming slowly discolored; following the growing stain back and down, we see that its source is smoke issuing from chimneys above huts clustered on a distant plateau. Whatever it is they burn produces oily soot; we can see traces of it on the snow.

Knut takes us then at an angle that leads away from the village toward the mountain of ice, its long valleys sliding deeper into shadow as we approach. Somewhere below are the breeding grounds.

We stop again. I pull up my field glasses, scanning the snowy contours of the mountain up to where mist shrouds the peak. As I focus in on that majestic stillness I wonder yet again what that snowy curtain might be hiding. I feel as if some omnipotent presence may be there, guarding the lair of the gods, and I remember with a shiver the book of Norse stories my father sent me on my third birthday, which I begged my nanny to read to me over and over until I had committed them to heart.

I tell myself these are childish fancies and am about to lower my glasses when something above the tree line, where the air is too thin to sustain life, stirs!

But when I look again, trying to bring whatever disturbed that hanging mist into focus, I can see nothing. Only when my eyes blur with the effort do I give it up. Perhaps a shadow has moved with a shifting cloud.

"Any sign of them, sir?" Per wonders. He is watching me with something more than curiosity; that tightness in his throat matches my own.

"Not a trace," I say shortly. "Let's move on."

"They're there alright," Helmut says, beady eyes glittering. "I can smell them."

Three other pairs of nostrils flare as the rest of us try to catch a whiff of whatever has excited the blood lust in Helmut. But our noses have been desensitized by the cold; perhaps the snuff Helmut continually packs up his, staining the nasal hairs but keeping the passages hot, has given him the advantage.

Helmut beams at our skepticism and takes over the lead at a nod from Knut. He changes our direction slightly, aiming for a snowy incline that rises between two jagged outcroppings. As we come closer those icy pillars seem to grow and thicken, finally looming overhead so awesomely they appear to be gates to some frozen paradise.

Underfoot the snow deepens, muffling our nail-clattering footsteps until the only sound in this gleaming wilderness is the susurration of our laboring breaths.

The pitch steepens as the incline narrows. Entering the shadow of the outcroppings, we step onto snow that

51

is frozen solid. We clasp hands to keep from falling, balancing one on another, occasionally clutching at the icy rock on either side of the trail.

And suddenly we are there. One moment we are struggling our way up, skidding against the rock; the next we are standing on a flattened ledge, staring through frosted pillars at a shallow ice pan that seems to flow for miles into, around, and through a series of low-lying, snow-covered hills that end at the open sea—a limitless sea stretching to the horizon, cold, gray and foreboding.

The sounds of our climbing die in diminishing whispers. Our breath steams for a time in small puffs, until that too evaporates; I wonder if the others feel the same anguish I do at its passing, the only evidence that anything here is alive, including ourselves.

This is how it must have been before time began.

The silence is deafening, an earaching silence that freezes the soul, signifying an icy wasteland in which nothing can live.

And yet—I become convinced that while we watch, something watches us. I feel hidden eyes upon us. I stir uneasily, not knowing what to do next.

Then an errant ray of sun pierces the cloud cover. And with it the expanse of ice beneath us sparkles as if inlaid with gems, millions of them, blue-white as fire. The shadows flee the sun and we see what we have been searching for.

They are stiff as sculpture carved from rock.

They seem not even to breathe. In another moment or two, if they remain still enough, they dare to hope that we, the intruders, will go away.

I know this as if I am there on the ledges with them. The part of me that remains at the pillars slowly raises the glasses, careful not to make too abrupt a move.

Only the eyes show life. However unblinking, those liquid brown eyes, fringed with lashes so long and curling they would be envied by coquettes, gleam with a fear so numbing my own heart aches.

I cannot hold any glance long. We look by turns deep into each other's souls—and whatever they see in mine gives them cause for dismay. I begin to count under my breath: two there, four here, a grouping of seven, ten, a cluster of twelve, twenty—hundreds, more than a thousand are gathered in what has been, and is no longer, a sanctuary.

My vision blurs. I harden my heart against whatever foolish and errant emotion is surfacing in me.

I remember a hunt for squirrel in the autumn ravine back of a friend's country home. How easily we slipped into its silence, carrying gleaming-barreled .22-caliber rifles, and stopped, listening for our quarry. A shrill chattering made his presence known. We spotted the flared brush of the squirrel's tail as he scolded us before skidding down the trunk and racing through the underbrush.

With a whoop and holler we were after him, the snapping of dead branches underfoot speeding the squirrel's flight. We treed him in a huge walnut. Though my friend offered me the shot, I pantomimed that I was out of breath, and he fired. The stilled creature plummeted down. The shot had been perfect, just in front of the furred ear, giving him what seemed a third eye.

We spotted another and the chase was on again. This time it was my shot. I put his tiny furrowed skull into the V-notch of my sights. Just as I went to squeeze the trigger, however, he complained bitterly, and the rifle moved as I fired.

Though he dropped like the other, bouncing off the leaf-strewn turf, he was still alive when we stood over him, continuing to scold me weakly.

"Finish him off," my friend said.

I tasted my breakfast, swallowed, shot, and shot once

more before the creature was stilled. My friend kicked the torn squirrel aside. I wanted to bury it, but the ground was like stone. Next time, I told myself, I would not flinch. But of course the next time had been off the coast of Lebanon, and my flinch, even at second-hand, had been felt all the way back to Washington.

"Captain Melman?" comes Knut's voice. I don't know how many times he has called.

"Yes?" I respond, clearing my throat, though not my memory, of this unwanted emotion.

"Those pelts are glorious," Knut says, and I am startled that so seemingly rough a seaman would use such a word. "Shall we take a sample or two?"

I refocus my glasses. I'm about to give Knut the order he seeks, when something in the midst of that immobile herd stirs with my own thought. I think I see a shimmer of color pass through the transfixed congregation. And those fear-stilled hearts immediately pulse as one!

The hills slide into motion. Skidding down the slopes, caroming one off another, bouncing in their haste like giant golden and white rubber balls, accompanied by yelpings and barkings and outcries so plaintive I have to stifle an answering cry in my own chest, the seals stampede along the ice toward the sea, rank upon rank upon rank of furred bodies scrambling in furious, headlong flight.

We are transfixed, unable to move. It seems an interminable distance to the water, but soon enough the first slithering bodies tumble in, sending up giant curtains of spray shredded as lace—and still the ice all the way back to the moving hills remains crowded.

Knut is the first to shake himself out of his trance. Reaching out for the *hakapik* that Helmut leans on, Knut kicks one end up and closes Per's hand around the handle. "Take him out to get one," he orders Helmut. "He can't miss in that crowd!"

Helmut shows stained teeth in a fearsome grin. Per looks to me, his pale eyes imploring, believing that we are kin, that whatever troubles him troubles me also. But I'm as impassive to his plea as the glacier whose shadow we stand in.

"Go on!" I cry, and Helmut yanks his end of the *hakapik,* pulling the stumbling Per down the slope.

Drawing in a sobbing breath in which grief and rage are intermingled, Per is forced to run, Helmut's nailed boots kicking up gouts of ice as they reach the flat, racing after the fleeing herd.

A number of seals, suddenly aware of danger, stop their headlong flight. Old patriarchs, lowing like bulls, flop into a half circle, tusks gleaming as they prepare to do battle. Mothers fling themselves on those pups unable to reach the water, protecting them with their own bodies.

Veering away from the roaring bulls, Helmut sprints toward a group of pups, last down from the frozen hills, now floundering, flippers scrabbling for purchase on the ice as they try to get away. One in particular is having a great deal of trouble; will he be able to swim if he reaches the water?

As he sees the pup falling behind the others, Helmut swerves again, digging in, bringing the lagging Per up even with him. Releasing the *hakapik,* Helmut shoves the pale young man onward, forcing him to run against the flow of the stampeding herd.

Per raises the *hakapik* shoulder high. I suck in my breath, fighting back an aberrant feeling that urges me to signal Per to stop. I will not disappoint my father.

A sudden blur fogs my glasses. I cannot be sure what is happening. Per comes up to the furry creature at a dead run, ready to strike in full stride. The *hakapik* swings forward—then stops in midair as if encountering a hidden barrier! Has Per had second thoughts midway through that deadly arc?

Per skids to a stop. As my glasses clear I make out the bewilderment on his face, as if he's unsure what has taken place. The seal pup continues by him in a frantic slither.

For a moment longer Per stands motionless; then, at a hoarsely encouraging cry from Helmut, he wheels and goes after the pup again.

It's unclear what causes him to trip. The snow pack seems smooth. But Per suddenly breaks stride, flails wildly about in an effort to keep his balance, then goes off in one direction while the *hakapik* goes flying in another. He hits the ice with so much force it seems almost as if he throws himself down out of terrible frustration and anger. That deadly crump, heard even at this distance, makes me wince, as if the pain is in my own bones.

The blur of color in my glasses I attribute to the intensity of my gaze and the turbulent emotions that threaten to overwhelm me. Blinking hard, I push by the open-mouthed Knut and go plunging down the slippery incline. The nail-studded boots squeal as I dig in, running now full out, not slowing as I pass the startled Helmut, decelerating only as I approach the fallen Per, wary of tripping on whatever it is that has flung him down.

But I see nothing: the ice is smooth, polished flat by the wind; if some obstacle has tripped him it has been kicked away. Far down the ice, the young seal gives a triumphant bark before plunging into the water—where a mother surfaces to guide him away.

Per is unconscious. His arms are above his head, and one of his legs is doubled under him. He looks more than ever as if drained of blood. I lift a lid; his pale eye is blank. I am wiping his pallid forehead with snow when Knut and Helmut arrive out of breath.

"Careful with his leg," I say. "It's probably broken."

While I lift Per at the waist, Knut cushions his head, and Helmut straightens the bent limb. Per cries out and comes to. But he looks at us as if we are strangers.

"You clumsy fool," Knut rages, using anger to cover his distress, "how did you manage to do this to yourself?"

"She tripped me," Per moans.

"She?" wonders Helmut.

"You tripped over your own feet!" Knut cries. "I shouldn't have let you come out on the ice!"

"Possibly his hair got in his eyes," Helmut says, twisting Per's long white hair in his gloved fist—the hair that the other crew members laugh at, privately, out of Knut's hearing.

"She tripped me," Per repeats. "Spit in my face and threw me down."

"She?" Helmut asks again, looking all around.

"He's not making sense," I say. "I'm afraid he's had a concussion."

"Maybe he ran into a sticky patch," Helmut suggests.

We all look. But our boots have chewed the ice for several feet in every direction. If there had been a rough patch it is impossible to tell now.

"It's my fault," Knut says, grieving. "It's against his nature to kill."

"We'll have to splint his leg," I say, wondering at this sensitivity in the burly Knut, made uneasy by what seems a mockery of the reason we are here. "Where's his *hakapik?* See if you can find it, Helmut." I look to the ship, then to the village: they seem equidistant. "I wonder if they have a doctor here?" I ask.

"You think his head is broken too?" Knut mourns.

I kneel by Per, brush his long hair back, looking for blood or bruises. There are none. But his eyes still seem crazed, and I shiver.

"That was a nasty fall," I say. "I can't see any damage, but the impact may have twisted his neck, put pressure on his brain that we can't see. It'll be best if we can find a doctor."

Helmut, who has been tramping the snow-sheeted ice in ever-widening half circles, is now a distance away. Suddenly he cries out, and plunging his hand into a small drift, pulls something up. It's the *hakapik,* broken in two.

"He threw it away," Knut says, justifying his earlier belief. "He couldn't bring himself to harm the creature."

Per, whose eyes are still unfocused, as if experiencing the recent past, manages to shake his head. "She took it from me," he says.

"It probably broke when he fell," I say to Helmut, who is examining the broken pieces.

"How did it get over there?" Helmut wonders.

"The ice is slick," I point out. "And that pup he was after could have hit it with a flipper."

Helmut does not seem convinced. But since there is no other rational explanation, he hands the broken *hakapik* to Knut, who without another word binds the two pieces on either side of Per's leg.

Taking care not to make any movement that will cause Per additional pain, Knut removes his greatcoat and slides it gently under him. Then using the coat as a makeshift stretcher, he stands at one end while Helmut and I take the other, and we begin carrying Per toward the village.

The going is slow and arduous. We stop frequently to rest, the journey made no easier by Per's incoherent babblings.

"Tell her I didn't mean any harm," Per keeps saying, over and over. "Tell her not to be angry."

"What's he talking about?" asks a worried Helmut, looking back the way we've come. "He acts as if someone's on the ice with us!"

58

"He's hallucinating," I say shortly, and I pour the remainder of our ration of brandy between the feverish Per's moving lips, hoping to silence him. His ravings make no sense, but he talks with such certainty that it makes all of us uneasy, as if something only he can see is actually there.

Long before we arrive at the village, dark figures begin gathering on the frozen hillsides to observe our progress.

"Why don't they come give us a hand?" I rage, unwilling to believe there can be people, even in so inhospitable a clime, without compassion.

Only when we are within hailing distance does that silent gathering stir; then a familiar figure appears and speaks a few words in a brutal dialect, and immediately a number of the islanders start forward to meet us, the ex-priest and his young guide in the lead.

"He fell and may be badly hurt," I say as they approach, still angry that help has not arrived sooner. "I hope you have a doctor here?"

"I do whatever doctoring's necessary," the ex-priest says.

"Father Delmain has performed miracles," Nicole says, motioning for us to put our burden down.

"Only saints and the blessed perform miracles," Father Delmain says sharply, but he allows Nicole to place his hands on the still-muttering Per's leg.

We watch in silence as he carefully explores Per's ankle and calf. Suddenly he stops, frowning, then sidles toward Per's face, putting his ear next to Per's lips.

"He may have a concussion, too," I say. "He's been hallucinating ever since he fell."

"Hallucinating?" Delmain demands, turning his face toward me.

"Says someone tripped him," Helmut offers, shaking his head, though he watches the blind ex-priest carefully. "And none of us within a hundred yards of him."

Delmain's hands go back to Per's leg and find the metal end of the *hakapik*. "I warned you not to try hunting here!" he whispers.

"It's my fault, Father," Knut says. "I wanted him to have the first kill."

Per stirs and moans. "She tripped me," he says.

"Mirabelle," Nicole says, her voice clear as the ringing of a chime.

"Mirabelle?" I ask.

"Ne le dis!" Delmain says, but she is already answering me.

"She is our guardian angel," Nicole says, speaking an English so perfect it must have been learned from a book. "Nothing can harm our seals while Mirabelle is present."

Delmain has his finger at her lips, too late.

"An angel?" Helmut mutters worriedly.

"A spirit," Nicole says.

"Let it be," I order Helmut. "You know there was nothing there—she's a fanciful child. Isn't that right, Father?"

Delmain turns his sightless eyes on me, but he's looking deep inside himself.

"Isn't that right, Father?" I repeat. "You were once a man of the cloth—surely you don't believe in spirits?"

Delmain seems to shrink inside his heavy garments, feeling at his chest for the cross that once hung there.

"As you say," he mutters at last. "It's a local superstition. A folk tale, nothing more."

7

PER SCREAMS AS Father Delmain snaps his leg back into place, then passes out while the broken parts of the *hakapik* are used as a splint.

"It will be best if we take him to the village," Father Delmain says. "The ship is farther away, and if he comes to before you get him there the pain may be unendurable."

"You have medicine for pain in your village?" I ask, feeling the sweat on my own brow turn cold as Nicole wipes the moisture off Per's.

"Tea," Nicole says.

I am about to protest when Delmain interjects. "It is a special tea, more soporific than any painkiller," he says.

I hesitate; then, as Per moans, I tell Knut to go back to the *Seljegeren,* instructing him to say nothing more than that Per has suffered an accident and we are taking him to the village for medical care.

Knut would have preferred that I send Helmut, but I am afraid that the talkative seaman would soon have our unlettered crew in turmoil over Per's hallucinations. Knut has had enough education himself to squeeze any superstitions out of his speech, and he understands that if our hunt is to succeed we must keep such disturbing fancies away from the men.

"And say nothing about this to any of the officers, either," I add.

"Not even Tor?" the startled Knut asks.

"It'll be best if he hears it directly from me," I say.

"Tell him only that the men are not to go ashore until I say otherwise."

"Aye, sir," Knut says, though he's puzzled. "He'll want to know when you'll be returning," he says then.

"When I'm certain Per will be alright," I say. And when I've gotten whatever information I can from the villagers, I add to myself.

"Aye, sir," Knut says again, this time touching his cap. He casts a lingering glance at the unconscious Per, then reluctantly starts back toward the ship.

The islanders, at a muttered word from Delmain, lift Per. With Nicole leading the way, and the ex-priest holding on to the makeshift stretcher, we set off toward the village.

Helmut and I bring up the rear. That weathered old hunter is unhappy; he does not like being forced into close proximity to these strange and sullen men, whose sidelong glances, when they think we aren't watching, seem filled with such hatred I feel my stomach turn. At the same time they have difficulty suppressing a kind of malevolent glee at our presence. I am determined to find out why.

The village is at the top of a slope surrounded by a barrier of huge rocks that must have taken an enormous amount of labor to drag into place. What are they guarding themselves against? I wonder. There are no other settlements for thousands of miles, and the newer maps seem to have forgotten this island's existence.

The streets are twisting, narrow, and rutted, barely wide enough for the islanders to carry Per without scraping the walls of the crudely built huts. No pedestrians are about. But inside, behind shuttered windows, I can make out shadowy figures watching us pass.

Ahead of us a broken steeple, as crudely built as the huts, stands under the darkening sky, looking as if some pressure from above has flattened it, perhaps from a thunderbolt during a violent storm—God's fist, my father would say. As we come out of the street into a small square, we see that the church doors have been boarded shut.

"Have your parishioners lost faith too?" I ask Delmain, jogging to catch up.

"Only hope," he replies shortly.

Across the square a hut larger than the others displays a faded sign. The drawing is of a seal balancing a tankard of ale. It is unquestionably the pub. The crushed snow leading to its doorway indicates where the villagers spend much of their time.

The windows are fogged with many breaths; a tattered sleeve wipes a pane clean as we pass, allowing us a momentary glimpse inside. These watchers are not so discreet: they stare at us avidly, with the same mixture of dislike and malevolent delight as the others.

The path leading to the church is virginal, marked only by footsteps leading to a small hut attached by a common wall. Nicole hurries ahead to open the door, and we stoop to enter.

Inside, Nicole is lighting a lantern against the gloom. The furniture consists solely of two chairs and a table; worn sealskins cover the uneven floor. In the smoky flicker of the lantern's oil-soaked wick, what appears to be the only decoration, a rude cross nailed to the rough stone wall, swims into view.

At Nicole's direction, the moaning Per is carried into a bedroom no larger than a monk's cell and placed on a pallet next to a rectangular window through which, against a deepening twilight, the brooding outlines of the glacier are seen.

Again, I feel the prickling at the nape of my neck; something up there is watching our every move. But when I step closer to the pane I see how ridiculous that notion is; nothing can live on that barren, glistening peak.

In the other room, Nicole, ignoring the islanders as they pass through on their way out, is adding what look like peat cakes to the fire in the iron stove; its sides become nearly transparent as the roaring heat changes the metal's color from gray to red.

Delmain, who impatiently acknowledges the last man's *adieu,* is filling a kettle from a bucket with a battered tin dipper. He shuffles to the stove, his right hand measuring its dimensions by feeling the radius of its warmth, then places the kettle precisely in the center of the lid.

"Tea to drink, and the leaves as a compress will soothe the pain," he says.

"Brandy might be better," Helmut suggests, as we hear Per moaning in the next room.

"That too," Delmain agrees. Taking a bottle from a shelf near the stove, he removes the cork with his teeth in a practiced gesture. But when he goes to pour some in a cup only a few drops spill out.

"Oh, *Pere Delmain,"* Nicole bursts out.

"I had trouble sleeping last night," he says defensively.

"I'll go to the pub for more," Helmut says.

"I'll do that," I say. "You stay with Per—when he comes to it might be best for him to see a familiar face."

I wait while Nicole warms a chipped clay pot with water from the now steaming kettle, then spoons in tea leaves from a nearly empty, old-fashioned tin large enough to have supplied them for the winter. She is animated, humming under her breath, excited by the accident and the presence of visitors. Though I am strangely reluctant to leave, I open the outside door, stopping at a word from Delmain.

"Tell them the brandy's for me," he says.

"Otherwise they may give you the bottle they have been saving," Nicole says when I start to protest.

"Hush, child," Delmain says. "There's no chance of that."

"I am no longer a child," Nicole informs him sweetly. "Today the blood came."

Everyone becomes very still; even Per's moaning stops, and Helmut appears in the bedroom doorway, awed as if in the presence of a miracle. Nicole is not embarrassed. Though her cheeks flush, it is with pride.

"I've lost track of the years," Delmain says, his manner suddenly agitated. "Are you now fourteen?"

"Sixteen," Nicole says.

That is late for puberty, I think, probably due to the arctic climate. Seeing Helmut eyeing the woman-child speculatively, I angrily motion him back into the room with Per. Then managing a smile, though I find it difficult to meet her transparently innocent gaze, I go out.

I find myself in a world grown suddenly cold. I hunch into my parka as the air, now the sun is down, bites to the bone. But the sky has kept its light, as if it has absorbed so much during the day that it will remain bright for hours.

In the distance I can see the *Seljegeren*. The broken ice in her wake will set up again with the drop in temperature. I worry about our being locked in and try to reassure myself that the warm day we have experienced is an early harbinger of spring.

At the pub door I hesitate. Through the thick walls I hear muffled voices raised in bibulous song. These dour folk singing? What is the occasion? Delmain has made it clear that he wishes we hadn't come. Maybe he speaks only for himself and not for the others, however much they defer to him in front of outsiders.

Without his intimidating presence maybe I can find out why they're behaving so strangely. What is there about our arrival that pleases them so much? I resolve to have only one drink—I have done without since Boston, and my head is as clear as my purpose—and pushing the heavy door open, I step inside.

They are in the midst of a clumsy, foot-shuffling dance. Old women and old men stamp and clap hands. The women lift ragged skirts above legging-wrapped ankles in a near-parody of coquettishness that the drink stimulates them to remember; while the men, in a great cracking of knee joints and flapping elbows, stoop and hoorah like arthritic roosters over these ancient hens. Around the walls a somewhat younger group—still older than myself by a generation—stamp and clap hands along with the dancers.

The cold enters with me. They become aware of my presence. Gradually the dancing stops and the voices trail off.

In the silence the fire can be heard roaring in a central stove. The air is smoky and stifling hot. The smell from the sweat-soaked clothing is so immediately rank that I come close to gagging. But I shove the door closed and walk without haste to the counter.

"Please don't stop because of me," I say to the room. But they are already walking to the benches around the smoke-stained walls, watching me with an anticipation that makes me uncomfortable. Their eyes, normally as faded as their dreams must be, are now bright with curiosity—and some other emotion decidedly unpleasant.

The pubkeeper, a gaunt man with a tobacco-stained beard that looks as if it has never been trimmed, moves in my direction.

"What are you celebrating?" I ask.

"Why, the return of the *Seljegeren*," he replies, as if surprised that I need to ask.

This confirmation of my suspicions only heightens my uneasiness. I manage a smile, however, and pulling my wallet from an inside pocket, I slap it on the bar. "Then let me contribute to the festivities," I say. "A round for the house."

I am unprepared for the response I get. "I cannot accept your money," the pubkeeper says, pushing my wallet back.

"Why not?" I ask.

He hesitates. A woman as gaunt as the pubkeeper, presumably his wife, joins him, red-faced from the dancing, behind the counter. "It'd be tampering with our luck to take money from such a welcome visitor," she says, forcing a smile. "But we'll certainly pour a round in your honor." She motions impatiently to the crowd, and her husband begins filling the mugs that are thrust at him in response.

"You know who I am?" I ask.

"Master of the *Seljegeren,* isn't that so?" she says. I nod uneasily. "And what's your pleasure, Captain Melman?" she asks.

"In a minute," I say, thinking she must have gotten my name from those who have accompanied the priest to the ship. "First, I have to send Delmain a bottle of brandy.'"

She hesitates, then pulling a ring of keys from her apron, stoops under the counter. A key scrapes in an iron lock. She stands again, holding a bottle without a label and a cap that seems homemade. At her beckoning finger one of the oldest men comes forward.

"Tell the priest this is the last," she says, handing him the bottle.

"I am told you have another, very old," I say.

The pub becomes silent, as if everyone there is afraid to breathe. The man with the brandy, several steps away, stands momentarily still, his head twisted back toward where I wait for an answer.

"Who told you that?" she demands at last.

"Someone mentioned there was a bottle being saved,"

I reply, not wanting to implicate the girl. "No one said why."

Those in the room seem at once relieved and disappointed. She turns and stares at her husband. He responds finally with a shrug. She holds up the key ring, searching through the keys individually, as if not sure what she will do when she finds the one she is seeking. She hesitates again when she gets to it: a key made of brass, of an ornate, ceremonial shape.

Again, she stoops underneath the counter. This time by the sound I am certain that the lock she is turning is rusty.

The bottle she puts on the counter has dust on it so thick the label can barely be read. It is a Napoleon cognac thirty years old, a ceramic seal marking it the choice of kings.

"That's a rare bottle," I say. She nods. "May I buy it?" I ask.

The pub becomes still again.

"It's not for sale," she says shortly.

"It's a shame to let a vintage like that go untasted," I say.

The pubkeeper seems about to speak, then falls silent as a blast of cold chills the room. Helmut stands in the open door, looking about worriedly, then hurries to join me.

"We need that brandy," he says.

"Has Per regained consciousness?" I ask, shamed that I have delayed so long.

"In a manner of speaking," Helmut says. "He can't remember anything about what happened."

"And what kind of happening would that be?" the pubkeeper asks with something more than curiosity.

"An accident," I say shortly. "Not being used to the ice he fell over his own feet. Better get the brandy to him," I tell Helmut.

"Cormac'll do it," the pubkeeper's wife says. "Hop to it, man," she shouts at the islander, that seemingly hypnotized old man who now comes to with a start. Clutching the bottle to his chest, he hurries out the door. "Let your man stay for a drink," she says then.

Helmut licks his cracked lips in anticipation. I haven't the heart to refuse him. And with my attention distracted, she's managed to put that bottle of ancient vintage away. Whatever they've been reluctant and yet eager to tell me has been delayed, at least for the moment.

At my nod, the pubkeeper's wife pulls another bottle from the shelf. Its label has long since peeled, and from it she pours a liquid of a greenish tinge into two battered, egg-sized tin cups. I salute the room and swallow the contents at a gulp—it is brackish as seaweed and sends a gust of heat through my mouth and nostrils that steams my eyes.

Helmut notices nothing out of the ordinary, grinning his pleasure as he too swallows it whole. He taps the cup back in her direction with a blunt finger, raising his thick brows and showing his furred tongue like a dog begging another treat.

I cover the cup before she can pour again. "Give us ale, please," I say.

She shrugs and pours two mugs full of a thick brown liquid. Helmut lowers his head and sucks in the foam, then grunts appreciatively.

"When you've finished that, go back to Per," I say, and swallow a draught of the warm brew, which is bitter yet refreshing after the other.

Helmut nods, but I can see by his sidelong glance that he's not pleased, and the level in his mug goes down slowly. He's examining the room. "Where's all the young'uns?" he asks. "Late in the day to be fishin', in't?"

"There are no fish," the pubkeeper says.

"The seals have eaten the waters clean for fifty miles in every direction," his wife says.

"Young ones gone to the mainland for livelihood," says Cormac, returning out of breath from the priest's hut, anxious not to miss whatever pleasure the villagers are anticipating.

"The young women too?" Helmut wonders.

"No sense them staying if the young men are gone," the pubkeeper's wife says.

"Would some of these here be widows then?" Helmut asks significantly.

"Some," she says.

"I suppose age don't change a woman's essential nature none," Helmut says, grinning at me as if suggesting that my desires are not all that far removed from his. "If anything, aging might improve it."

"You won't have time to find out," I tell him. "We'll be out on the ice again first thing in the morning."

"You're going to hunt the seals in spite of what happened?" the pubkeeper asks incredulously.

"Why should we let an accident stop us?" I ask, not really expecting an answer.

Then: "It was no accident," a voice hoarse from too many tumblers of the local whiskey says. By following the turning heads I finally see him—a man old before his time, whose head shakes with the tremors of drink, a head with skin so tight the skull underneath can be seen. His hollowed eyes, yellowing and veined, are fixed upon mine.

"I don't know what you heard," I tell him forcefully. "But you mustn't take any of that seriously. The young man who fell has a vivid imagination, and to cover up his own clumsiness he concocted this story about a vindictive spirit . . ."

"No one can harm the seals when she is about," the drinker says, interrupting.

I hear Helmut suck in his breath. "But obviously that's impossible," I say as politely as I can, not wanting to insult the man but knowing that I cannnot allow such a statement to pass unchallenged in front of the superstitious Helmut.

"I was crippled myself on our last hunt here," the drinker tremulously insists. "When I fell and could not get up again she came to me and whispered in my ear— 'Tell everyone to stop the killing or there will be worse to come,' she said."

"She?" I ask, in the hush.

"Mirabelle," the man replies. "Dead as many years as I've been alive. She was pale as the falling snow. But she was there."

"You actually saw her?" Helmut asks, his drink forgotten.

"Aye," the man says. "Though there was a strong wind, and no one could be seen through the blizzard as more than shadows running every which way after the herd, I could make out her scarf—her scarf was as full of color as a rainbow."

"And that's how you know it was her, this Mirabelle?" I ask skeptically, wishing I had sent Helmut away.

"Mirabelle loved color and wove that scarf herself," calls an old woman from a corner of the pub.

"Per insists he heard a voice and saw a flash of color," Helmut reminds me, his eyes growing increasingly wide.

"But the rest of us heard and saw nothing!" I remind him.

"Only those who try to kill the seals ever hear her," Cormac says. "It's a whisper soft as the wind."

"An angel's whisper," an old woman agrees.

Those in the pub mutter knowingly, exasperated at this nonbeliever in their midst. They want to convince me that this improbable story, no doubt embellished with every telling, is true.

Helmut shrinks back against the bar. If I'm going to negate this folk tale's effect, I have to provoke these islanders further. "Why do you call her an angel when she's ruining your livelihood?" I ask.

"She has reason," an old man in the crowd mutters.

"What reason?" I ask.

"She was driven from the village," an old woman behind Cormac says. "Along with her poet."

"Her poet?" I ask.

"A Protestant from the mainland named Macafee," another old woman says, her eyes shining with memory. "He had curly black hair and wore a bead in his ear and played a strange, three-stringed instrument."

"He sang his own verses for bread and a pillow," adds the man beside her.

"All the village lasses were much taken with him," Cormac says with a remembered bitterness.

"So different he was from the tongue-tied, ill-mannered local lads," the old woman behind him agrees.

"But it was Mirabelle who caught his roving eye, and it was Mirabelle who turned his head," the drinker says.

The pub is still, its patrons leaning forward, rapt, as if hearing the story for the first time, as if hoping to come upon some hitherto undisclosed fact that will explain what has remained all these years unexplainable.

"Mirabelle was the village beauty," Cormac goes on. "A foundling child, perhaps left by a visitor from another island, but a flower among weeds, as full of moods as the weather, bright one day and dark the next, her laughter like a running spring, a temper sudden as storm, driving every lad to distraction. The competition for her favor was fierce and unyielding, each convinced he was the one chosen . . . until she asked for help about the seals. Telling us that the slaughter of innocent creatures was a sin against nature. When we refused to give up the hunt she had nothing more to do with us."

"And then the poet came," I say, gripped in spite of myself by this village tale.

"I need something to soothe my throat," the drinker quavers, plucking at his Adam's apple with a hand like a claw.

The pubkeeper pours a full cup, handing it silently over the counter. It is passed from hand to mottled hand until it reaches the drinker, who gulps it down noisily.

"Macafee was penniless and without prospects, a beggar who could offer her nothing," the drinker continues with a rasp. "The Father cautioned her that she risked damnation if she lived with him out of wedlock, for no priest would sanctify their relationship."

"But she would not listen," Cormac adds. "The priest suggested that if Macafee converted to the faith he would be welcomed to the village. Macafee refused. Mirabelle would not let him embrace a faith founded in blood, he said."

"It was not her lack of faith that disturbed the village," an old man interrupts. "It was her condemnation of our ways!"

"And so you took matters into your own hands?" I ask, though not sure I want to hear more.

"We told them they couldn't stay," the drinker finally says, admitting the inadmissible.

"And the priest did nothing?" I demand, surprised at how outraged I am by this ancient wrong.

"He offered them sanctuary in the church," another old woman answers. "But Mirabelle said the outdoors would become their church.

"But where could they go?" I ask, wondering at a commitment strong enough to prevail against such odds.

"It was summer," Cormac says defensively. "They could have gone to the mainland."

"But they did not?" I ask, though I know the answer is bound to distress me.

"They went to the mountain," answers the first old woman, her face suffused with a shame she can never forget.

"The mountain," Helmut repeats, echoing my own awe and dismay.

"And they lived there how long?" I ask, caught up in spite of myself. Whatever happened so many years ago has no doubt been exaggerated over time, becoming so familiar to these villagers that they recite it almost in unison. But for some reason the tale is having as profound an effect upon me as upon the stricken Helmut.

"He did not survive the winter," the old woman answers at last.

An almost unbearable sadness rises in me. What kind of merciless fate would destroy so vital, if foolish, a young man in his prime?

"What did he die of?" I ask, wondering why I insist on pursuing this. This morbid fascination, I tell myself, must be due to the heated, near-stifling atmosphere of the smoky room.

The drinker's head tremor is suddenly worse. Though he wants to tell me, he is having difficulty answering.

"Was he sick?" I ask. "Did he starve or freeze or . . .?"

"There'd been some kind of accident," the pubkeeper says significantly.

"When the priest came back down from the mountain," his wife adds in the waiting silence, "he told the villagers Macafee was dead."

"No one asked him how?" I say incredulously.

"We could not press him then," Cormac says. "He was suffering from snow blindness. Later he said God would make any judgments that needed to be made."

"And you accepted that?" I ask, dismayed.

Cormac shrugs. "How could we not?" he asks in turn. "With the priest never getting his sight back, and the captain taken back to his ship in chains, raving like a madman?"

"The captain?" I ask, stunned, though I know immediately who he is talking about.

"Captain Melman, master of the *Seljegeren*," the pubkeeper's wife says, and I see now that this is what they've been so eager to tell me since I first arrived.

"How was my father—Captain Melman—involved?" I manage at last.

"He'd gone with the priest up the mountain to reason with Macafee, to try to get him to stop interfering with the hunt," Cormac says.

"And what about her?" I ask, struggling to understand what I am being told, and why. "The young woman."

"Mirabelle is still with us, as you have already discovered," the drinker replies.

Those in this crowded, overheated room release their held breaths, sighing as if one.

In spite of myself, I shiver. Though my face is hot as fire, my heart is cold.

8

I BEGIN TO feel lightheaded. I tell myself that it is a combination of the liquor I have drunk and the closeness of the air in the pub, but I know, deep down, in that increasingly remote corner of my soul where no self-delusion is permitted, that learning of my father's involvement in the tragic story that has been recounted here fills me with a sense of foreboding so ominous and dark it makes me giddy. Every fiber of my being warns me to flee this village at once, to set sail and never look back.

Instead, against all my instincts of self-preservation, I take the time to thank the pubkeeper and his wife for their hospitality and the others for telling me what I now wish I hadn't heard, then grab Helmut by the elbow and escort him outside.

"Keep watch with Per," I tell him. "Say nothing to him about the old man's tale. Do not question him further about his accident, leave that to me. If the priest wants to know why I have not returned with you, say only that I have urgent business aboard ship."

Helmut, who is himself trying to come to grips with what we have just heard, makes an effort to concentrate on what I am saying.

"You are going back to the *Seljegeren?*" he asks uncertainly. "By yourself?"

"The path is clear, the ice is thick, and there's a three-quarter moon," I say shortly. "If you're worried about missing the hunt, I'll send a man to relieve you before morning."

"That's alright, sir," Helmut says quickly. "I don't mind staying. I'll be happy to hang about till Per recovers."

I study him for a moment. His grin, usually overbearing and self-confident, is now tentative and ingratiating, and he shuffles nervously in the snow while waiting for my answer. I am right to keep him away from the others, I think. Though he is the *Seljegeren*'s best hunter, we will simply have to make do without him.

"Right," I say, and after waiting to make sure he goes directly to the priest's hut, I plunge down the trail back toward the ship.

I feel the brutal cold only remotely. The alcohol roaring through my veins produces a sufficient, if false, warmth for me to accept the frost against my overheated skin as a welcome relief.

I set a rapid pace—it's as if I'm escaping some terrible fate. Another few minutes in that pub and all might have been lost. I was beginning to accept that which is unacceptable, to think I could understand that which is clearly incomprehensible—in short, I feel that I've come close to losing my mind.

I'm confused as to why. The story the villagers told might be based on fact, but with each telling down through the years it has taken on the reverberations of myth. And to have given up their main source of income because of a superstitious dread is tragic.

But I'm a rational being; why should I believe the unbelievable? I've almost succumbed to mass hysteria . . . there's something about this place—its remoteness, its surrealistic landscape, even the fact that it's close to the magnetic pole—that plays havoc with the mind. Is it only imagination that makes me feel the tidal pulls?

Above me the moon, not quite full and pale as death,

rises from behind the mountain to wash the icescape in an unearthly glow. In the distance I make out the *Seljegeren*, shimmering dreamlike as it seems to float above the ice that actually holds it fast. All about me, while clouds the color of coal scud across the moon, shadows leap out of hiding, ominous as assassins.

I come to an abrupt stop, heart thudding against my rib cage, only to see the shadows disappear like malicious ghosts in a game meant to drive me mad. I am no longer warm. I begin to shiver uncontrollably. I hurry forward, afraid my resolve may weaken and my limbs freeze if I stand too long in one spot. Once before I allowed outside factors to so overwhelm me that a momentary indecision grew into a near-permanent confusion. I do not intend to let it happen again.

What would Eileen make of this? These peculiar islanders attribute present bad luck to the past. It's a collective guilt. They're wasting their lives and the lives of their descendants in senseless atonement.

But why hasn't the priest put them straight? I wonder. What happened to cause him to lose his faith, and what so deranged my father that force had to be used to get him back to his ship?

I'm anxious to confront Tor. He may have the answers I seek. But the *Seljegeren* seems as distant as before, as if I'm not making any headway. Again I increase my pace, swinging my arms high, digging my cleats into the ice to lengthen my stride, my breath clouding with the extra exertion.

Something seems not quite right. The crunch of my boots is out of synch, reaching my ears moments late—as if someone behind matches me stride for stride!

I whirl about. Just for a moment I think I have indeed glimpsed someone—or some*thing*—stalking me, and then I realize, as I release my held breath, that a gleam of moonlight has reflected off a shard of ice before disappearing into the limitless night.

I am absolutely alone in this vast, frozen stillness. I know that. And yet something deep inside myself, beyond rationality, has me convinced that someone is there!

I curse myself for letting nerves get the best of me. I am about to go on when a shift of wind brings a sweetness to my nostrils, like a faded perfume. Somewhere night flowers must be blooming, I tell myself—until I remember that it is hardly spring.

Then faintly, out of the night, I hear a melancholy singing. It comes from the mountain, which by a trick of the uncertain moonlight looms closer, its forested peak glimmering through the frosty haze. The song, unknown to me, is so poignant, so sorrowful, that I can feel my heart close to breaking.

I change course and head in that direction. I am suddenly terribly anxious to find whoever sings so sadly. I am meant to console her, I think, perhaps for all time. Only when a shot rings out, echoing from the *Seljegeren* to the distant peak and ricocheting back, am I startled out of a hypnotic, dreamlike state. I am instantly full of fear. How could I have been overcome so easily?

A blue fire bursts in the starry heavens. The ice, empty for a hundred yards in every direction, is illuminated by a dazzling light.

I hear shouts and make out a cluster of men at the ship's rail. What are they pointing at? Then I see a figure dashing out from behind the *Seljegeren*'s bow, heading full speed toward the glacier! A few men drop hand over hand down knotted ropes to the ice. But whoever is running away is fleet of foot—they'll never catch him.

It's up to me. Without stopping to consider whether the fugitive is armed or not, I'm off and running too, angling to head the other off before the parachuting flare burns out and he disappears forever into the treacherous dark.

I am almost upon him before he becomes aware of my pounding cleats. He isn't expecting a pursuer from this direction. He turns to see who it is—too late. I reach him just as the descending flare hits the ice. In the fading glow I recognize the startled, wide-eyed face of the young radio officer, Nils.

I fling myself at him. He goes down, as do I.

At the impact, the breath is knocked out of both of us. Nils regains his wind first and attempts to squirm from under my weight. I grab his foot as he tries to stand and yank him back down. As we wrestle along the slippery ice he writhes and bucks like some trapped animal, his breath coming in hoarse, agonized sobs.

"Stop it, Nils—this is Captain Melman!" I get out between gasps for air myself. I think he understands, for though he continues to flail about he is not trying to hurt me so much as to get away.

Tor and the party from the ship reach us then. They separate us, none too gently, and pretend surprise when Tor holds the lantern so the sickly light falls upon my face.

"It's the captain. Excuse us, sir," one of the men, a huge Boston black, says, letting go after nearly wrenching my arm from its socket.

But Tor makes no apologies. He meets my glance only briefly before turning to deal with Nils, who is struggling in the grip of two men, an unsavory pair of Greeks whose only English is the profanity they are using on Nils.

Handing his lantern to the black man, Tor goes to Nils, who seems possessed of a lunatic strength, lifting first one and then the other Greek off the ice. After studying him for a moment, Tor hits the young officer with all his might.

Nils slumps. The two Greeks, now grinning, continue to hold him upright.

"What are you doing?" I shout, aghast that Tor would strike someone defenseless.

"He's raving mad," Tor replies, not even looking at me. "I'm trying to shock him back to his senses."

I grab the lantern from the black man, shoulder past Tor, and shine the light on Nils. He is coming to, muttering something I can't understand, staring past us into the shadow-ridden night. Blood on his lip, cracked by Tor's blow, is already congealing in the cold.

"What is it, Nils?" I demand, leaning close. "What's happened? What's troubling you?"

He begins humming under his breath, like a radio transmitter between signals. I make out hints of a melody. A chill that has nothing to do with the cold spreads through my body.

"Where did you learn that, Nils?" I ask. He does not even pause for breath. I grab his unkempt hair, forcing him to look at me. "That song—how do you know it?"

"I heard it," he stammers when his eyes focus at last.

"*Where* did you hear it?" I demand, shaking him.

"The . . . radio," he answers finally.

"You've got the radio working?" I ask, looking at Tor. "Have you gotten in touch with my father?"

"We got the mast up and the power generated," Tor replies. "But there's some kind of magnetic field interfering with the signal—all we can get is static and echoes . . ."

"Echoes?" I repeat.

"Ghost voices . . . singing," Nils says.

"There are distortions at the top end of the band," Tor explains. "He picked up some broadcast signals—"

"She . . . was singing," Nils interrupts.

"He let his imagination run away with him," Tor adds with disgust. "He got scared, said something was pre-

81

venting the transmission—the next thing anyone knows he's over the side and gone!"

But I am hardly listening. I let go of Nils and peer into the moon-bathed darkness in the direction I have come. I am aware of the acoustical tricks this landscape can play. I have heard a song similar to the one Nils hums, without benefit of radio. I had attributed it to my imagination. Was I wrong? Or can the human ear pick up radio waves?

"Listen!" Nils suddenly shouts.

The quiet is broken by a muffled hum I finally identify as coming from the ship's generators. Nils is listening hard, straining up on his toes, head cocked, eyes slanted in the direction of the glacier.

"Don't you hear it?" he demands of his captors, then of me.

For a moment—a brief, unsettling moment—I think I do hear a snatch of the song I heard before, a plaintive melody drifting down from the mountain.

The wind, I tell myself, though the night is still. Up there on that formidable peak the wind soughs through the ice-laden fir branches, the sound floating down to us through some kind of acoustical funnel, made into melody by minds attuned to rationality.

"There!" Nils cries, rocking forward and back as if keeping some ethereal beat. "You hear it, don't you?" And he hums a fragment before holding his breath again.

Everyone looks at everyone else, unwilling to trust the evidence of their own ears, afraid if they admit to having heard anything they will be singled out as unstable or worse. Or is it possible that I am the only one besides Nils who hears anything at all, even on a nonexistent breeze?

Tor is staring at me with an intensity that is unsettling. Does he suspect that I have become irrational too?

"Captain?" Nils is pleading with me, hoping for confirmation, unwilling to be thought mad. "You hear it, don't you?"

"Take him back to the ship," I order, turning away from those beggar's eyes. "Lock him up. We can't chance him harming himself—the poor fellow's out of his mind."

As the men, relieved of their concern that this lonely nightscape might be spawning madness, hurry to do as I order, I put a hand out to detain Tor.

"Let them go ahead," I say. "I have something that needs discussing."

"Aye, Captain," Tor says, freeing himself from my grip. "And I too." He is so tense he seems to vibrate like a mast in a restless sea.

"You first," I say, as we fall in some distance behind the others. "Mine will keep."

"You have noticed the temperature drop?" he demands, and I nod. "It's gotten so cold the channel behind us is freezing up," he says. "Another night like this and we'll be locked in so solid we won't be able to get out for the devil knows how long—I recommend we lift anchor and break out while we still can!"

"We're not leaving till we have our quota of skins," I say.

"No use having them if you can't get them out," Tor says.

"It won't be winter forever," I say, managing to remain calm, though I'm shaken by his vehemence. "Eventually the ice will melt—it always has . . ."

"But you've seen what happened to Per, and now Nils," Tor says. "It could happen to any of us, even you!" We have stopped and now stand face to face, Tor almost shouting.

"Is that what happened to my father?" I demand, and now I too am trembling with tension, as if underneath my feet the icepack shifts with some cataclysmic movement in the oceanic deeps.

Tor's face has gone pale. He does not answer.

"They told me in the village that he had to be carried back to the ship," I say. "You were there, weren't you? You had him bound. Was that the sickness you mentioned? Was he out of his mind, like Per and Nils and . . . me? That's right, Tor," I say, throwing caution to the freezing wind, "I heard what Nils heard. And so did you, I'd stake my life on it!"

"No," Tor says, spitting the word out. "I never heard anything, this time or last. It's for those who are high-strung, these whispers and songs. Something in this atmosphere stretches the nerves tight as ropes on storm-filled sails, till you imagine you hear . . ."

"What?" I prompt, as he falls silent. "What did my father imagine, Tor?"

"It's not for me to say," Tor responds at last.

"You must say!" I shout, so loud the men ahead of us break stride to look back. I wave them on. "Your loyalty is commendable but out of place," I hiss. "Whatever happened before was so frightening you tried everything to keep us from coming here. Now you're moving heaven and earth to get us to leave. Well, I'm telling you we're not going until our holds are crammed to bursting with sealskin. Now tell me what I need to know to make that possible!"

The lines in his weathered face deepen, but whether with anger or sorrow it's impossible to tell. He moistens his lips as if needing lubrication to let the words slip past.

"All I know," he manages at last, "is that the captain—your father—stayed on the glacier overnight. When we got him down he wasn't talking sense. We couldn't sail, he said, until she arrived. He'd promised to take her back with us . . ."

"She?" I ask.

"The poet's wife," Tor says at last.

"And the poet?" I ask, shaken.

Tor shrugs. He either can't answer, or won't.

"How long did you wait?" I ask.

"Not an hour," Tor replies. "If we were going to get back to Boston in time we couldn't delay—"

"In time for what?" I ask.

"Why, your birth," Tor replies, as if I should have known. "I knew that in his right mind your father would never forgive himself if he wasn't there!"

I stare at this practical old sailor, still upset after thirty years. "And when my father came to his senses," I can't help asking, "was he grateful?"

Tor takes a deep breath. "The subject never came up," he says. "Your mother gave birth prematurely. He never talked about the island again, and neither did I."

9

I DO NOT sleep well. I am restless, partly in anticipation
of the coming hunt and partly because I cannot make
sense of what may have taken place during the *Seljeger-
en*'s last voyage here.

When I finally drop off, after trying to dull my raw
nerves with one rum and then another and another, I am
troubled by dreams.

I wander in a barren landscape, overwhelmed by a
feeling of loss. But it is unclear whether I am lost or
searching for someone who is. I call out a name in an
unfamiliar language. Figures appear, wreathed in mist. I
recognize my father as I remember him from childhood
and my mother as a young woman, weeping bitterly. I go
to console her. But my father steps between us, barring
my way with a *hakapik*. My fiancée, Eileen, appears,
wrapped in a sleek sealskin fur, slowly parting it to reveal
herself naked underneath. I rush toward her and find the
hakapik in my hand. I try to hold back—too late, I stick
her deep. Blood fountains from between her legs. I kneel
and drink thirstily . . .

I awake, sweating and nauseated, thirst unslaked. I
drink what is left of the rum to take the bitter taste from
my tongue, and eventually I fall off again.

Now I am in a rude church shaped like a ship, kneeling
in a confessional, speaking of someone else's sins as if
they're my own. I rise and shake the lattice screen,
pressing close to see Father Delmain on the other side,
young and with brilliant eyes that pierce me to my

quaking soul! "You are guilty!" he cries. Though I deny it he will not listen, and I flee his punishing eyes, running out under a gloomy sky and colliding with a young man who has a glimmering pearl in his earlobe. The impact knocks him down, and when I stoop to pick him up he is all bones. I drop that moldy skeleton with a soundless cry and turn to flee again, the pearl somehow clutched in my hand, and am confronted by a breathtakingly beautiful, sea-eyed, flame-haired young woman whose mouth is opened in an O of rage so huge that I am swallowed by it whole and fall, fall, fall down an endless throat until I am awakened by a scream that diminishes . . .

I sit up, drenched in my own sweat. Someone has whistled down the speaking tube. "Yes?" I breathe hoarsely, picking it up.

"Bridge, Captain," the man on watch says. "You asked to be awakened before dawn."

"Right," I say. "Thank you. Give me five minutes and then wake the morning watch."

I stumble into the bathroom and am startled by the hollow-eyed creature in the aluminum mirror. With the week's growth of beard, I have become my father's youthful double. Avoiding those accusing eyes, I remind myself that my feeling of guilt is a residue of that terrible dream.

I shave with extra care, like a pagan priest readying himself for bloody ritual, feeling somehow that how I look during the hunt is important, as if my appearance will affect my performance. I vow to make the first kill.

A knock on the door brings the officers' mess steward, a thick-necked sailor from Ireland pressed into service when the Chinese man who'd been with the *Seljegeren* forever quit the night my father was hospitalized. Finn carries the tray awkwardly in two calloused hands, his slitted eyes looking anxiously about for a place to set it.

"Right here," I say, making room on my desk by pushing aside the old logs I have been studying.

Finn puts the tray down, removes the napkin from the plate of hard rolls and lingonberry jam, and pours steaming liquid simultaneously from the silver pots of coffee and milk until it overflows into the saucer.

"You don't much like being steward, do you, Finn?" I ask, emptying the saucer into the washbasin.

"I'd rather work on deck, true enough, sir," he replies, and finds his way blocked as I stand in the doorway.

"And the hunt?" I ask. "You'd like that too?"

"It's part of the job, isn't it?" he says.

"You don't have any reservations about it?" I ask. My questions are casual, but I am intensely curious about the answers, wondering whether the seaman feels any of the apprehension I have been experiencing since our arrival at this island.

"I'd like to get it over with, if that's what you mean, sir," he says.

"Because of the . . . atmosphere?" I ask.

"Because it's bloody hard work and if you don't get your quota before the sun goes down it's bloody cold too," he says, both impatient and puzzled by this interrogation, perhaps afraid these questions will reveal his ignorance—or mine, more frightening if he thought I wouldn't be able to get us out of this isolated spot.

"Well, we won't have any trouble getting our quotas here," I say to reassure him. "We should have it by mid-afternoon—"

"I hope we have it before that, Captain, if you don't mind my saying so," Finn interrupts. "There's a storm on the mountain bad as any I've seen."

I put my coffee down untasted, grab my parka, and head topside, fighting back doubts and troubling premonitions.

On deck I hesitate. The sun is just coming up, rising like some ancient, fire-hammered disk from an infernal forge deep in the earth, reddening the sky, while below the blue-sheened ice glows with its reflection. Is this a natural phenomenon or a portent of disaster?

I look to the mountain—and take an inadvertent step back. A curtain of sleet, a roiling, seething mass of pelting hail and high winds, obscures the peak. Within the storm I see flashes of lightning and even at this distance hear the rumble and crack of thunder—the hawk and spit of a god's displeasure.

All else is clear. The turbulence blanketing the glacier must have been created by some peculiarity of the atmosphere—how else could so much sleeted rain pour from so clear a sky? Tor arrives at the rail beside me, barehanded in spite of the cold.

"It might be wise to postpone the hunt," he says.

"That storm's nowhere near us, and there's not a trace of wind," I reply testily.

"Wind could come up out of nowhere, like before," Tor reminds me.

"I'm not postponing because of coulds or probablys," I say. "If it worries you, stay and keep watch from here, signal us if the storm starts moving."

Tor grips the rail as if he means to tear it from the deck. "You agreed I was to be in charge!"

"The circumstances are different," I point out, doing a poor job of controlling my temper. "I'll change my mind a hundred times over if I think it's in our best interest!"

Tor's face works, as if he's discarding angry words that rush to mind. "How is an inexperienced officer leading us in our best interest?" he demands at last.

I flush. "You've been against this hunt from the start," I remind him. "It's more of a risk putting someone with no enthusiasm in charge!"

We stand glowering, face to face, so close our frosty breaths intermingle. I have no doubt mine stinks of last night's liquor; his reeks of tobacco smoked during long hours of wakeful brooding.

Behind us, while we've argued, the men have gathered on the aft deck, huddling into their cold weather gear, sullen at being awakened early.

"Good luck to you," Tor mutters finally, paying no attention to the skin he has left on the freezing metal as he pulls his hands away from the rail. "God knows you'll need it."

"Tor," I say, and he swings back, his heavy eyebrows knotting as he hears my changed tone, ready to reject any sympathy. "When you were here before," I ask, averting my eyes from his bloody fingers, "did you ever meet Mirabelle?"

"Once," he says reluctantly, as if not sure he ought to answer. "When they came down to protest the hunt," he goes on, as I wait him out.

"What did she look like?" I ask.

His face changes, becoming almost reverent as he sees her in his mind's eye. But then he catches himself and answers warily: "Hard to tell, with her bundled against the cold—"

"Was her hair red?" I ask.

"She had it covered with a scarf," Tor replies.

"What kind of scarf?" I ask.

"Knitted," Tor answers, "out of multicolored yarns."

"What color were her eyes?" I press him eagerly.

"They reflected the snow," Tor says.

"Well, were they round or narrow, wide apart or close set?" I continue, impatient with his lack of descriptive powers.

"Wide apart," Tor replies, puzzling at this seemingly random questioning. "Not round, not narrow either—"

"Doe-eyed?" I interrupt. "Like a young deer, would you say?"

"Yes," he frowns. "You could say that. Or like a seal pup's, except for the color . . ."

"Is it possible her eyes were green, like kelp?" I demand.

"It's possible," Tor shrugs. "There's so much reflected light here it squeezes most of the color out—"

But I'm no longer listening, instead remembering with a mixture of excitement and dismay the wide-set, sea-green eyes of the young woman in my dreams. It's impossible; I'm being influenced by the superstition of the islanders and the aberrant behavior of two of my own crew.

Tor is staring at me.

"That is how Mirabelle was described in the village," I lie. "I was curious whether your description matched theirs. Now if you'll make sure those assigned to the hunting party are outfitted properly," I go on, "I'd appreciate it. I'll be back in a few minutes."

For a moment I think Tor is going to disobey. We lock stares, his stubborn, mine unyielding, and then Tor turns on his heel and strides toward the crew, only his bloody fists clenched at his sides revealing his anger.

Taking a relieved breath as I recover my sense of purpose, I climb the ladder to the wheelhouse.

The duty officer, Lars, who has been watching us from the windows, now leans over the shoulder of the crewman fussing with the radio, a dark man with the kinky hair and hooked nose of an East Indian. He must be suffering in this cold, I can't help thinking, though I hardly have time to worry over the crew's discomfort.

"Isn't the damned thing working yet?" I demand.

"Every component in it is checking out," the East Indian says in accented English. "But all that is coming through is static."

"Anyone talk to Nils this morning?" I ask Lars.

"I try," Lars replies. "He says nothing understandable—only sings."

I repress a shiver. "Make sure everyone keeps away from him," I say after a moment. "Sooner or later he's bound to need something, and then he'll have to ask for it, won't he?"

Lars nods doubtfully. But I am already at the storage lockers. I unlock the one identified with a Captain's Use Only sign. It contains, along with personal gear, explosives and guns.

I recognize the *hakapik* that my father used. The handle is slick with oil from his palms. I heft it with a quickening heart. It should give me the confidence he always displayed.

Down on the aft deck, the hunting party is ready. Knut has lined them up in uneven rows of three men each. There are eleven of us, counting Knut and myself. They watch me approach, but only for a moment. Then their eyes turn back toward the mountain.

I look too—the storm has not abated. If anything, it has grown in intensity. Though I cannot be sure, it may also have moved slightly since I last observed it. But even if it has started inching down the mountain, its pace is so glacially slow I'm certain we have more than enough time to get the job done.

"Where is Tor?" I ask.

"Per asked to see him," Knut replies.

"He's come to his senses then?" I ask, delighted.

"I'm not sure," Knut says, after a brief hesitation. "He claims that *she* spoke to him again."

"Is that so?" I reply uneasily. "What did she say this time?"

"That we mustn't harm the seals," Knut replies, embarrassed at having to repeat it.

"Are the men ready?" I demand, hurriedly changing

92

the subject, unwilling to risk dampening the crew's enthusiasm further.

"As we'll ever be, aye, sir," Knut replies.

"Then let's get on with it," I say, and swinging over the rail, I climb down the ice-encrusted rope ladder to the pack.

Knut stands at the rail, giving each man a final check and then an encouraging slap as they come over the side. They move stiffly, but only from the cold, I believe. There is a growing excitement as they gather on the ice, waiting for Knut, who comes down last.

"Fifty dollars to the first man who spots the herd," I tell Knut. As he passes it on to the men, I examine the terrain we will have to traverse.

It's like a lunar landscape, an unending stretch of frozen tundra that seems to undulate with the movement of the sea it covers. In the distance, beyond some hillocks of snow that seem to have been pushed into grotesque shapes by undersea forces, there is a long, slick promontory of ice scrubbed clean by some errant wind. Beyond that is the inlet where we saw the herd.

I take a breath and set out in double time.

Almost immediately I hear the first cleats digging into the ice after me. The air is filled with ribald jokes and coarse laughter.

By now the sun is high enough to take the last shadows off the ice, and I pull my yellow-tinted goggles down from my watch cap to soften the anticipated glare. No sooner do we near the promontory, however, than we encounter a thickening haze like a succession of gauze curtains. The moisture brushes my face like icy, finely spun cobwebs, streaking my goggles, which I must continually wipe to keep my vision clear. Though the day is not appreciably warmer, the rapid pace has me sweating profusely. When we arrive at the promontory's edge, I stop to catch my breath and allow the men to catch theirs.

As the men crowd in I motion for silence. We need to move cautiously now. The sound of our trek may carry, alerting the herd. Our breaths steam and I become aware of the rank odor of the men, who use the cold as an excuse not to bathe.

I glance at the mountain—that curious storm has definitely moved—and then look back the way we have come.

In the distance the *Seljegeren* is partially obscured by the haze we have moved through, and it appears wavery as a vision in the diffused light from the cheerless and now unseen sun. A slight wind stirs along the ice, dusting our tracks with a covering of snow. Soon there will be no sign that anyone ever passed this way.

Cautiously, I move around the elongated finger of land and stop again, overwhelmed by the panorama before me. Icy spires glisten like pipes from some celestial organ. A deep groaning prolongs the illusion, and I shiver until I see that these profound chords are being created by the wind blowing across holes in the frozen rock, a hymn resounding in nature's cathedral.

I am enormously moved, and I am debating whether to drop to my knees in a reflex of a remembered faith when I become aware that many eyes are upon me.

I suck in my breath. The seals are all over the hills, perched, as before, on ledge and outcropping, again stiff as if sculpted from snow—except for the eyes, which are brown, deep-set, long-lashed . . . and anxious.

I am unable to move. Then I hear cleats squeaking over the ice as the men move around the promontory to join me. I glance beyond the spires toward the glacier: that curtain of sleet seems surprisingly closer, its pace having quickened since last I looked. I must decide instantly whether to continue or go back, else find myself without option to do either.

"Follow me!" I cry, before any surfacing doubts cripple my resolve, and making sure I have a firm grip on my father's *hakapik*, I set off at a dead run.

I take a direction that will put us between the herd and the open water, which can be glimpsed, cold and steel gray, about a hundred yards off to our right.

A tremor, like the beginnings of an earthquake, runs along the hillsides. Almost as soon as I hear the pounding of the men's boots behind me, the seals are in flight also, tumbling down the outcroppings, an avalanche of bodies, barking out of fury and fear, fins scrabbling as they pull themselves headlong across the ice.

I lengthen my stride, careless of the uneven footing, thinking of nothing except the selection of my prey. Ahead of me I make out—with some difficulty, as I am running now into a stiffening breeze in which flurries of snow sting my skin and blur my glasses—a handsome young bull pup.

He is sleek as a torpedo and as strong, belly muscles elongating like steel cables as he stretches himself out over the ice, desperate to reach the open sea. His fur is glistening and thick, a pelt that will fetch top price, or make a superb trophy for my father.

I begin to gain on him. He looks back, and then, surprising me, stops. Propping himself up on his flippers, he blows into the pouch below his nose. A hood red as anger rises to helmet his head and intimidate his enemy, me. Only his eyes give him away. They are shiny with fear.

So sudden is his turnabout that I am by him before I can stop. I stumble, swerve, regain my balance, and come back at him, charging, the *hakapik* held high.

My heart is pounding with a feeling that surges beyond excitement. I am sobbing for breath, and for whatever is being submerged by this lust for the kill that overwhelms all other feeling.

All about me Knut and the others are running in the midst of the fleeing herd. I close out of my mind any consideration of what the swish and hollow *thuks* of the swinging *hakapiks* meeting their targets mean.

Skulls fragile as glass shatter. Bodies writhe and twist and flop about on the reddening ice. Hoarse cries of triumph mingle with yelps of anguish and despair. Hardening my heart, I swing my own weapon in a deadly arc.

The hooked blade enters the bull pup's skull as easily as a knife slicing cheese. The frightened beast rises as if propelled from springs, and I can feel the impact of iron meeting bone all the way to my elbows. His neck muscles whip sideways, and so unexpected is that paroxysm that my feet slide out from under me and I am flung to the ice.

I do not know whether the scream comes from his throat or mine. Under me the ice becomes wet with a slippery substance that I identify, after an agonizingly long moment, as blood. I cling to the still vibrating *hakapik* with one hand and push to get up with the other.

I stand uncertainly, then almost fall again. Somehow, in his death throes, the bull pup is yanking me toward the water. But I do not want to let go of the *hakapik* for fear of losing my kill, symbol of my manhood, proof that I am my father's son!

I dig in my heels, trying to muscle the bull pup back the other way. As I turn toward the mountain a gust of wind, so bitterly cold and strong it must have come from the depths of the glacier itself, blows into my face, bringing with it a shower of ice that blinds me, shattering my goggles. At the same moment the ice underfoot buckles and cracks with a report like a sail blown out of its frame.

As I claw my eyes to clear my vision I make out that

the slab of ice on which I stand has broken apart from the main mass!

I glance hastily about and see that three of the hunting party have been, like me, out too far and are also on broken ice. They begin scrambling to get back, jumping frantically from slab to floating slab.

One man skids on his leap, tumbling into the water, taking another with him. They surface briefly and go under again. Though crewmen immediately probe the icy waters with *hakapik*s the two do not reappear.

Another man falls and immerses one leg trying to get up. He pulls it out and runs for safety. He's in great trouble, I know—within minutes, unless he can reach shelter, that leg will be frozen.

I am horrified to see his stiffening leg give way. Helplessly, I watch him slide into the water.

I become aware then that the slab I am on is floating toward the open sea! For almost too long I stand transfixed, watching that terrifying gap widen, staring into its murky depths, as if some watery demon's lair is going to be revealed at any moment. Then I come to my senses, take three frantic steps, and leap with every bit of strength I have left.

I land sprawling full length on the main icepack, clutching at nonexistent handholds, feeling myself, under the push of the gale-force winds that have come up, sliding back toward the open gap.

I believe I am done for. Then something stops me. Against my feet is a soft, yielding barrier . . . a hillock of snow, I think.

I twist to look. The seal I have slain is pinned to the ice with my bloody *hakapik*! Swallowing my revulsion I struggle to my feet and stand swaying, bent almost double against the wind, peering about for the others. But I can see nothing through these curtains of sleet and hail now pounding the ice.

I stumble forward, calling for the men. I lose all sense of direction. Which way is the ship, which way the open water?

I begin walking in ever-widening circles, struggling to make headway against the storm, which seems to be blowing from every direction simultaneously. I am caught in the kind of maelstrom that seems to blow up out of nowhere in these arctic regions. But how can I have so miscalculated this raging squall's arrival?

I stop yelling for the men. My fading voice is lost in the howls of the storm. I need all my energy merely to stand upright.

Suddenly I stumble and sprawl over something at my feet. Again the dead seal! I am in an embrace with my victim, whose glazed eyes peer straight into mine. It's as if he can see directly into my mind's innermost depths.

I have never experienced such anguish. Rolling off that furred body, I stand and grab the *hakapik*'s handle, trying to shake it loose. It will not move.

Sobbing with fear, anger, and revulsion, I yank with all my strength—and so unexpected is the sudden release that I stumble backward and fall. My head strikes the ice pack. I feel myself drifting into unconsciousness, at the same time sliding slowly and inexorably toward the open sea.

This time I am done for, I tell myself. Though no longer a believer, I ask God to forgive my sins. Then just before I pass out I see, through the storm, someone approaching—it is the Angel of Death, I think, coming for my immortal soul.

10

I DON'T KNOW how long I remain unconscious. At first, when I come to, I have difficulty seeing. Then, as my vision clears, I realize that I am still on the ice, the water only inches away. But I am wedged up against the *hakapik*, which is somehow imbedded in the ice. Its upright handle has stopped my progress. And bending over me is a green-eyed young woman of such melancholy beauty my heart becomes swollen with longing.

The woman in my dream! She shields my upturned face from the pelting snow with her shawl, which, though faded, seems to have been woven out of every color in the spectrum.

"Who are you?" I ask hoarsely. "Where did you come from?"

She does not answer but instead stands and motions for me to do the same. Using the *hakapik* to brace myself, I struggle to my feet. Dizzied by the effort, I sway and almost fall. She catches me, holds me upright. I reach out my hand in gratitude, and her eyes suddenly go wide with horror.

As I follow her terrified gaze, I see that my gloves are coated with blood. She takes several steps back, her face full of loathing, and turns to flee.

"Don't leave me!" I plead. But she has already disappeared into the blizzard.

Crying out, I plunge into the raging storm after her, believing that she is abandoning me as punishment for having killed the seal, desperately afraid that unless I catch her I will never get the chance to make amends.

Flashes of color from her shawl, appearing intermittently from within the milky downpour, are my only guide. As we leave the flatland and begin to climb I realize we are at the foot of the glacier. But it's no use turning back. The village is already too far. I can never reach it on my own.

I lose all track of time. I can't tell how long or how far we climb. But I guess we are very high up when I begin gasping for breath, unable to get enough of the thinning, sleet-drenched, ghostly air into my straining lungs. I have long since lost all feeling in face, fingers, and toes, and I am no longer able even to blink my eyelids, which are stiff with frozen tears.

A misplaced step and I fall. My energy is spent—I can never get up. I burrow into the snow pack to escape the punishing wind and the memory of my misdeeds, searching for a comforting, mindless warmth.

I find it. My eyes close as I begin sinking into a blessedly dreamless sleep.

A blow awakens me. My eyes snap open to find her crouching over me, ready to strike again. She motions impatiently for me to rise. I shake my head.

"I can't go any further," I try to tell her, but the words remain frozen in my throat. She motions me up again. "Let me sleep," I moan, closing my eyes.

Suddenly I feel my face being slapped. I am continually hit from side to side until my ears ring.

I crawl away. But she comes after me, grabbing at the hood of my parka to lift me to my knees. Then, tying one end of her shawl around my arm and wrapping the other about her wrist, she yanks me upright, and putting her shoulder under the tightened cloth, pulls me on into the shrieking storm.

I stumble after her for what seems like hours. I fall

and she lifts me to my feet, again shouldering the cloth to half lift me along this impossible climb. Suddenly she stops.

I drop, exhausted, to one knee. Ahead, immense boulders block our path. We can go no further, I think. I slump gratefully, willing to die on the spot rather than attempt any more.

But once again she forces me to my feet and pushes me, stumbling, along the rock, until suddenly I am pitched forward into space.

For a long, heart-stopping moment I do not know what is happening. Then as my shoulders constrict, I realize I am plummeting headfirst along an icy chute that tunnels down through the rock! My body twists to the left and then whips suddenly right. I'm being flung about so rapidly I'm unable to get my half-frozen arms up and in front of me.

I come rocketing out into daylight and drop like a stone. A huge drift of snow cushions my fall. As I come up sputtering, I sense rather than see her drop into the snow beside me.

I wipe my eyes and discover that we are in a hollow protected by giant, tomblike monoliths. The howling wind is faint here, the sleet deflecting off the towering rocks, the snow drifting like powder down into this sheltered place. The air is as still as if we've been shielded under a paperweight's glass.

Across the way, at first difficult to make out because of the peculiar half-light created by the distant storm, a small hut is nestled into the crevice of a giant rock.

I begin crawling toward it, anxious for warmth—but my strength rapidly diminishes and I collapse, weeping bitterly, sinking once again into darkness, this one unwelcomed.

I awake in so much pain I am certain I can never survive it. It's as if red-hot needles are stitching unendurable patterns all over my body. My hands and feet are so swollen I am afraid they will burst. My sinuses ache, and everything my throbbing eyes contemplate is suffused with a nauseous shade of yellow.

Then I realize I am staring into a blazing fire. Though I am lying very close to it I can feel no heat. I am, in fact, terribly cold. I hug myself for warmth and become aware that I am lying naked next to a stone fireplace on the rough floor of a hut, covered only by mounds of melting snow. I begin shaking uncontrollably and wish aloud to die.

The door opens and she comes in, a wavery, indistinct figure against the light. She has a wooden bucket heaped with snow in each hand.

"Where are we?" I demand, barely recognizing that hoarse croak as my own voice. "Who are you? What is this place?"

She does not answer, instead begins heaping snow over my corpselike skin. I try to roll away but she is quicker, putting a cruel knee into each of my inner elbows to hold me in place.

"Lie still," she whispers fiercely. "If the blood comes back too quickly you could lose your limbs!"

I shudder and do as she asks. I know enough about frostbite to know she is right. But the pain is almost unbearable. The cold has penetrated so deeply I think my heart is frozen too.

She begins massaging my body with handfuls of snow. As my skin burns I try to move out from under her weight but can't. My fingers and toes feel as if they are being held to fire. My heart begins to pound so heavily I am afraid it will burst out of my chest.

I pray that I might black out again. But it is not to be. Instead I feel something hot between my legs. Dreadfully ashamed, I close my eyes.

"What is it?" she demands. "What's wrong?"

I have wet myself. Moaning, driven to distraction by the pain and humiliation, I somehow gather enough strength to arch my body and buck her off. Rolling over and over toward the door, I lurch to my feet and stumble outside. I break into a shambling run toward the tunneled rock, hoping to climb back into the storm where I can hide from her accusing eyes forever.

No more than halfway across the clearing, however, I trip and fall. Before I can get up she is on me, then half carries, half drags me back to the hut, wrestling me inside.

I am in no condition to fight her off. My entire body is seized by a chill so profound I know that I am very near death.

She knows it too. For a moment she hesitates, as if debating whether to accept what seems inevitable, as if ready to allow me to go to what the priest would call my final accounting in peace.

But then her eyes gleam fiercely, reflecting the dying fire's glow. She picks up every piece of available wood, throwing it onto the fire until the flames roar.

Dragging seal skins from somewhere under the hearth, she makes a bed of them close to the fireplace. As she rolls me under those furred covers I curl in on myself like an infant, my teeth chattering so hard that, afraid they will splinter, I bite down on my arm.

Watching me, her stern expression softens. Suddenly she slips out of her ragged garments. I no more than glimpse her body, full-figured but with skin so milky pale it seems almost transparent, before she is under the covers with me.

She holds me close, her flesh firm and scented as ripening fruit. Immediately I feel a heat transferring itself from her body to mine, suffusing me with warmth. Gradually my trembling stops.

I put my face to the hollow of her neck and shoulder,

inching down until I am pillowed by her breast. A delicate odor emanates from her, and I recognize the perfume of those winter flowers I'd smelled earlier from the glacier.

The pain of my returning circulation is now almost bearable. Those needles which have bristled out of my skin produce only a tingling sensation. Feeling has come back to all parts of my numbed body. I am exceedingly grateful.

Then a wave of horror sweeps over me. I am responding to her sexually!

I groan an apology and try to put distance between us. "I'm sorry, I can't help myself," I whisper, ashamed.

But she doesn't let go. She looks deep into my eyes as if reading my anguished soul, then holds me even more tightly, murmuring encouragements into my burning ear. I sigh, releasing the accumulated tensions of the past weeks. I begin thrusting against her, feeling her strong legs spread to encompass me, and I sink deep inside her.

The blood pounds through my veins, bringing heat to all my nerve endings, and sweat starts from every pore, drenching us both with hot rain. Both of us glow with the fire of my passion.

Except for an occasional encouraging murmur she is otherwise silent, a perfect companion, accepting me without question, anticipating my every movement with a matching response. It's as if we have known each other's most intimate, secret natures forever.

I rock and plunge beside the fireside hearth like someone possessed. I am mindless of everything except the love that I feel. This woman has brought me from the edge of death to this life-giving place and has taken me to new heights of passion and joy, making me want to please her more than anyone I have ever known.

"I love you," I whisper hoarsely. "I love you!" And with that I spasm, arching like a bow drawn to its outermost limit, then release and fall back, exhausted, my diminishing penis spraying what is left of my seed down the inside of my contracting thighs.

She leans over me, cool mouth at my ear, urging me to sleep. My eyelids close in spite of themselves. I drift down and away, carried by webs of gossamer into regions of unimaginable bliss, where sweet music rocks me deeper into a welcome oblivion.

I awake in the midst of a nightmare. I have been rocketed into the future to find the hut a ruin, spider webs over charred roof beams, wind howling down what is left of the fireplace chimney, stirring funereal ashes that have been cold for years.

I howl and sit up. Quick as an eye blink the awful vision passes. She is there by the crackling fire, her hair highlighted by the flickering light, its color matching the flames. She's stirring a pot fragrant with steaming herbs. In an instant she is at my side.

"What is it?" she asks, concerned eyes pale as the sea.

"Nothing," I say. "A bad dream, that's all."

"Go back to sleep," she says, and begins wiping my brow with a worn lace handkerchief she takes from her ragged sleeve.

"I prefer to be awake," I say, smiling and reaching for her.

"Please don't touch me again," she says, evading my grasp.

I stare, open-mouthed. Her sweet, open countenance becomes transformed. Her eyes blaze and her face works with anger.

"I don't understand," I stammer, taken by surprise. "I thought—since we—just now—" I make a helpless gesture, unable to find words.

"It was to save your life," she says. "I thought I saw,

I *felt*, a remorse in you, a secret kindness, that made it worthwhile—now I'm not so sure!"

It takes me a long moment to absorb this. "What do you mean?" I ask, confused.

"You've killed a helpless creature," she says. "And for no other reason than the money its fur brings. The fur's not even used for warmth anymore, only vanity! And that's reason enough for you to kill again, isn't it?"

Of a sudden I remember my mother's fur, hanging unused in the cedar-lined closet for so many years. I remember then the *hakapik*'s cleaving the pup's skull, and conflicting emotions threaten to overwhelm me.

"It's a way to manage nature," I say, repeating my father's words as a way to expunge the unwanted rush of shame I feel.

"Nature manages well enough on its own!" she says.

"If the herds continue to propagate unchecked," I continue stubbornly, "they'll clean these seas of fish—the fishermen here have already lost their livelihood." Though the words are not my own, I have no reason to disbelieve them.

"It's long past time for them to have moved on and found better ways to earn a living," she says sharply, though her face betrays a hidden sympathy.

"If you feel that strongly, why haven't you left?" I demand.

"I would like to," she replies wistfully. "But I promised Captain Melman I'd wait."

I stare at her, uncomprehending. "I am Captain Melman," I say.

The steam from the fragrant pot has obscured her features; she brushes the vapors aside to show her large eyes, startled and questioning.

"It can't be," she says.

"Come to the *Seljegeren* with me and I'll show you my papers," I say.

"That's impossible," she cries. "The *Seljegeren* is Johann's—Captain Melman's—ship! He would never have given it up!"

"Johann?" I demand incredulously. "Johann is my father's name!"

"Your father?" she gasps. She crosses her hands over her breasts to contain an emotion that threatens to overwhelm her. "I should have known," she murmurs at last. "I can see him in you, very plain!"

"You know my father?" I ask, suddenly shaken by a jealousy so powerful I am about to explode with anguish and rage. Then I am struck by a discrepancy that should have been obvious from the start. "But how can that be?" I ask uneasily, barely able to get the words out. "He hasn't been here for more years than you've been alive!"

"I am older than you think," she says, and she touches her face as if feeling for the wrinkles that ought to be there . . . but are not.

"Who are you?" I ask shakily.

"Mirabelle," she replies, and the mists from the pot rise again, shimmering about her pensive features.

"That's impossible," I say, barely above a whisper. "In the village they mentioned someone named Mirabelle who ran off with a poet named Macafee—you must be their daughter . . .?"

"I'm Macafee's wife, at least in spirit," she interrupts bitterly. "Because only God sanctified our marriage, Johann—Captain Melman—thought he had the right to claim me. I only submitted because I believed Macafee would release me from my vows . . . and then Johann . . . Johann lied—your father lied!"

Outside, through the frosted window, I can see it has grown dark. In the flickering light of the dying fire she seems as insubstantial as a shadow. Only her keening of grief and disillusionment, a sound so knife-sharp it cuts me to the heart, seems real.

I must be hallucinating. The exhausting climb after that savage hunt into the rarefied air of this sanctuary has plunged me into a state where the most dreadful imaginings seem real. Throwing my covers aside, I try to get up but fall back on the skins, lightheaded.

She comes out of the shadows, kneeling by my side again, putting her cool palm on my fevered brow.

She is real! I tell myself. And seeing her close, her lovely features firm and unlined, I cannot imagine she is more than twenty. Yet what she is telling me can hardly be true . . . unless . . . Have I somehow fallen into another dimension, where past coexists with present?

"I've got to get back to the ship," I say, struggling to get up, to flee, to try and discover which of us is mad, which sane. "I have to see whether my men survived the storm—"

"You mustn't agitate yourself," she says. "You're ill and in no condition to make the trip back now." She rises, goes to the fireplace, fills a wooden bowl from the steaming pot, and brings it back to my couch. "Drink this," she says, holding a fragrant spoonful to my cracked and swollen mouth.

"What is it?" I ask, fearing to taste anything whose aroma I do not recognize from the hands of someone who may wish me or my kin harm.

"A soup made of moss and dried seaweed," she says. "Macafee gave me the recipe—it'll bring the fever down, make you stronger."

I am unable to refuse her anything. I swallow until the bowl is empty, then fall back, once more exhausted. As she pulls the covers over me, bending so near I again smell her wildflower fragrance, I wonder if those hypnotic eyes have cast me under a spell, for I cannot believe she is capable of lying.

108

"Where is Macafee now?" I ask, thinking that it's important for me to discover what happened.

"Dead," she replies, and whatever she sees in her mind's eye makes her cringe.

"How?" I persist, though I dread the answer.

"For love of me," she says, beginning to weep. "No more questions," she continues, before I can speak again. "Sleep," she commands. "When you wake, you'll be strong enough to return to your ship. Get in touch with your father, tell him I'm still waiting, as he asked. He must release me from my promise, release you from your promise . . . Now sleep," she repeats, putting her finger to my lips to silence the hundred questions I am burning to ask, especially about promises, hers and mine. "Sleep."

And I do.

11

I OPEN MY eyes at the sound of a muffled banging, slow as a funeral drum. For a long moment I'm not sure whether I'm awake or dreaming. Cobwebs hang like shrouds from the charred ceiling beams, dust lies thick on the splintering table and bent chairs, rust pits the blackened kettle that hangs askew in the cold, broken fireplace—those disconnected images flashing into my consciousness during the worst of my fever, which I attributed to an inflamed imagination, are now before me, as fixed in place as an old photograph.

As the cold in this pitilessly gray daylight stipples my exposed arm with gooseflesh, I shiver and realize that I am completely naked and fully conscious under the shabby fur covers, lying in a room whose state of disrepair could not have been accomplished in a single night.

"Mirabelle?" I call, wondering why she has allowed the fire to die and gone out leaving the door unlatched. It continues to bang remorselessly in the wind. There is no answer.

I get up slowly, trying to avoid a repetition of the lightheadedness that has left me dizzy and faint, and discover my clothing standing mannikin-stiff and frozen solid on the hearth. My skin roughening in protest at the biting cold, I wrap myself in a fur, go to the door, and peer out into the clearing.

"Mirabelle?" I shout. My voice echoes off the glacier-like rock, ricocheting around the frozen clearing before dwindling into the empty air.

I step outside and stare in disbelief. The snow on the ground reveals only one set of tracks—by the size and the cleat marks mine. The merest dusting of snow sits in my footsteps; not enough could have fallen through the long night to cover hers. They must be here someplace, I tell myself—there is no way I could have gotten through the storm and found this remotely isolated, secret clearing by myself.

My next thought is that she has herself covered her tracks, not wanting me to know where she has gone.

"Mirabelle!" I shout, and dropping to my hands and knees I scramble about, clawing at the snow like someone possessed. But there is no sign of her passage anywhere, coming or going.

The fur slips from my shoulders. The cold seeps into my naked bones. I can hardly search for her in this state of confusion and undress. I hurry back inside to thaw my clothes.

But when I poke the ashes, they disintegrate at my touch. The fireplace is cold as death. Didn't I doze off in front of a blazing fire only hours before? Why is there not so much as a glowing coal? Putting aside my growing uneasiness, I set about building a fire.

There are only a few scraps of wood at the bottom of the cobwebbed, dust-laden bin. I stack them over a small pile of splinters and shavings, hoping they will prove adequate.

Scattered over the hearth are old matches. I scrape a sulphur tip over the stone. The head disintegrates. I strike another and then another without producing so much as a spark.

They are either too cold or too damp . . . or too old. Putting that anxious thought aside, I warm a match in my hand. When finally struck, it flickers long enough for me to light a splinter. Shielding the tiny glow with trembling hands, I blow gently until the shavings smoke and finally burst into flame.

Once the larger kindling begins to burn I stack my clothing close to the warmth, paying special attention to my gloves, underclothing, socks, and shoes. My fingers and toes have ugly patches of yellowish white where the blood has ceased to circulate. I must thaw them now or risk losing them.

My stomach rumbles. I examine the kettle, hoping to eat what is left of last night's soup. But an inedible crust covers the bottom—the pot looks as if it hasn't been used for years! Refusing to consider what that might mean, I take the kettle outside.

"Mirabelle!" I bellow, emptying my lungs in an outburst of anger and frustration . . . and fear.

The air is still and cold. Though I can see the sun in the filmy sky above the towering, frozen rock, that pale disc seems without heat, as if its gaseous furnaces have long since burnt out.

Shivering, I scrub the rusting metal clean with snow, then stack it full and hurry back inside. Hanging the pot by its bent handle, I add the remainder of the wood to the fire under it. I turn the now-softening clothes, and then I massage my extremities until the pain tells me the blood once more flows, however painful and slow. Then I search the cabin for food.

Clumped in the bottom of a glass jar I find brown granules that may once have been honey or sugar. A fraying cardboard packet yields dirt-flecked salt. A battered tin box contains a chunk of greenish mold covering a quarter loaf of bread so old it is hard as stone. A ceramic crock holds a discolored substance that may once have been cheese.

Then, in a chipped earthenware bowl, I make an electrifying discovery. Yellowing paper that had once been waxed contains some dried greenish-colored strands that taste to my cautious tongue like the seaweed soup Mirabelle made!

Hurrying back to the pot, I drop in the dried weed and stir it about the now-bubbling water, hoping to prove that last night's vivid experience was not a hallucination.

I venture a taste. It is so disgusting I spit it out immediately, barely able to keep from vomiting. Then I force myself to drink it a few sips at a time, knowing that I need the sustenance.

When I can stomach no more, I go back to prowling the cluttered room. Eventually, high on a corner shelf, I spot a thick old book, its once elegant leather binding cracked and worn. What remains of its gold leaf imprint identifies it as a *Holy Bible*.

As I turn the pages dust rises to my nostrils. I sneeze.

The very sound frightens me: my father claims sneezing opens us up to the devil. "Bless me!" I mutter, my hand on the holy book, and feel at once foolish but relieved.

I continue riffling through the brittle, fading pages. A folded paper slips out and drifts to the floor. As it settles I sense the impact, as if a weight of such magnitude has dropped that the earth trembles.

Stooping to pick up that piece of flimsy, I hesitate, a feeling of such dread coming over me that I am dizzied. All my nerve endings are vibrating, warning me to let the paper lie, to put the holy book back, to dress and leave this hut instantly.

But my curiosity is not to be denied. I take the paper, yellow and flaking with age, unfold it carefully, then hold it to the dim light spilling in through the window. However indistinct, I immediately recognize that bold scrawl.

My dearest Mirabelle,
I command you to wait here for my return. I have
convinced Macafee that it is better for you to return

to civilization with me than to remain here under such primitive conditions.

I know you wanted to tell him yourself. But it's best that I told him, better, in fact, if the two of you never see each other again. He cares for your happiness too much to deny you your freedom. Once you are aboard my ship and we are sailing toward our new life together your terrible feelings of guilt will drop away like so many leaves from an Autumn tree. I assure you Spring will once again return, and our love will blossom then. Be patient. Wait. Remember that a love like ours must never be denied— otherwise the gods will see to it that we suffer through all eternity.

Yours forever,
Johann

I am stunned. I am as disoriented as someone in an embryonic state, a disembodied spirit who has not yet been given birth. I was swimming in my mother's womb when my father wrote these passionate words.

Had my mother not told him about me? Or had Mirabelle so infatuated him that he was willing to scuttle his responsibilities as husband and father no matter what the consequences? Yet Mirabelle had not come home with him. He'd been forced to leave her behind, and she'd been waiting all this time for him to return.

What had happened to cause Tor to keep him from her? Why had he never tried to come back? Tor knows. And the priest as well. What was so forbidding about this affair that neither man finds it possible to talk?

As I stand in the middle of the room, confused and upset, other questions race through my mind. Why am I accepting the presence of Mirabelle as real? This hut has not been lived in for years! If someone was with me last night there is no sign of it now.

114

But how can I have been hallucinating? No fevered imagination could have reproduced these events in such vivid detail. No apparition could have led me up so treacherous a mountain to so hidden a place. Had this Mirabelle materialized from some halfway netherworld only long enough to save my life, pass a message to my father, then return to her own time?

My blood runs cold at the thought. Even under my fur covering I shiver. I pick up my clothes, anxious to dress and get away from these disturbing thoughts.

But my undergarments are still damp. I don't dare risk putting them next to my skin. But if I stay here much longer I'll never make it down the mountain before dark. And I don't relish the idea of spending another night in this desolate place.

I clutch the fur's warmth closer. This animal's skin is designed to survive arctic conditions. If I can somehow shape it into a covering, I could not ask for better winter gear.

I make another search of the cabin. Under a chair next to the wall, half hidden in a corner, I find a ball of yarn stuck through with a variety of needles and pins. Under its coating of dust that yarn has the same colors as Mirabelle's scarf; whether coincidence or proof of the unprovable is not as important to me at the moment as getting away from here with all possible speed.

I find a blackened kitchen knife in a warped drawer and cut slits in the fur for my arms and legs, then use the pins to close the pelt at my midriff and neck. My wool stockings and my knit cap, my shoes, and my gloves are now dry enough to use; I have difficulty getting my parka over the fur but finally manage it well enough.

The fire is almost out. I tip the kettle to douse what is left, my nose wrinkling in disgust at the smell of scorching seaweed. I hasten to the door, eager to at last leave this place, which seems to my anxious eyes to actually vibrate with its passionate and disturbing memories.

But with the door halfway open I hesitate. Though I try to convince myself to let the past lie undisturbed, I return inside. Though aware I'm risking even further confusions between past and present in my already disoriented mind, I pick up the Bible. Removing the fragile note from the brittle pages, I carefully wrap it in the paper the seaweed had been in. Thrusting it deep into an inside pocket of my parka, I finally step out into the clearing.

Behind me I hear a muted groan. The short hairs on my neck bristle. I resist turning around. Though I tell myself it's old timber stretching under the warming sun, it sounds to my anxious ears like someone mourning loss. I hurry to put distance between myself and the cabin.

When I reach the frozen spires I am brought up short. Where is the tunnel through which I have entered this clearing, once so welcome a shelter, now so ominous and foreboding? These huge boulders look impenetrable, crushed together as if thrown aside by some giant, careless hand. I peer into one dark crevice after another. There's no sign of daylight anywhere.

I circle the enclosure until I'm back where I started. I retreat to the middle of the clearing. Hearing my breath coming short, I caution myself not to panic. Squinting at the sky, I see that the pale, distant sun has risen to a point opposite the tallest spires, casting irregular shadows across the crusted snow all the way back to the cabin.

I try to remember how these spires have looked from the opposite side like giant fingers upthrust through the glacier's peak. My guide had disappeared between index finger and thumb.

By examining the shadows, I discern similar shapes.

Moving amongst the outer rocks, I discover a path leading to a narrow crevice I have not noticed before. As I peer inside the black hole, I make out a faint illumination at the distant top, possibly the glint of sun on snow.

It is considerably harder climbing up than it was plummeting down. But I am able, by digging my snow cleats into the rock and at the same time feeling for handholds on the sides, to work my way out until I am finally standing, panting for breath, on the topmost slope of the mountain again.

I can see most of the island. Several miles down and to my right the village lies in shadow, charcoal smoke from its chimneys rising crooked as a primitive drawing into the gauzelike air. Below and to my left is the *Seljegeren*, fixed solidly in the now-frozen channel we made by entering, a faint blue sheen the only indication that a sea runs underneath. From the ship's funnels an oily smoke gushes—they must be very cold to burn so rich a fuel, I think.

Tiny figures are gathering on deck. It is difficult, through this hazy atmosphere and without my lost binoculars, to make out what they are doing. Then I see a number of them, dark specks peppering the ice pack, leaving the ship.

I wait a moment longer to make out their direction, then go into shock as I see they are making their way toward the sealing grounds! I funnel my hands and shout a warning as loud as I can. Though the chance of them hearing me is remote, I am hoping that those strange acoustical echoes I was subjected to earlier will now work in my favor.

The line doesn't falter. My voice is immediately absorbed by the spongelike atmosphere; if there are any echoes they disappear into the shimmering air.

How can they be so stupid? Are they unaware of what happened during yesterday's disastrous hunt? I can't be the only one who's aware that some force greater than ourselves is protecting the seals. Upset by what seems flagrantly idiotic behavior, I ignore my weakened condition and plunge down the icy slopes on a course designed to intercept them, afraid that this new expedition may produce an even more calamitous result.

My anger fuels my energy; my pumping adrenalin takes me at a half run through the stand of frost-tipped evergreens and almost halfway down the mountain before I pull up at the sight of a glittering patch of ice that lies in full sunlight just ahead.

I know better than to go pell-mell over that treacherous crust—its bottomless center may be soft, and a misstep could send me plummeting to the heart of the glacier, buried alive, never to be seen again!

Fast using up what strength I have left, I climb back to the edge of the forest and search for an appropriate stick. I find a broken tree limb jutting out of the snow. It measures about seven feet in length, sufficient for my purpose.

I edge back out on the mountainside, probing for solid footing before each step forward. Occasionally I pause, gasping for breath in the rarefied atmosphere, sweating underneath my layered garments, looking to make sure we remain on intersecting courses.

I see the men more clearly. They have reached the finger of land that lies between them and the breeding grounds and are stopping, apparently to rest.

I shout and wave my arms. On a sudden inspiration, I take off my parka, put it on the branch, and wave it back and forth like a battle flag, crying out with all the power in my lungs.

None of the men look up. They are sitting in small groups while they wait for their leader—at this distance I cannot recognize who that is—to come back from reconnoitering the herd.

118

The seals are in their accustomed places, lining the ledges and abutments that overlook the ice pack, as tranquil and oblivious to the looming danger as if the stampeding of the day before has been stricken from their memory.

How I wish for a rifle now. A few warning shots would be enough to scatter the herd. Without that, there seems little I can do to prevent the impending slaughter, which would result, for the men as well, in a tragedy of monumental proportions.

But I cannot stand idly by. Whether the events of the preceding night are hallucination or not, whether Mirabelle is a spiritual visitation or the creation of a shame-ridden mind, if I am to make amends, for my father and for myself, I must do whatever I can to head the men off.

I am about to push on, desperately hoping I can get close enough to the men to be either heard or seen, when I hear a loud whisper off to my left.

I look quickly there in time to see a hummock of snow slipping off a formerly hidden ledge—as startling a revelation as if a magician's white cape has performed a miracle.

Have my shouts caused that layer to slide? Avalanche conditions are created when sudden weather changes put drifts of wet snow atop hard-frozen crusts. Any disturbance can dislodge them. Is that the situation here?

A gust of wind sends a hazy curtain of snow whirling along the now-exposed ledge—it can't be, I tell myself; this rainbowing color I see is in my own vision, a result of too much squinting against the glare.

Below me a puff of white dust, like smoke from an explosion, jumps high in the air where the layer of snow crashes to a stop not far from the resting men.

They look up, startled. Again I shout, waving the parka—but because they are looking into the sun, they still do not see me.

The man in charge is Tor, wearing hooded gear as protection against sudden storms, now returning from his reconnaissance. The men get to their feet, shrugging aside the slide as of no significance. They pick up their weapons, prepared to go on.

I tumble down to the newly opened ledge and run along it, chasing that twirling funnel of snow full speed until my path is blocked by a huge snowdrift. Atop it the funnel continues to dance, dervishlike, just out of my frustrated reach. I am about to climb over it when a packet of snow is blown full into my face.

As I wipe my eyes, temporarily blinded, I hear another whisper. My vision clears in time for me to witness another fall of snow. Huge rumpled sheets pour off the mountainside, raising enormous clouds where they hit the base of the slope, blocking the men's path to the breeding grounds.

Ahead of me, where the drift has been, a giant boulder is exposed. The huge rock teeters on the edge of the trail, held in place by a few tendrils of ice, tilting in the direction of the men far below who are now staring upward in fear and shock. I drop my parka and race to the boulder, wedging the stick underneath, desperately trying to keep it in place.

That funnel of wind and sleet has disappeared. I get between the rock and the front slope, frantically scooping up snow and ice as a barrier. I glance about continually, full of anxiety about whether there is someone, or some*thing*, with me in this wilderness.

But there seems to be nothing. Even the gusts of wind have died down. Shadows do appear to move at the periphery of my vision, but when I turn to confront them head-on they disappear.

When I pause, leaning against the boulder to get my breath, I am thunderstruck to feel it tremble.

At first, I do not trust my own senses. My strained muscles must be giving way, a reaction to my exertions.

Then I feel it again: that rock is definitely shifting, as if someone on the other side pushes against it!

Without thought, digging in for a foothold as best as I can, I press with all my might in the other direction. Now I can definitely feel it—the rock is slowly, inexorably, moving, bending me an inch at a time backward over the abyss.

I hear those ribbons of ice, all that is holding the boulder in place, crack. My snow-packed cleats begin to lose their footing. My feet slip out from under me.

I begin sliding backward downhill, clutching futilely at jutting rocks, my momentum increasing until the terrain is a blur. At the same time, above me the boulder breaks free. It plunges off the ledge, the entire mountainside shuddering with each impact as it bounces down the crusted slopes.

In another moment I will be crushed. With what little maneuverability I can manage I am just able to twist to one side before the boulder plunges past. But I continue to skid sideways in the direction of the cliff's edge.

Unable to stop, I slide past it and fall through space for an eternity. Then I am enveloped in snow, a drift cushioning my body though the air is driven from my lungs.

As I lie dazed and in darkness I feel more than hear the boulder continuing to thunder down the slope like a runaway train. I moan in anguish at the thought of the havoc that will be wreaked if the men can't get out of the way before the growing avalanche arrives.

I struggle up and out of the drift just in time to hear what I have been dreading—the familiar screams of men frightened beyond endurance.

12

By the time I get to the base of the mountain, those men who have managed to scramble to safety are helping those not so lucky. I count three who lie sprawled in the snow, moaning with broken limbs; two who are silent, crushed underneath that boulder's awesome weight; and four being pulled up from underneath a deep covering of snow, their faces gray and slack-jawed with shock, their location identified only by the *hakapiks* they have managed to thrust upward while falling.

"Is that everyone?" I demand of Tor, who is shouting instructions to the able-bodied survivors.

Tor turns, startled. "Was that you up there?" he asks, after taking a puzzled moment to observe the makeshift garment I am clothed in.

"Never mind that now—is everyone accounted for?" I ask in turn.

Tor hesitates, then does a hasty count. "Two still missing," he says.

"Then get your search organized," I say, "and better be quick about it—if they're buried under snow they won't live five minutes!"

Though still full of questions, Tor gives me a partial, somewhat mocking salute and returns to the men. While those who can begin plunging about in ever-widening circles, I follow the boulder's track, which looks like nothing so much as a fossilized dinosaur's bone-studded tail. Precious minutes speed away before I spot indentations in the crust, one on either side, where men have leaped to get out of the plunging boulder's path only to be smothered by the following rush of snow.

"Get people up here!" I shout, and dropping to my knees by one of the indentations, I work furiously to uncover whoever might be underneath.

Help arrives just in time. Both men, the apprentice helmsman and the Portuguese, are still alive, though barely, with eyes frozen shut, like moles emerging from an icy underground. Tor and I straddle them like frantic lovers, breathing our hot breaths into their cold lungs, slamming their rigid chests with our fists, hoping to start sluggish hearts.

At almost the same moment, each near-dead man sucks in air, the rasps in their throats like files on steel. Their eyes bulge under their frosted lids as they struggle to open them, whimpering like frightened animals when they cannot.

"This is Captain Melman," I say. "Don't worry— once we get you to the ship we'll be able to steam your eyes open with hot cloths."

The young helmsman stiffens. "Captain Melman?" he whispers. "You couldn't have survived that storm?"

"I'm not a ghost," I assure him, helping him to his feet.

"None of those who went out with you came back," the youth says.

"None?" I repeat dumbly.

"All dead," Tor confirms, staring at me accusingly.

"Knut, too?" I manage finally.

"He fell on his own *hakapik*," Tor replies.

"That's impossible," I protest, shocked. "He knew how to handle himself—Knut was our best hunter, next to Helmut . . ."

"That's as may be," Tor replies. "But the ice around him was slick as soap—he either tripped over his own feet, or did himself in."

"Knut wasn't clumsy, or suicidal," I insist.

"You're not suggesting someone pushed him?" Tor asks.

I turn away for a moment, fearful and heartsick about what might have taken place under cover of that blinding storm. "Better send someone back to the ship for help," I order at last. "We'll never manage by ourselves."

Tor considers this for longer than I like, as if not sure it's necessary or wise to obey me any longer. Then he turns and shouts in a strange, guttural tongue at one of the few able-bodied men left. The man, probably an Arab, who wears a ragged scarf of an exotic design covering his face, nods and sets off at a trot back down the trail.

I manage to get those who are still alive back on their feet, using *hakapiks* for makeshift splints and crutches, and start them hobbling toward the ship. Because of my own weakened condition I put myself between the two blinded men: with our arms linked, they hold me up while I guide them over the ice pan.

We look like survivors of war. As we straggle onward, companions in misery, I see a party of men leaving the *Seljegeren*, heading for us at a run. Some pull sleds and others carry blankets, knowing that shock lowers the body's temperature to a dangerous level. The wounded give a feeble cheer and try to hurry their own faltering steps.

The rescue party, led by Lars, reaches us within the half hour. Though Lars stares wonderingly at the fur I am wrapped in, I do not wish to talk in front of the men. He has remembered to bring rum. We greedily swallow the dark, sweetly burning liquid, then collapse into the sleds, burrowing under blankets, almost immediately half asleep from the warmth that spreads through us from the inside out.

I do not awaken until they are hoisting us back on

deck, using squealing, oil-deprived pulleys to haul us up, sleds and all. The shouts of Tor and the other officers instructing the shipboard crew to get the wounded below penetrate the furry cocoon I am in. I sit up, causing my sled to sway dangerously.

For a moment, I think the man handling the ropes is going to let me spill over the side to the ice twenty feet below. It is the Arab, his face still wrapped in the scarf, whose eyes, black as a demon's, study me for longer than I like. Then the moment passes, and using his *hakapik* he hooks the ropes and swings the sled safely onto the deck.

Though every nerve and sinew in my body cries out for rest, I struggle to my feet, pushing aside the hand of whoever is reaching to help me. Then I recognize Per, haggard and pale, braced on a single crutch.

"Should you be up?" I ask, peering closely at him.

"I heard you survived the storm, Captain," Per stammers.

"I was fortunate," I say, apologetic and somehow ashamed. "I'm sorry about Knut, and the others."

"I warned him not to go," Per says, suppressing a sob.

"That's enough, Per," Tor says, stepping forward. "Get back below now."

"Let him be!" I say. "He's not suffering from nerves, or a hyperactive imagination, or arctic madness, or anything else that anyone may be telling him. Per *was* tripped and thrown to the ice. That voice Nils heard *is* real. There *is* someone out there in the wilderness. It's Mirabelle. I saw her. I talked to her. She saved my life!"

Per's colorless eyes glisten, as if he wants to believe but is afraid to.

"Next I suppose you'll be telling us it was her, and not you, that pushed the boulder down on the men," Tor says heavily.

"Of course it wasn't me!" I cry, shaken by the accusation and suddenly uncertain, memory blurred as to just what happened up on the slopes. I did not actually see anyone else up there, and if those errant winds and heavy falls of snow have made me believe otherwise it will buttress Tor's conviction that I am out of my mind.

"I think you'd better get below yourself, Captain," Tor says, after it becomes clear that I am having difficulty finding words to deny what he is implying. "You've been through quite an ordeal. It's amazing that you're still on your feet." Behind him, the crew watch us closely.

"I'm not crazy!" I whisper, hard pressed to keep my voice down. "Mirabelle exists! There's evidence to prove that what I've been saying is true . . ."

"What evidence?" Tor wonders as I fall silent.

"A letter," I reply, and then I realize, in a panic, that I've left it behind. "It's in my parka, up where the boulder fell—did any of you men find my parka?" I ask, my voice rising as the onlookers begin to mutter amongst themselves.

They look at one another, then back at me, shaking their heads.

"Send a search party back to look for it," I demand of Tor. He stares at me for an agonizingly long moment, then beckons to a sturdy young Scandinavian petty officer. "Take two men and see what you can find," he tells him. "The rest of you get about your tasks," he suddenly roars, and the others hesitate before they scatter—a sign that our authority is diminishing.

"Now, wouldn't you like some hot soup, and enough soap and water to get that black off your face?" Tor asks, overly solicitous.

I put my hand to my face, feel the slickness, then smell the mucous substance on my fingertips.

"Seal oil," I explain. "She covered me with it to protect me from snowburn."

"Now you're aboard ship you won't need it," Tor responds.

"I'm only staying long enough to get in touch with my father," I say. "Then I'm heading back out to look for her."

"You're not strong enough to make that trek again," Tor says.

"I'll use the helicopter," I say, seeing that the smithy has replaced the straightened blades. Before Tor can give me further argument, I head for the wheelhouse ladder. As I mount those slippery rungs, every step seeming more difficult than the last, it's as if I'm pulling against all the gravitational power that the earth possesses. I dread the conversation that I must have with my father now.

In the radio shack, a supple-fingered crewman, Sparks, the radio officer's English assistant, is winding thin wire to an aerial lead. He looks up in astonishment.

"Why isn't the radio working?" I demand without preamble.

"We're still getting echoes of our own transmission," Sparks says. "After what happened to Nils, the first mate thought it best to keep it off until we can get a clearer reception."

"Did he?" I mutter, hastily sitting before my legs collapse. "Well, let's see what we can pick up now, all right?"

"Aye, sir," Sparks says after a moment, and flicks the appropriate switches. A low hum comes from the speaker.

"Turn up the volume," I say.

The hum grows louder as Sparks complies. As he changes frequencies, we hear static and growls. He makes further adjustments, and suddenly we hear a hollow wailing, forlorn as a lost soul. I shiver in recognition and dread—it is probably the voice that sent Nils fleeing into the night. Even with the distortion produced by the tinny speaker, I recognize it as coming from Mirabelle!

". . . Melman . . . man," the voice moans, echoing itself. "Captain . . . tain . . . Melman . . . man. Why . . . ay . . . ay . . . haven't you . . . ou . . . ou . . . come back . . . back . . . back?"

Sparks is sitting rigid with fear, with his arm extended. "Do you hear that?" he whispers, dismayed.

Behind us someone has come into the radio shack. Without looking I know it is Tor. Ignoring him, I grab the microphone and press the button to transmit. "This is Melman," I say hoarsely into the mike. "Is that you, Mirabelle? Please identify yourself. Over."

Static comes from the speaker.

"Mirabelle, where are you? Please answer. Over," I call urgently.

". . . losssssttt . . ." we hear finally, before the word disappears into static again.

"Mirabelle?" I demand, full of anxiety.

"There's nothing out there," Tor says from behind, "except for a magnetic force field that blocks our signal and throws it back. Isn't that right, Sparks?"

"What else could it be?" Sparks says. But his voice is full of doubt.

"Mirabelle?" I call again. "Is that you? Please identify yourself. Tell me where you are. This is Captain Melman. Over."

" . . . losssttt . . ." comes that shivery moan again.

"I'll meet you at the cabin," I say into the mike. "Can you hear me? Go to the mountain cabin. Over."

Static. I am about to try again when Tor's gnarled hand reaches between Sparks and myself for the dial.

"What are you doing?" I demand, outraged, flinging his hand away so hard he is thrown up against Sparks.

"All frequencies are the same," Tor insists, his face darkening. "You're getting echoes and distortions—"

"Didn't you hear her voice?" I say. "Sparks heard—didn't you, Sparks?"

"I heard . . . something," Sparks admits, hugging his fear.

A hair-raising moan comes from the speaker.

"Hear that?" I ask, trying to adjust the dials.

"Hear what?" Tor asks. "That's just a mechanical distortion. Right, Sparks?"

"Nothing human makes a sound like that," Sparks manages at last.

I can feel my racing blood run cold. "She's alive," I insist, my mind refusing to accept the other possibility.

"It's a magnetic field producing static and howls," Tor repeats, equally stubborn.

"Mirabelle?" I call shakily into the mike. "Are you out there? This is Jason. Please answer. Identify yourself. Where are you? Over."

Static. And then we hear something else, a hissing that's hard to identify. Then I faintly make out ". . . Jaaasssonnn? . . . not . . . Jaasson . . . Johannnnn . . ."

"It's an echo of your own transmission," Tor insists.

But I am scarcely listening. "She wants my father," I say, grieved and bewildered. "My father promised he'd come back—and it was you, Tor, caused him to break his promise!"

Blood surges and recedes in Tor's face on the tides of his anger, leaving him pale and shaking. "You've taken leave of your senses, boy!" he whispers. "The far north can do that to men, I've seen it before—"

"With my father?" I ask, but Tor does not even pause for breath.

"Lars!" he bellows, and the sturdy mate appears in the radio shack entry so fast he must have been standing close. "You and Sparks are witnesses—I'm declaring the captain incompetent and taking command!"

"You don't dare!" I cry, disbelieving, pushing to my feet.

"It's for your own good," Tor says, unyielding. "You're a menace to yourself—not to mention this ship and crew."

"Stand aside," I say to Lars, who is blocking my way. "Don't be misled by this foolish old man—you can be hanged for mutiny!"

"Take note how he's dressed," Tor says. "We'll get statements from the men he tried to kill—"

"I saved their lives!" I cry, outraged.

"—and hope that he'll come to his senses before we have to use them against him," Tor continues, calmer now that his decision has been made.

"I am perfectly rational," I say, inwardly cursing my quavering voice. "You've said yourself there's something unnatural about this island. Well, now I'm telling you it's the spirit of Mirabelle that's haunting this place, and she—*it*—will do anything to protect the seals. Think what happened to Per, and to Nils, and to Knut, and how that storm came out of nowhere—"

"Being this close to the pole affects some men more than others," Tor mutters to Lars. "Now take him below!"

"Aye, sir," Lars says, and grabs my arm none too gently. "I'd appreciate it if you'd come quietly, sir."

"Sparks," I plead. "Get in touch with my father— he'll confirm that what I'm saying is true!"

Sparks hesitates, then looks to Tor. But Tor ignores him, grabbing my other arm to help push me out. I despair whether Sparks will do what I ask. He's young enough to believe that Tor's experience in these waters overrides whatever brief authority I have had as captain.

130

13

I AM LOCKED in my cabin, a prisoner on my own ship.

Before Tor turns the key I demand that he at least send for the ex-priest Delmain, who will, I am convinced, confirm that it is his old Bible I found in that mountain hut. If my description of Mirabelle matches that of the young woman he knew, he will have to admit that I couldn't have simply conjured her angry spirit up out of my own imagination.

But Tor repeats his suggestion that I rest, after which I might be able to discuss my situation with more rationality. I almost break my fist on the closing door.

I begin to understand what being caged means. However much I rage and storm about, there is no one to take notice.

I listen at the door, hoping to hear some susceptible crew member in the corridor that I might call to and intimidate or bribe to release me. But the steel-bolted thickness allows no sound to penetrate.

Through the porthole all I can see is that unending frozen expanse, now glittering under an unclouded sun. I push open the glass, but find the opening too small to squeeze through. Before I can vent my fury by shouting challenges to whatever faceless, uncaring God watches from the infinite sky, I hear delighted cries from the deck. Tor has seen fit to pass out another rum ration. Why? Does he hope to keep the crew occupied while he schemes how to break the *Seljegeren* out of the ice? If this warming trend continues, that should not prove difficult.

I will not leave without seeing Mirabelle, I vow to myself, alarmed; I must think of a way to find her before the ship sails. It would be unforgivable to abandon her without an explanation—that would be twice by members of the same family; the Melmans would be cursed through all eternity.

But I can do nothing from this locked cabin. Somehow I must get them to open the door, then seize whatever opportunity offers itself to escape. I take the speaking tube and whistle up to the bridge.

"I want hot food and a rum," I tell Lars, the officer on duty.

"It may take a while, Captain," Lars replies hesitantly. "The cook's . . . indisposed . . . I don't know who we'd have available would know how to use the galley stoves."

"Get Per," I say quickly—perhaps too quickly. "He's helped the cook before, and God knows he's not fit for anything else . . ."

"I'll see to it," Lars says after another hesitation, and I can only hope my request is innocuous enough that he won't feel compelled to check with Tor.

I search my cabin for a weapon. Though it shouldn't prove difficult to intimidate Per, I doubt if they'll allow him to visit me alone. I'll need something other than my bare hands. But except for an iron paperweight, a portion of a Viking ship's anchor my father sent to me on the occasion of my naval commission, there is nothing—someone, probably Tor, has removed my pistol and knife.

Shoving the iron weight under my blankets, I sit on my bunk to await developments. The room seems overly warm. I have trouble keeping my eyes open. I pick up the speaking tube again. "At least send me the rum," I say when Lars responds.

"Aye, sir," he replies. "Soon."

I rest my head on the pillow, just for a moment. The moment stretches. Though I bite my lips and pull my cheeks to keep awake, I drift into a dreamless sleep.

I begin to smell flowers. It's a remembered scent, a winter bloom of recent memory. I struggle to open my eyes, afraid that if I don't wake completely I am doomed to sleep forever. A moan escapes my chapped lips.

Someone in the room stirs. There's a slither of steps and a soft cool hand touches my warm brow.

"*Que se passe-t-il?*" a gentle voice asks. "Do you dream?"

My eyes snap open and I swim into dazzling green pools. For an instant I think I am drowning in Mirabelle's eyes. Then I recognize Nicole.

"*Pere* Delmain!" she says urgently, lifting her head. "I don't think he knows who I am."

A murmuring like a distant, angry sea I identify as two voices in hushed and agitated consultation. When it ceases, heavier footsteps bring Delmain, guided by Tor, to my bedside.

"You survived," Delmain says. "Praise God."

"*C'est un miracle!*" Nicole says.

"I suppose you would have to call it that," I say, "since I was rescued by someone who according to Tor cannot exist."

"You believe you saw Mirabelle?" the priest asks, sightless eyes burning into mine.

"Who else could it be?" I ask.

"What did I tell you?" Tor demands of the priest.

"Describe her," Delmain says, ignoring him.

"She has eyes so pale the color is like the sea seen through ice," I say. "Her hair shines like gold in firelight. Her skin is pale as milk with a spray of freckles on nose, arm, and thigh. Though she smiles infrequently, when she does it is like a ray of sun on a cloudy day . . . her teeth are faultless, except for a tiny gap in front—"

The priest shrinks within his frayed cowl. "What age?" he asks.

"No more than twenty-two," I answer.

"You were told how she looked by someone in the village," Delmain guesses. But he is worried.

"Only that she was beautiful and headstrong," I say.

"Somewhere in your father's papers you found a written description," Delmain says.

"No," I say.

"In the hut you somehow stumbled on, God knows how, there was a picture of her," Delmain says.

"No," I repeat.

"He had a vision, *Pere*," Nicole says sweetly, interrupting. "He is blessed."

"There has to be another explanation," Delmain mutters.

"She is three-dimensional, made of flesh and blood," I insist. "We spent the night together—I can't be mistaken about that!"

"I am told that you were very ill," Delmain says, increasingly upset. "Your own spirit may have left your corporeal shell and entered another plane, where it encountered hers—"

"Surely you're not encouraging his delusions?" Tor protests.

"I caught glimpses of her later, on the glacier," I say excitedly, thinking that at last I have found someone I can convince; I may even be able to make an ally of the priest. "She broke that boulder loose to stop the hunt."

"It is something she would do," Nicole agrees.

"No woman would be strong enough to tip over a boulder that size," Tor growls.

134

"And no spirit either," Delmain agrees. But he is uncertain.

"The boulder didn't fall by itself," I say.

"Those of us watching saw you pushing it," Tor says.

"What you saw was me trying to hold it back!" I say, furious that still no one believes me. "Why would I want to harm the men?"

"You also wish to prevent them from hunting the seals," Nicole suggests.

"Admit it," Tor says, when I'm unable to respond. "You were shouting at them to turn back—acting crazed, as if you'd forgotten why we came here in the first place!"

"When we return, I'll make it up to the men out of my own pocket," I hear myself saying. What is happening to me? I wonder in shock. Have I, without being aware of it, come to a decision regarding the seals? But how can I face my father without a quota of pelts? Yet a hunt is impossible so long as Mirabelle guards the seals.

"You intend to go back empty-handed?" Tor presses.

"Not quite," I reply, desperate to resolve this inner confusion I find nearly unendurable. "I intend to take Mirabelle, or her bones, if it comes to that, back with us, to keep my father's promise!"

The cabin becomes graveyard quiet.

"You can't know what your father promised," Delmain mutters unsteadily.

"I read the note he wrote to her—the note I found in your Bible, Father," I say. "How did it get there?"

"You actually have this note?" Delmain asks, taking in a shuddering breath.

"I lost it on the trail," I am forced to admit. "But you know it exists, don't you? Be careful how you answer," I warn him, when I sense that he may be preparing to lie. "Some of the crew were sent to look for it—they may be bringing it back even now."

"They returned some time ago," Tor growls, and for the first time he seems unsure of himself.

"And you didn't tell me?" I ask, startled and angered. "Did they find it or not?"

Tor does not answer. He steps to the doorway, beckoning to someone in the corridor. It is the young ensign, his cheeks and nose reddened and peeling by exposure to the sun's glare. He is carrying the wrapped letter.

"Give that to me!" I cry, terribly excited. At Tor's reluctant nod, the ensign hands it over.

I unwrap the oilskin with trembling fingers. The letter is intact. "Do you recognize this, Father?" I demand, placing his hand on the frayed pages. He snatches it away as if the words burn him.

Carefully, I open the brittle pages; triumphant, I'm about to read it aloud, when to my horror the paper begins to disintegrate. I try to hold the shredding bits together, only to see them drift to the floor, little more than dust by the time they settle.

"What is it?" the blind priest demands, sensing by our sudden intake of breaths that something startling has occurred.

"There was a letter, *Pere*," Nicole whispers.

"Was?" Delmain asks, now as frightened as the rest of us.

"It . . . disappeared," Nicole says.

"Nonsense," Tor interjects harshly. "With paper that old it's no wonder it fell apart in his hands."

"But there was a letter," the priest says.

"You can't deny it!" I say triumphantly to Tor.

"It proves nothing," Tor says, but he's uncertain.

"It proves I was not hallucinating about Mirabelle's hut," I say. "And Father Delmain knows my father promised to take Mirabelle back with him—don't you, Father? Why didn't you speak up when Tor had him bound and gagged and dragged aboard ship? What didn't you want him talking about? You were with him up on the glacier, weren't you?"

"That's when I lost my sight," the shaken old priest answers.

"But not your tongue," I can't resist pointing out.

"There are some things that can only be said to God," the priest replies, and groping with his hand for Nicole's arm, he stumbles toward the door.

They almost collide with an unshaven crewman, the broken-nosed lout with decaying teeth who has been assigned kitchen duties because he has no other skills. He is carrying a tray with a bottle of rum and steaming mugs of tea. He cannot take his eyes off Nicole. That innocent smiles at him as she leaves, and I shiver at his grinning response.

"Put those here," I command sharply, and the crewman jerks his head to face me. He brings the tray to my table. I take one sip and spit it out. "What is this slop?" I demand.

"I couldn't find the fresh tea so I used what was left in the pot," he replies, and I turn aside to avoid his breath.

"Take this drunken sot off kitchen duty," I say to Tor, irritated almost beyond reason. "I told the third mate to assign Per to the galley—surely I am entitled to a decent meal on my own ship?"

"Aye, Captain," Tor says, apparently deciding it best to humor me. "I'll see to it personally." Following the others out, he pulls the door shut behind him. I hear the key turn.

Again, I am left caged and powerless. A swallow of rum heats my brain and produces a surge of energy, but soon the lack of food and the distress engendered by yet another failure to get anyone to believe me leave me weak and trembling.

Faintly, from above decks, I can hear the crew's rough banter as they drink. Apparently Tor has passed out a double or even triple rum ration. They sound increasingly harsh and edgy, like troops kept inactive too long, spoiling for a fight.

Their voices grow louder and more raucous. Suddenly there is a tramping of heavy boots approaching the wheelhouse, followed by a call for silence. Someone shouts out something—a request of some sort. Tor answers—and there are whistles and cheers as the men disperse, clattering down the iron ladders to their sleeping quarters.

I grab the speaking tube and whistle up to the bridge.

"What's going on up there?" I demand.

"Tor's granting the men shore leave," Lars replies.

"All of them?" I ask, astonished, as I hear the men making a great hullabaloo, shouting promises of unsurpassed hellraising once they reach the village.

"All who wish to," Lars says.

"That won't do," I shout, dismayed. "I'm countermanding his order—the men stay on board ship until I say otherwise! Understand?"

"Aye, sir," Lars finally responds.

I can hear the crew beginning to disembark, going over the side, clambering down the ladder to the ice.

"Where is Tor?" I demand. "I want to talk to him, now!"

"I'm not sure where he is," Lars says hesitantly.

I'm about to accuse him of lying or worse, when I hear a knock. The key turns in my door. It opens to admit Tor, carrying a steaming bowl of fish stew.

"The meal you requested," Tor says.

"Why are you letting all the men go ashore at once?" I demand, ignoring the food. "They'll make a shambles of the village!"

"There's no way I can pick and choose," Tor says. "It's all or none—the mood they're in they'll go with permission or without."

138

"You see what comes of flaunting authority?" I rage. "I'll stop them myself!"

I start for the door. Tor blocks my way. "Believe me, it's no use, you couldn't stop them if you wanted to," he says. "They've been through freak storms and unnatural avalanches, seen friends killed in mysterious accidents, believe their captain's out of his mind—no matter what consequences you threaten them with or what rewards you offer they won't believe you. All they can think about is getting drunk, and no one better stand in their way!"

"At least warn the priest they're coming," I say. "He can make sure the villagers stay out of sight."

"They've dealt with crews on shore leave before," Tor replies.

"How long ago?" I ask.

Tor shrugs.

I let my shoulders slump, as if finally defeated, and return to my bunk. Sitting, I slip my hand as unobtrusively as possible under my blankets.

"You agitate yourself unnecessarily," Tor says. "The men will only go to the pub—they can't do too much damage there."

I find the iron weight and surreptitiously curl my fingers around it. As Tor turns for the door I lunge at him, aiming a blow at the back of his head.

At the last moment Tor steps to one side, flinging an arm like a steel bar back across my chest, stopping me in mid-stride. Because I have intended only to stun him, I do not have the momentum I should, and when his elbow slams back into my solar plexus I crumple, my breath whooshing out, my arm flailing rubberlike in air, the iron paperweight dropping from my nerveless hand to the floor.

Tor lifts me back to my bunk. He indicates the stew. "Better eat—you'll need more strength than you've got to pull off something like that," he says, more pitying than sarcastic. Stooping, Tor picks up the iron, judges its weight, looks at me appraisingly, then once more heads for the door.

"By the way," he says before stepping out, "you were right about Per. Turns out he's an excellent cook. He's making some pudding, says it's from an old Norwegian recipe, used to soothe brain fevers. I'll send some down when it cools."

14

FOR A LONG while I stand at the porthole, watching the men straggling across the ice, walking into the setting sun.

Some pause now and again to drink from bottles they must have pilfered from the ship's stores; the broken-toothed lout looks up and sees me peering out—he nudges his mates, and even at this distance their raucous laughter has an edge that stretches my already taut nerves to the breaking point.

Despairing, I turn away and go to sit on my bunk, cold-sweated head in my trembling hands. Eventually, though I have no appetite, I recognize the truth of what Tor has said, and I force myself to eat the congealing stew.

Though it is hard going down and hardly the treat Tor has promised, I feel some of my strength returning. But Tor will hardly give me another opportunity to attack him, and so I resign myself to spending the night a prisoner.

No sooner do I come to this conclusion, however, than I hear a knock at my door—so tentative that I am not sure I have heard it at all.

"Yes?" I whisper hoarsely at the door jamb.

Slowly the key twists in the lock. The door opens to reveal Per, a tray held awkwardly in his hands, the crutch jammed up under one shoulder. Before I can move or say anything, the rangy Lars moves into position behind him, ready for any trouble I might make.

"Couldn't you at least have carried that for him?" I ask.

"He insisted on doing it himself," Lars replies apologetically.

"I wanted to personally make sure you understand that the pudding has to cool and thicken before it can be eaten," Per says.

"He didn't trust anyone else to deliver the message," Lars says.

"I have to go on night watch soon and I didn't want to leave it in the galley where anyone might get at it," Per explains.

"You using cripples to stand watches now?" I ask Lars, annoyed.

"We're short-handed," Lars replies defensively. "Those of us left need rest, so we'll be able to handle things when the crew returns."

I sniff dubiously at the pudding bowl's thickening yellow contents.

"This will help my brain fever?" I ask sardonically.

"It will soothe a troubled spirit, yes, sir," Per replies.

"That's what it did for you?" I ask. Per nods. "I take it then that you no longer believe you saw anything out on the ice?" I continue. "You tripped over your own feet, is that what you think now?"

Though his pale face turns red, Per does not seem offended. "I was a victim of my own imagination, yes sir," he says.

"And what about Nils?" I demand. "Have you fed him enough of this medicinal glue to bring him peace of mind also?"

"Nils is still a basket case, beggin' your pardon, sir," Lars says.

"Better give him my portion then," I say, shoving the bowl back. "I'm not willing to give up my so-called delusions just yet."

Per takes a stumbling step backward, pivoting on his crutch so that he will not have to accept the bowl. "I beg you to try it, sir," he pleads. "You will not be sorry, I assure you."

Though I wonder at his vehemence, I watch without further protest as he places the bowl back on my table. Lars holds the door open as Per maneuvers past the raised sill.

Per turns, gives me a half salute with his free arm, and smiling apologetically, shuts the door. I listen expectantly, my hopes briefly raised. But I know them to be false when the key clicks forcefully in the lock.

Outside, the sun has disappeared below the horizon, and the sky, like my own bruised flesh, is mottled with purple and black. I can no longer make out the men, who by now must be climbing the narrow, rutted slopes into the village. I shudder with resurgent anger at what they are likely to do, and turn from the darkening glass, which reflects my brooding countenance in so distorted a manner I am reminded again of how like I am to my father.

I pace the narrow cabin, sit and stand, and sit again. I am too troubled to read, and my own thoughts fill me with so much dread that I think if I am not already out of my mind this forced inactivity will soon push me over the edge.

I pick up the pudding and examine it under my lamp. Would they have added some tranquilizing substance to prevent any future escape attempts? I stare at the thickening custard—an innocuous yellow with a caramelized glaze—and put a forefinger in for a taste. I can discern no foreign substance, though the amount of sugar used would probably hide most drugs.

But I am suddenly aware of a metallic aftertaste. Angered that Per could have become Tor's dupe so willingly, I slam the bowl down with so much force the already chipped ceramic shatters.

Pudding spreads over my table like a covering of farmyard muck. I shrink from the mess and go to the sink for a towel. As I push the custard into a dust pan, avoiding the broken glass, I spot a foreign object surfacing. The outline is of an iron key!

I do not believe what I am seeing, attributing it to a hallucinatory case of wishful thinking. And then I realize that Per, with his urgent pleas for me to try his pudding, has risked his own freedom to give me mine.

Moving with deliberate speed, I rinse the key at my sink. Making sure the metal is dry, I hasten to the door. Listening to make sure that no one is in the corridor, I insert the key.

It goes halfway in and stops. What is wrong? For an instant I panic. Then I understand that the outside key has been left in the lock. Cautiously I probe from my end, afraid if I thrust too hard the key will fall to the iron deck with a clatter someone may hear.

The key drops. To my anxious ears that clang resounds loud as a gong admitting miscreants through the gates of hell. I wait, holding my breath, ready to abandon all hope should this last effort prove unsuccessful. Eventually I decide that my luck is holding: no one seems to have heard.

Quickly I open the door, retrieve the fallen key, place it back in the outside lock, then pull the door shut again.

I am not quite ready to leave. I rub what is left of the seal oil into the exposed areas of my skin. Its odor is rank but bearable. Its dark overlay will not only keep my pale face from shining in the dark but will almost certainly prevent the sensitive areas around my eyes, lips, and nose from cracking open again in the cold, dry, outside air.

I knot the laces of my boots together and sling them around my neck—I don't want those ice cleats to reverberate throughout the ship, announcing my departure—

and take one final moment to consider what else I might do to facilitate my escape.

My eye falls on my disheveled bunk. I find extra blankets and pillows and rearrange them into the semblance of a sleeping figure. Should the ever-wary Tor send someone down to check, it will look to a casual eye as if their mad captain, his stomach full and his demons momentarily subdued, finally sleeps.

One last thing. I whistle up the speaking tube to the bridge.

"Yes, Captain?" As I have hoped, it is Per who answers.

"I just want to thank you for the pudding," I drawl, making my voice sleepy.

"I'm glad you liked it, sir," Per responds.

"I've not been myself lately," I continue, "but maybe after some rest I'll be able to think more clearly."

"That's what happened to me, sir," Per replies, and I guess that he's not alone.

"I hope to sleep now," I say, "and I'd appreciate it if I'm not disturbed. Would you pass that on to the officers?"

"Everyone's turned in except the first mate," Per replies. "He's just outside, on the flying bridge—would you like a word with him, sir?"

I can picture Tor standing at the outside rail, peering into the milky arctic night, brooding over past and present events, wondering, as I do, whether it's possible for the two to coexist simultaneously. If Tor is lost in thought, I may have a chance to elude his penetrating gaze—slipping from the ship's shadow to that of the glacier while his attention is directed inward.

"Just tell him what I told you," I say. "When it's convenient—when he comes back inside."

"I'll see to it, sir," Per replies.

I cap the speaking tube and move swiftly to the door.

With the crew ashore and the officers sleeping, it should not prove too difficult to move through the ship without raising an alarm.

I inch the door open to survey the empty corridor, then slip outside, locking the door so all seems as it was before.

It's slippery climbing the iron ladders in my stocking feet, but I am soon on deck, where I stand in the shadow of an overhang, letting my eyes grow accustomed to the dark.

The night is achingly cold. Those few stars visible flicker like chunks of white fire; perhaps remnants of volcanic explosions that flung them deep into the boundless sky, where they have hung cooling for millions of years. Somewhere below the horizon the moon remains invisible, but it illuminates the ice pack, causing it to glow in a peculiar manner, as if some ghostly population thrives under the glossy surface.

Here on deck, all is so quiet that I can hear the trembling squeal of the iron cables shrinking in the cold. In the dimly lighted wheelhouse I see Per with his crutch standing three-legged at the frosted windows. Outside, I eventually make out a spare, hunched figure at the flying bridge rail: Tor, his back to me, is staring out over the transparent ice in the direction of the village.

I edge out onto the open, keeping bulkhead and mast between us. My destination is the aft rail, where the anchor chain, dropped to provide a stability that turned out to be unnecessary, should provide easy access to the pack.

I hesitate by the helicopter, which looks, in these cold shadows, like some prehistoric bird sleeping head under wing. But this modern machine is of no use in dealing with supernatural occurrences, and I regret that I troubled to bring it along.

The chain is rigid, its rusted links sheathed in ice, the

anchor itself frozen deep in the pack. Carefully, I put on my boots, double-knotting the laces so that no random string will trip me. Then I swing over the side.

Straddling the chain, I feel the cold penetrate even through the fur I am swaddled in, my privates aching with an intensity that reaches all the way up into my sinuses. Squinting against the sudden pain, I do a half roll, clinging with only my hands and crossed ankles, and begin sliding rapidly down. Suddenly I smack up against a wooden shield; the sound cracks like a whip through the freezing night air. I have forgotten about the rat guards made of barrel covers, put up whenever the anchor is lowered.

Clinging with all my strength to the swaying chain, I hear the links pop loud as gunshots as my weight straightens them out of the ice's grip.

I am done for, I think. Tor cannot help but hear.

And yes, above me, on the deck, I hear the sound of approaching footsteps! Uncrossing my ankles, I hang full-length from the chain, frantically kicking my body forward and back, and manage to swing my legs over the rat guard to the links beyond, where I lock my ankles again.

Mouthing a silent prayer that I will have enough momentum, I let go my hands, and allowing my body to fall backward into space I arch down and then up like an acrobat, managing, at the last minute, to grasp the chain beyond the barrel cover. I scrunch up to that wooden shield, making myself as small as I can, gasping silently for breath.

Distantly, I hear Per's voice: "What is it?"

"I thought I heard something," Tor replies, so close I feel I can reach out and touch him.

"Shall I rouse the other officers?" Per asks after a moment.

There is a worrisome silence while Tor hesitates. Then:

"No, let them sleep," he calls back, and I listen gratefully to his receding footsteps.

"It's probably the drop in temperature," Per says from the bridge. "All that metal popping can sound like a firing range."

Tor's reply then is indistinguishable, because the moment I hear his footsteps on the bridge ladder I resume my slide down the anchor chain, anxious to put distance between myself and the deck. The nearer I get to the bottom the more my speed increases. Apparently my gloves and booted feet have warmed the ice enough to pick up moisture, lessening the friction of my passage until I am rocketing toward the ice pack below.

I try to brake with my boots, to no avail. When I hit the pack, I roll to lessen the impact. But my legs jacknife up into my stomach and chest, forcing the air out of my lungs. I lie helpless, half unconscious, fighting for breath, afraid that this time it's inevitable that Tor has heard.

Gradually my wind comes back. I feel over my legs and chest. No bones seem broken. I struggle to my feet, and standing in the ship's shadow, listen.

I hear nothing from above. I start away from the ship at a ninety-degree angle, planning, when I have traveled a sufficient distance, to circle back and head for the mountain.

But as I get to the shadows cast by the glacier's slopes and make my turn with the *Seljegeren* no longer impeding my view, the frosted moon suddenly slides from behind the mountain's peak and illuminates the entire plain.

The landscape springs into view as if floodlighted by an enormous lamp. I look down—and see a sight that I will never forget to my dying day.

Under the ice are three of the men lost on that ill-fated hunt. They are floating face upward, eyes closed as if in a dreamless sleep, mouths open as if the water streaming through is part of their natural habitat, arms and legs extended and partially intertwined so that they form a kind of misshapen star, while a half dozen young seals nudge and push and tug them along toward the open sea.

Before I can will myself to move or shout or pound on the frozen shield between us they have slowly wheeled past and gone, into the murk beyond.

With brimming eyes I look up, ready to ask heaven's pardon for leading them to their deaths—and I discover that the sky has a reflected glow, shining as if polished, except where it is smudged like a schoolboy's slate with a careless hand.

The smudges are smoke from the village chimneys, and now I make out the huts crouched in the shadow of the glacier. I can see all the village clearly, though it's as if through the wrong end of a telescope. At the same time I hear, remotely as if over long-distance wires, hoarse voices singing a raunchy ballad off-key. It's my crew, mean drunk.

And then, above the hand-clapping and laughter as the obscene song ends, I hear the breathless cry of a young girl: Nicole!

15

WITHOUT HESITATION I change direction and head for the village, running as if in a dream. The cold light glimmers off the ice pack. My cleats give out tiny shrieks, as if bloodthirsty creatures snap at my heels. The cold funnels up my nose, causing my brain to ache. But I do not slacken my pace. Those drunken songs are not good-natured.

When I reach the rutted path that leads up the slope to the village, I am forced to slow. My breath, coming short and fast, smokes like dry ice between my chapped lips.

From up ahead I hear an out-of-tune fiddle whining a lover's lament. But the raucous laughter accompanying it sounds ominously out of place.

All of the huts—except one—are dark. The pub is brightly lit, as if every lamp and candle in the village has been brought inside. I look toward the boarded-up church; neither it nor the ex-priest's hut show any signs of life. I pray that Delmain is with Nicole.

I fling the pub's door open. The heat billows out as if I have opened a furnace. Inside it stinks of sweat and fermented grain and rancid malt—and something else I have not smelled since those terrible scents carried on the hot winds off the coast of Lebanon.

The glowering faces turning toward me burn with more than alcohol. Smoke from pipes and hand-rolled cigarettes clouds the room with the sickeningly sweet scent of hashish. I hesitate in the doorway to let some of the stench dissipate.

As the clean, cold outside air flows inside, the fiddle, a warped instrument played by a villager old enough to have known Mirabelle, stops. Some of the crew are dancing with each other, since village women able to shuffle about are in short supply. Now they stop too, arms clasped around one another, caught in mid-motion as if posed for a photograph.

In a corner of the room I spot Nicole. Surrounded by deckhands puffing smoke at her, she's helplessly trying to wave those hallucinatory clouds away, holding her breath as long as she can but periodically forced to inhale in great gulps.

A volcanic anger rumbles in me. Where is the priest? I spot him then, slumped on a corner bench, his sightless eyes rolled up into his skull, unconscious either from drink or hash or a combination of both.

"Either come in or get the hell out!" someone yells. "But shut the damned door!"

They haven't recognized me. I walk straight for the cornering men. They are too busy tormenting Nicole to notice my entrance. I shoulder between them and grasp Nicole by her slender wrist.

"You don't belong in here," I say, pulling her out of the startled circle.

"We can't leave *Pere* Delmain!" she cries.

The men are staring angrily. Gradually recognition spreads over their reddened faces. I'm reluctant to delay our departure. But it's obvious that Nicole won't leave without her charge. I release her and go back for the priest.

A crewman steps in front of me. I recognize the kitchen helper, his lips parted in a wet grin, revealing the broken tooth.

"I thought you was confined to quarters," he says.

"You can see I'm not," I reply shortly and go to move around him. Again he steps into my path.

"We was told the first mate was assuming command because you was . . . indisposed," he says.

"You were told wrong," I say. "Now stand aside."

All in the pub have become silent. Around us the encircling men have shuffled a step closer, leaning in, intent on our confrontation. In this constricted space I smell the kitchen helper's stomach-turning breath. Keeping my gaze locked upon his evasive one, I decide that only a bold move will get us out of the pub unharmed.

Gently, so as not to startle or provoke the man into a reflex action he is not yet ready to take, I reach out my hand, and breaking the primary rule of command that an officer must never physically touch a seaman, I bunch his coat material into my fist and move him roughly to one side.

His face loses its color. But he remains fixed where I've planted him.

"You're in my way," I explain, and go to where the priest lies slumped on the bench.

As the men around us exhale, disappointed, I try to stand Father Delmain upright. It's as if he's made of rubber. He's heavier than I thought and seemingly boneless. Nicole, who's darted under someone's elbow into the circle, manages to get one of his limp arms around her surprisingly strong shoulders and lifts him in unison with me.

The men reluctantly step out of our way. The priest's feet drag across the scarred floor, making our progress toward the door painfully slow.

The kitchen helper, straightening his parka, trots after us and gets in front of me again, forcing us to stop. Though I fear the worst, I glare at him unflinchingly.

"Let us give you a hand with him, sir," he slurs, falsely ingratiating, motioning to a short, pig-snouted man whose red beard looks as if it has been dipped in burnt grease to join him.

152

I hesitate, reluctant to leave the pub in their company. But it will hardly do to remain here.

I look to the villagers for help. They turn their curious glances away, burying their shamed faces in foaming steins, inhaling sour wine out of cracked mugs, unwilling to face up to what these drunken sailors may have in mind.

"Come on, mate," the other urges his companion as he steps forward to take one of the priest's arms.

The other glances at me, as if for permission, then half diffidently, half aggressively edges me aside and takes the priest's other arm. The two set the priest on his rubbery feet, somehow keeping his legs from buckling, and look to Nicole.

"Which way, sweetheart?" the kitchen helper asks, as if there has never been a problem between any of us.

"Never mind the endearments," I snap, trying to keep what little control I have over this potentially volatile situation. "I'll show you the way."

"Been there before, have you, Cap'n?" he asks, and actually winks.

"She's a child!" I protest furiously, but realizing we can't stay here, I push Nicole through the crowded room to get her out.

"You forget, Captain, I've passed blood," Nicole says so sweetly my heart aches, as I hold the door open for her.

"You see, Cap'n?" the kitchen man murmurs, as they carry the priest past. "They know when they're ready."

Again I flame with anger. But Nicole, as if sensing how near to the edge I am, steps close to the priest to divert their attention, and putting her hand under Delmain's chin, lifts his head.

His blank eyes roll obscenely, but the only sound he makes is a sudden snore. "Can you keep his head up?" Nicole asks. "I'm afraid he may hurt his neck."

"That's easy," the kitchen man says, and grabs Delmain's hair with his free hand.

Though both Nicole and I wince, the priest doesn't seem to mind. He begins, in fact, to hum tonelessly under his breath. I motion for Nicole to go first and the others to follow. I bring up the rear, my mind racing to think of a way to deal with these drunken scum when the next confrontation, which is inevitable, comes.

As we march across the ice-covered square toward the hut adjacent to the boarded-up church, I realize that the night is growing dark. A cloud no wider than an unraveling scarf, drifting down from the glacier, is obscuring the frozen moon.

The uneven path lies suddenly in shadow. It is hardly wide enough for two to walk abreast. The crewmen supporting the priest curse as first one and then the other must slog through the crusted snowdrifts on either side.

"Watch your language there!" I snap.

Their voices drop as they mutter under their breaths with so much anger I begin looking about for something with which to defend myself. Even a rock or a ball of ice will be better than nothing.

But when I try to scoop ice out of the snow the crust is unyielding. Though I kick at the ruts in the path they do not give, jarring my legs until I realize that my own bones will break first.

The church looms closer. In another moment we will be at the priest's hut. I push around the men to confer with Nicole. But she has run ahead to open the door, unaware of the lust that burns just under the surface in these drunken men!

She has the candles lit when we carry the priest, now stiff as some religious icon, across the threshold. Nicole draws the blankets aside and the deckhands drop him on his cot none too gently. Delmain complains wordlessly, then resumes his intermittent humming, as if trying to remember an old tune.

"That's thirsty work," the red-bearded one grunts.

"A drink wouldn't be refused, that's certain," the kitchen man agrees.

"Look in the cupboards there," I say before Nicole can respond. As the two of them follow my suggestion, I lean across the restless priest, pretending to help Nicole tuck the blankets in. "When we leave, bar the door behind us," I whisper. "And don't open it no matter what you hear!"

"There's a bottle, but it's empty," the kitchen man complains, tossing the one he's found aside. His companion bangs the cupboard doors, disappointed.

I leave the puzzled Nicole, and taking each by an elbow push them toward the door, lowering my voice confidentially. "I want to talk to you two privately for a moment," I say. "It's a matter of great importance."

While they are considering this, I nudge them all the way outside. Then I lean back in, motioning urgently to Nicole before pulling the door shut.

"I can't tell you how much I appreciate your help," I say, confronting the two men, who are both rubbing elbows where I have gripped them. "Come along with me to the pub. I'll buy drinks and we can talk."

They look at each other, then back to me. "We fancy staying here for a bit," the kitchen man says. His companion nods. They move forward, but I am between them and the door.

I listen hard. Have I heard the bolt slide home? "That's out of the question," I say. "I'm ordering you to come with me, now!"

"So you can slip back and diddle her yourself, I suppose?" the kitchen man asks.

I react without thinking, backhanding him across his leering face. He stares, rheumy eyes unbelieving. Touching a splayed finger to his bloody lip, he examines the smear with profound concern. His companion watches thoughtfully, as if not sure what he should do.

I know the blow is coming before he throws it. His eyes narrow a fraction of a second before; I duck, and because he is too sodden with drink to have any coordination, his fist shoots past my face and thuds against the door. As he yowls I put my shoulder into his chest and shove him into his friend, who shouts "hey!" as they tangle up in each other and go down in a heap.

I turn quickly and try the door. It's locked. "Who is it?" Nicole calls anxiously from inside.

"Don't open under any circumstances!" I manage to cry, just as I feel unfriendly hands on my shoulders.

I thrust both my elbows backward. But this time they anticipate me, and the hard blows to my kidneys buckle my legs.

I fall to my knees. With better footing the boots kicking at me from either side might do considerable damage. But they slip on the ice and I come up under their legs with stiffened arms, sending them sprawling.

Immediately I set off down the path toward the village square. Behind me they curse and come after. Because of the pain in my lower back I can't run very fast. I hear them gaining. At least, I think hopelessly, I'm drawing them away from Nicole.

Then I become aware that except for my tortured breath and my digging cleats the night is profoundly silent. I risk a glance back over my shoulder. What I see causes me to skid to a stop. They are heading back toward the priest's hut—and one of them has unsheathed a seafarer's hatchet!

In a moment the sound of splintering wood reverberates throughout the square. I hesitate, unsure what to do. Before I can run to the pub and convince someone to help it may be too late. Yet how can I overcome two men, each by himself more powerful than me?

Full of anxiety and dread, I stumble along the rutted path toward the hut, only dimly aware that a cold wind has arisen out of nowhere, attributing the sudden penetrating chill to my own deep-seated fear.

"You cowardly scum!" I shout, almost inarticulate with rage. Suddenly I'm forced to shield my eyes. Sudden gusts of wind whip stinging pellets of ice off the surrounding snowbanks. "If you don't stop," I yell, making a funnel of my hands, "I'll make it my business to see to it you both hang!"

That stops them. But only momentarily. "Everyone knows you've gone out of your mind," the kitchen man sneers. "We'll say you locked the girl up for your own uses and by the time we rescued her it was too late . . ."

Sobbing with frustration, I rush at them headlong. Both take fresh grips on their hatchets, their feet spread, setting themselves to strike. Something underfoot catches my left boot and sends me tumbling up against a snowbank. They laugh and move forward, separating to come at me from either side.

I claw at the crusted bank, trying to get up and retreat at the same time, and trip over my tangled feet. As they laugh again I scramble away desperately on hands and knees, looking for some spot where I can't be cornered, where I can make enough of a stand to eliminate at least one of them, hoping that the other, left alone, will give the matter up.

"Let's put an end to this," the kitchen man mutters. "Get behind him!"

The other leaps to obey. I shrink back as he mounts the snowbank and jumps down behind me, blocking my retreat. I turn again to find the kitchen man advancing, testing the hatchet's edge with a calloused thumb.

Mouthing a silent prayer, I lunge forward. The kitchen man raises the weapon high, ready to strike.

At that moment, in the lowering sky, the scarflike cloud is ripped apart by an unexpected, howling gust of wind, and the moon bursts through like a giant egg spilling out of its nest.

The three of us, like mimes in a deadly play, freeze in place. All about us shadows flee as if blown by a vagrant wind, and we are suddenly illuminated by an unearthly light.

The man in front shields his eyes, looking about for the source of that surreal glow, disbelieving that it could be coming from so wintry a moon. Behind me the other's features are as pallid as those of someone caught in fearful anticipation of his own death.

While the two, mesmerized, stare upward, my own eye is caught by something that gleams from a nearby snowbank—I squint to make out what that is half hidden by the frozen crust. The cold hairs on my neck rise. It is the *hakapik* I lost, days before, out on the ice! There's no doubt it's mine—I recognize the special strap on its handle, and the blood congealed on its barbed end.

How can it have gotten here? We're miles from the sealing grounds. Has some nocturnal creature carried it all this way, finally dropping it as useless? But the snowbank is untracked, and surely no human would have brought a weapon this far only to abandon it.

Another gust of wind whips snow into my face, stinging me out of my awestruck contemplations.

I plunge headlong up over the snowbank. I dig for the weapon while the two men whirl to see what I am up to.

They do not delay an instant. With a shriek of fury, the kitchen man comes racing at me, lifting his hatchet, his companion only a step behind. I wait, bringing up the *hakapik* as if to block the coming blow. But at the last possible moment, I drop to my knees, jamming the *hakapik*'s deadly point horizontally into the snowbank on my left, holding the shaft leg-high across the path. The onrushing man hits the metal bar in full stride.

The impact almost tears my arms from their sockets. Bones crack. The man screams and skids forward on his face. Almost certainly his leg is broken.

But I have no time to consider him. I yank with all my strength to free the still-vibrating *hakapik* and twist to confront the second deckhand. He is so close on me I can see his bulging eyes. Another two steps and he will split my skull.

I brace myself for the impact. And in that instant, like a lightning flash illuminating a shadowed inner terrain, I know, with the force of divine revelation, how that cornered seal bull pup felt watching the instrument of his coming death bearing down on him. It is a feeling beyond terror, a despair over a fate that destroys without purpose, a rage at the inscrutability of the universe.

It's as if I've been given a moment in which time stops, a pause that stretches for an eternity, so that my mind, working at the speed of light, is able to consider and reject alternatives and contemplate past mistakes and failed endeavors, giving me the opportunity to absorb the profoundest truth of all: Thou Shalt Not Kill . . . Any Living Thing.

And then, as I resignedly await my end, begging forgiveness for wasted lives, praying for the intertwined souls of killed and killers, grieving for myself and for the unthinking man with murder in his heart bearing down on me, a dervish wind that has been dancing along the snowbank suddenly whirls off the crust, pelting ice full into the charging deckhand's face. He stumbles, off balance. Howling, he drops to his knees, throwing his hands up to protect himself, losing his hatchet. Though he leans back as far as he can, his momentum carries him skidding forward.

The hook I have been holding skewers his hands and brings them up just under his straining chin. Except for the *hakapik* bracing him upright and the blood beginning to run down the handle, when he comes to rest he looks like nothing so much as a penitent at prayer.

Horrified, I go to examine him. His eyes look up beseechingly out of his blood-flecked face—he is alive!

"I'll send someone to help you," I begin, when the door of the hut behind me opens.

The priest is standing there, supported by Nicole. "Mirabelle?" Delmain whispers hoarsely. "Are you there?"

The chill I feel has nothing to do with the outside cold. A sound unlike any I have ever heard, an eerie moaning starting from the very deepest part of the register and moving up to one so keeningly high I am afraid my eardrums will burst, holds me spellbound with terror.

It is gone so quickly I would not be sure it has existed at all, except for a funnel of snow suddenly rising in the village square. Before any of us can move, the miniature whirlwind races toward the pub. Even at this distance we hear the rattling of shutters and glass shattering as the pub's windows are blown in.

"Mirabelle!" the priest shouts, and he tries to run in that direction, only to stumble and fall.

I help Nicole pick the frantic man up. "Get him inside," I tell her. "I'm going after her."

"No!" the priest says, recognizing my voice. "Let her go!"

I pry his importuning hands from my arms.

"She's going somewhere no human can survive!" the priest cries, like a man possessed, stumbling after me.

From the damaged pub, villagers and crewmen are pouring out into the square, looking toward the commotion. I dart between the church and one of the huts, heading out the back of the village, hoping to reach the mountain slopes before anyone can cut me off.

"Somebody stop him!" the priest shouts. "If he isn't stopped, God only knows what will happen to us then!"

Those words send a tremor through me so profound I stumble and almost fall. I catch myself against the corner of a hut, gasping for breath. I hear shouts as first one and then another and another man head in my direction.

I set off again at a dead run. This time nothing will stop me. I must find Mirabelle, whether she is dead or alive, a living woman or a pile of bones, a vengeful specter or a troubled spirit. I will have the truth from her, no matter what the cost to my father—and yes, to myself.

16

FOR LONGER THAN I think I have stamina for, I run along the uneven, slippery trail that winds toward the base of the glacier, the crewmen in furious pursuit. Whether the priest's damning cry has spurred them on, or they have some idea that capturing their deranged captain will bring them riches or revenge, I don't know. But considering the amount of liquor and hash they've consumed they show a remarkable persistence.

My own endurance starts to dissipate. At a steep and tortuous bend in the slope I cling to a frozen spire, giddied by my exertions and the lack of oxygen in the thinning air.

My panting soon ceases, but my head continues to swim. Though the frozen moon illuminates every rock and crevice they waver in my vision. I begin to imagine a myriad of wraithlike figures emerging from hiding places all along the slopes.

I am frightened. But I no longer care whether this is real or hallucination. I will not go back. I know that flesh or bones, alive or dead, Mirabelle is somewhere on this mountain.

Below me the men are still in full cry. I examine the giant icicle I am clinging to. It is cracked at its base. I kick at the fissure with my cleated boots. Finally it topples, thudding into the softening snow.

The icy spire remains intact. I struggle with it up the slope, grateful that whenever I pause for breath the wavering shadows retreat, as if they are as afraid of me as I am of them.

Around the next bend I find a boulder balanced precariously at the trail's edge. I wedge the slippery spire underneath, then lean my entire weight on it, hoping to lever the boulder free before the spire shatters.

I hear a loud crack. I collapse into the snow, disheartened, thinking I have failed. But when I look up the boulder has moved. Released from its bindings of ice, it's tilted over the edge. Struggling to my feet, I put my back against the boulder and dig my heels in. Its vast bulk trembles. I sprawl forward just as it plunges over.

"Watch out below!" I shout with all the power I can push out of my lungs.

The earth shakes underfoot as the boulder picks up momentum, dislodging ice formations on its thundering path downward. Above its increasingly loud roar shouts and yells waft up to me as the men scramble out of the way. There is a final enormous crash like trains colliding—and then a reverberating silence.

When at last I hear men's voices calling to one another I turn and begin climbing again. It will take them some time, I think, before they can find a way around the unexpected barrier; time enough to put distance between us.

But almost immediately I run into an obstacle of my own. From above, near the tree line, as I emerge from under an icicled overhang onto an open trail, I hear a crack as loud as a gun shot. Looking up, I see a giant slab of ice toppling off its base. Pushing snow ahead of itself down the mountain, it picks up speed, heading directly toward me!

I duck back under the overhang and watch in disbelief as the sky turns a blinding white. Though the muffled roar eventually subsides, the color does not change. The avalanche has turned my refuge into a giant cave. It's as if I'm engulfed in an enormous cocoon.

Trying not to panic, I burrow like a worm into the huge drift, which is loose and dry as talcum powder, finally managing to wriggle my way out before it can settle and solidify and seal me in forever.

As I stand, shivering with relief and brushing the snow off before it can soak through my makeshift garments, I become aware that I'm in the midst of an unfamiliar terrain. The trail I've been following has disappeared, as have all the familiar landmarks. And an enormous pile of snow is blocking me from heading back the way I have come. The only path left open is along the side of the gigantic drift, which, though it's blocking my pursuers, also keeps me from continuing my climb. Telling myself that I should be able to find a continuation of the trail I have been following somewhere above, I edge cautiously out upon the snow's crust.

All seems solid enough. Soon I'm moving quickly again, peering over the seemingly endless landscape for a place where I can turn and head up.

Those ghostly shadows have disappeared. My earlier assumption that they might be manifestations of the spirit world I now attribute to my aberrant, hyperactive imagination, heated by the kind of emotional overload that brought me home from Lebanon. But this time I'll not retreat or allow my will to freeze. This time I'll have Mirabelle's secret. I'll prove once and for all that I'm not insane.

I reach the end of the piled-up drift. As I start to move above it, I hear a whoosh and slither. Another slide! I fall back out of the way just as a new wall of snow tumbles across my path.

Again I'm blocked from moving upward. Again banks of snow have piled before me in such a way that I can move only in one direction. Can this be inadvertent? I shiver again. But if this is a supernatural intervention, I tell myself, it's leading me toward the confrontation I have sworn to have.

Swallowing my dread, I set out once more. Protected from the north wind, I angle over the crest of a hill toward a stand of trees in the distance.

As I draw nearer, those frosted woods seem somehow familiar. I stop short, trying to remember. Can these be the pines overlooking the sealing grounds? If so, it can't be coincidence. I shut my eyes to clear my chaotic thoughts.

When I open them again I wish I hadn't. Lights seem to be flickering through the snow-laden pine branches, as if people holding lanterns gather in that wintry forest for purposes I shudder to guess at.

But what people? I ask myself. Those few left on the *Seljegeren* would not leave the ship unmanned. The villagers are too old to have gotten here before me; the crewmen on my trail are too drunk to catch up.

Once again, thoughts of the netherworld congeal my blood. I force myself to move forward at a crouch, keeping whatever cover I can find between myself and the trees, hoping against hope that Mirabelle will not turn out to be some*thing* from beyond the grave. But I'm determined to have my say however she manifests herself.

Drawing nearer, I drop to my stomach and crawl forward on elbows and knees. Those gleams of light are too bright for kerosene lanterns, and candles, however large, could hardly burn unprotected, however airless the night has suddenly become. No, these lights are unearthly, I reluctantly tell myself. They are as insubstantial as fireflies—is there a species unheard of that is able to live in the arctic North?—or am I witnessing a gathering of spirits who glow with unholy fire?

I begin to hear voices, remote as those wailings on the

shortwave radio. They seem to be coming from places more distant than can be imagined—echoes from another dimension.

Trembling with anticipation and dread, I continue to inch forward. Snow is working itself down my collar and under my garments. But I think of nothing other than how to persuade Mirabelle to let me get close, close enough to determine whether she is flesh and blood, a creation of my disturbed imagination . . . or something indescribable.

By the time I reach the inner ring of trees I am sweating profusely. I clasp the rough bark of a tree and pull myself cautiously to my feet, breathing shallowly so as to make no sound. I wait a moment to make sure my presence has remained undetected; then, moving my head only, my heart pounding so rapidly I fear its drumming must be heard, I peer around the tree into the clearing.

For a wondrous moment I think that I have achieved the impossible—I believe that what I am seeing is a magical conclave, that I am a privileged witness of spiritual, otherworldly beings in a riotous proceeding.

And then—then I am overwhelmed by a feeling of such frustration that I pound my fists against the tree trunk, groaning with so much disappointment I wish my heart would stop.

Those flickering lights are still there. But they are not held by human hands. They are dazzles of heavenly fire. Flashes of northern lights, the aurora borealis, are pouring from the frozen sky, showering down through the long-needled, frosted branches and dancing up off the mirroring snow.

I stand transfixed, hoping for some sign of Mirabelle's presence in that awesome display; then I turn away, tears of wonder and dismay turning bitter cold in my eyes. I am indeed deranged, quick to convert nature's spectacular realities into personal fantasy, a mentally unstable wretch who belongs neither in this world or that. A cliff lies only a few hundred yards beyond, dropping vertically to spiny ledges far below. Just as I wonder what it would be like to run as fast and as hard as I can to the edge and over, an unmistakable voice calls out.

"Jason," she whispers.

I stop breathing. I tell myself that I am alone. What I have heard is the wind soughing through the pines. Yet—

"Jason," comes the tantalizing whisper again. "Over here."

Carefully I turn in a slow circle. The stand of trees has turned dark. The northern lights have dimmed. The moon has disappeared. The stars are fading, the sky to the east chalked with that peculiar sheen seen only just before dawn.

No one is there. I have heard nothing. The silence is as deep as that which must exist in the reaches of outer space. I have listened only to my own inner ear reproducing the lilting accents with which Mirabelle once pronounced my name. I am alone in this wooded ravine, giddied by the lack of oxygen and my terrible anxieties.

Then, at the periphery of my vision, against the trees, I see a glimmer of color. I whip my head around—it's no longer there. I hesitate. Thinking I know the spot where the color has disappeared, I rush forward, dodging around one tree and then another and another—and find nothing.

I slump against a tree, exhausted and depressed. My breath rasps painfully in my throat.

"Mirabelle, where are you?" I demand hopelessly of the wilderness.

Her name reverberates in the wintry hush. Despondent, I sink to my knees, my head bowed. And then, before I can pray God's forgiveness for believing in the unbelievable, before the last echoes have faded completely away, I think I hear laughter.

But how can I be sure? I can't trust any of my senses.

"Mirabelle?" I call again.

Deep in the stand of trees a branch trembles, its burden of snow slipping to the ground. Quickly I stand and move in that direction.

"Mirabelle," I say, forcing my voice to remain calm and reasonable, "there'll be no more hunting here, now or ever. I promise."

The light is changing. Somewhere below us, at the edge of the sea, the sun's first rays brighten the sluggish waters and gradually creep up to the ice pack, causing it to shine.

"I know you're here somewhere," I say, turning in a slow circle. "You made yourself known to me once. Please show yourself now!"

Light from the rising sun continues its climb until it illuminates the glacier's peak. The pine tips start to glow.

"The *Seljegeren* will sail at first thaw," I say. "If you have a message for my father, please tell me now!"

The thin morning haze drifting through this wintry grove is bejeweled by the risen sun. I turn away from its blinding radiance—and she appears before me so unexpectedly, in a sudden dazzle of sunlight, that I recoil.

"Ah, *mon cher,* you're not afraid of me, surely?" she asks.

"You startled me," I tell her when I'm able to talk, my heart filling my throat for fear she will disappear again. "I was beginning to think you didn't exist—that I imagined you."

"You believe you have so powerful an imagination?" she asks mockingly. "You have so much ego that you believe you can create someone who hasn't existed before, like God? I think only poets have this power, *mon ami,* and you're not a poet, are you?"

"I've discovered I'm not meant for killing either," I say, shielding my eyes for a clearer glimpse. "I want to make amends. Tell me what I can do. Don't stay angry. I've been through a lot trying to find you—"

"What is it you want?" she asks, but she has softened somewhat.

"You," I dare to say. "Or if I can't have that," I hasten to add when she flinches, "some token that will prove to the others I'm not mad." I take a surreptitious step nearer.

"Why do you need to prove anything to anyone?" she asks, moving back and forth, restless as a doe sensing danger. "It's enough if you believe, isn't it?"

"They'll lock me up again," I say, keeping very still, afraid that she's taking it into her mind to flee. "And I won't be able to prevent them from hunting!"

She frowns, thinking. I do not move a muscle. "But what do I have that would prove anything to those . . . those cretins?" she demands finally.

"Your scarf?" I ask, and very carefully I edge forward again.

"My scarf?" she repeats, and strokes the faded, frayed wool possessively. "Very well," she says at last, and slowly, reluctantly, she unwraps the scarf from about her neck and shoulders. "But I must have it back. The yarn was a present from your father." She holds the frayed cloth out to me.

For a held breath's time I am too stunned by jealousy to move. Then very carefully, not wanting to startle her, I move closer. She waits with a smile, mysterious as a sphinx, her expression difficult to read in the shifting light.

I take hold of the frayed end. It seems that we are, for the moment at least, bound across time or whatever divides us by the cloth we hold stretched in our two hands.

"Come back to America with me," I say, hoping against hope that this lovely wild creature will agree and spare me the necessity of taking her by force.

"To Bos-ton?" Mirabelle asks, smiling, accenting the last syllable. I nod, afraid that if I speak I will break her dreamy concentration. "That is where your father said he would take me," she says, "after burning his chart, so that no one could ever find this island again. And I would have my choice, he said, between living there and living in Norway . . ."

"You can't have known my father!" I burst out. I cannot bear to think of this young woman with that bent and crabbed old man. And what she's telling me goes against the evidence of my own eyes, or any known law of nature. "You're living someone else's life—your mother's, probably, who told you how some sealing captain abandoned her and left you this scarf as a memento . . ."

"It's you who's living someone else's life," she interrupts with great calm. "I assure you it was me your father abandoned."

"But that can't be!" I protest, even more agitated as I try to reconcile what I want to believe with what I know to be unbelievable. "How can time stop for you and continue for everyone else?"

"Because I never left the glacier," she replies, with what she obviously assumes is irrefutable logic.

I stare in awe at her glowing beauty and begin to wonder whether in fact her skin seems so transparent because of age or because it is a tribute to the freshness of youth.

I move another step toward her. The once-colorful scarf remains taut—she has taken a step back.

"Let me hold you once more," I plead. "Let me prove to myself once and for all that you're real."

"I thought I proved that to you once," she says warily.

"I was running a fever," I say. "I could have been hallucinating."

She waits for me then as I fold the remaining length of the scarf until I am looking directly into her eyes. They are deeper than I remember, the color of a sun-drenched sea. I lean forward and kiss her parted lips. They are as cold as ice. But that must be from exposure to this arctic air, I tell myself. She does not pull away. And I can feel her lithe, muscular body, though it is also stiff with cold under her worn sealskin garment, responding to mine.

"Come with me," I beg, hoarse with longing. "Leave this place. I'll see you get the finest care."

"What kind of care?" she asks, frowning.

"Doctors who can bring you back to yourself," I say. "They'll convince you we're of the same generation— you'll see it's me you loved, not my father!"

"You don't understand, do you?" she says so sadly that my own heart aches. "I can't go anywhere until your father returns. I promised I'd wait."

"He can't come back," I try to explain. "He's crippled and old. If you want to see him again you'll have to return with me to Boston!"

"It's here I promised to meet him," she insists.

"Why is where you meet so important?" I ask.

"Not important," she corrects me. "Necessary."

Her hand is so cold my own flesh shivers. But she is flesh and blood, I tell myself, not an apparition.

"You're hurting me," she says.

"I'm sorry," I apologize. But I don't let go. I intend to take her to the *Seljegeren* by force if necessary.

"What are you doing?" she asks, alarmed, as I try to lead her away.

"Taking you back with me," I reply, tightening my grip.

"But I told you that's impossible," she says.

"We'll see about that," I say, hardening my resolve

against giving in to an argument I consider irrational. I suddenly grab her arms and lock them behind her. She gasps with surprise and hurt. Though her face is in shadow I see her skin turn the color of ice.

I flinch in sympathy. Inadvertently, my grip loosens. And before I know what is happening, she has pulled the scarf from me.

I lunge for the cloth. She evades my grasp. As I stare dumbfounded at my empty hands, she slips away and runs, fleet as any creature in this wilderness, through the woods and out the mouth of the ravine.

With a start, I come out of my trancelike state and take off after her. "You've misunderstood!" I shout. "I'm not like my father. Come back!" But she doesn't hear. And as I run out of words and breath and into the sunlit snowscape, the glare is blinding. She is a fleeting shadow against the risen sun.

Barely slackening my pace, I fumble for my goggles and put them on. The smoke-tinted lenses provide immediate relief—but my eyes are so teary I can make out nothing except the colors in the scarf she is carrying.

I begin to have trouble keeping up. Her seeming weightlessness allows her to run over the spongy surface with ease, while I sink periodically into the snow's softening crust.

She puts more distance between us. At a frozen ridge intersecting the undulating contour of the slope she is running along she stops and turns. Waving the scarf as if in farewell, she then rounds the corner and disappears. Heartsick, I struggle onward, praying that the footing on the other side of the ridge will enable me to pick up speed again. Finally, gasping for breath, I arrive at the spot where I have last seen her. I round the corner—and there is no sign of her anywhere.

Sucking air into my tortured lungs, I lift my goggles

and sleeve my eyes, then scan the slope all the way to the horizon.

She is nowhere in sight. How can this be? On this side the glacier slopes in a series of gentle undulations, a wide-stretching snowscape in which not even a small creature could hide. And yet there is nothing in view!

Stooping to the snow, I look for her footprints. The winds on this permanently shaded slope seem to have swept the surface down to a sheen of ice. For anxious moments I begin to believe that she has left no trace.

Then bending closer I make out what look like periodic dullings of the ice sheen. The marks of her passage? Her sealskin boots could have left these opaque brushings, I tell myself. I will follow them wherever they lead.

It is slow, slippery, enervating work. The trail takes me on a winding course that I realize, when I pause to get my bearings, is eventually going to provide a panoramic view of the ice plain stretching to the open sea. I am in fact approaching a spot where I will be able to see both the sealing grounds and the *Seljegeren*.

But as I approach the icy promontory, the tracks take a sudden turn. I am led on a parallel course up a steepening slope. The footing becomes more difficult. In order to keep going I am forced to drop to all fours.

And then I am stopped by a wall of ice that towers before me.

The tracks—her tracks, I am convinced—march right up to that sheer bluff and end in mid-stride, as if she intended to walk directly—as if she *had* walked directly—into the heart of the glacier itself!

Taking off my glove, I run my bare hand over the freezing surface that rises like a heavily starched curtain into the lowering mist, hoping to find a hidden seam, some opening that will allow me to slip through to whatever passage might lie inside. But the surface is smooth and impenetrable as opaque glass.

It's impossible for her to have simply vanished. Where can she have gone? I look up, straight into the mid-morning sun, wondering if she could indeed have disappeared into this thin mountain air, a spirit given flesh only by my deranged imaginings.

I remain on my knees, weakened more by my fears than my exertions, trying desperately to recall words with which I might address God. But I have been so long without Him that my mind remains blank.

A droning sound, which at first I take to be myself giving voice to melancholy, a kind of metaphysical *om,* intrudes on my consciousness. As it grows louder I realize it is somewhere outside myself. I struggle to my feet and look for its source.

At last I see it, a distant speck in the brilliant sky, growing larger as it approaches, until it is close enough to be identified. A plane! It banks just before reaching the mountain peak, its ski-equipped pontoons glinting in the sun, the shriek of its jet-assisted engines like the cry of a predatory bird. The plane begins gliding downward on a path that will take it to a landing on the ice pan near the *Seljegeren.*

"Mirabelle!" I shout. "Someone else has discovered this island—come with me before it's too late! Can you hear me, Mirabelle?"

The only answer is the echo of my own voice. If she hears, she gives no sign.

17

By THE TIME I work myself down the icy slopes to the plateau overhanging the ice flats, where I have an unimpeded view of the ship, the plane is already landing. It has screamed down from the glacier, passing over the *Seljegeren* once, and now, having banked, whispers back from the open sea, settling down on the shallow ice pan like a hawk with claws extended, skidding over the pitted surface, throwing up slush. As its speed slackens, it taxis in a wide circle to pull up alongside the ship.

The man stepping painfully down from the door over the wing is bent with rheumatism but still powerful enough to quicken my heart with a remembered awe. My father must have heard or guessed that the *Seljegeren* had sailed into forbidden waters. Apparently no power in heaven or his living hell was able to stop him from flying out to discover why.

He lifts a hand to help another passenger down—and my breath stops. Eileen is tall and graceful, bundled in an enormous silken fur that glistens like stirred cream in the sunlight. Why is she here? To doctor my father? Or me? Tor is climbing down the ship's ladder to greet the newcomers. He is no doubt telling them that I have fled the ship and gone somewhere on the glacier. They turn and stare in my direction.

I duck behind a mound of snow, though it's unlikely they'll be able to spot me without binoculars. I don't want to take any chances. If they find me now they'll lock me up again. Eileen, because of her training and my background, will naturally assume I'm irrational. Only my father will know otherwise. And he will not want me raising questions the answers to which can only cause him pain and humiliation.

Somehow I have to get my father alone. I am trying to think how when I notice something happening along the trail leading toward the village. A few crewmen have stumbled into view, rubbing the drunken sleep from their eyes, scooping snow into parched mouths, one and then another stopping to be sick after the night's debauch. Probably the scream of the jet has reverberated down through the valley, bringing them awake and outside, alarmed as to who their visitors might be.

Straggling behind are the two who have attacked me, bandaged and limping, prodded along the path by the sturdier villagers. An enraged cry echoes down from the glacier then. Those on the ice pan look up. I follow their glances and see, on the gleaming slopes between us, those who have been pursuing me.

They are a long way off, tiny figures working their way around the barriers the avalanche has left. That blood-curdling yell was frustration—they are caught at mid-point, not knowing whether to climb after me or return to the ship.

And then, in the farther distance, I spot two additional figures toiling up the slope. One of them is wearing dark garments—the priest. His smaller companion is undoubtedly Nicole.

What does Delmain have in mind? Nicole is not leading him toward the others but following a path that will take them to the stand of pines where I have encountered Mirabelle. Has he been lying to throw me off the track? Does he secretly believe in some kind of miraculous incarnation? If so, what does he intend to do—exorcise the spirit, or commune with it?

In any case, Mirabelle is no longer there. Though I

would like to spare them the arduous climb, at this distance there is no way I can direct them to the spot where she disappeared. My more immediate concern is how to divert the others away from the ship. Only if I'm alone with my father can I force him to tell me what actually happened so many years ago; only he will know whether I am his rival or a self-deluded fool, inheritor of a family curse.

The sun is now almost directly overhead. The sky is cloudless. I can feel the day appreciably warming. The snow conditions are beginning to change. The snowbank I am crouching behind has settled some few inches even as I wait; listening, I hear the whispers and drips of melting snow.

I reach my gloved hand into the bank. It is multilayered and soggy with half-frozen moisture. Underneath is a strata of still-solid ice, a slippery underpinning that will not hold the loose upper tiers for long—a condition ripe for further avalanche.

I move out from my hiding place and examine the sheer slope leading down toward the *Seljegeren*. On closer look, the softening snow is porous, absorbing the warmth like an enormous sponge.

What will set it off? A thunderclap or an explosion— but the storm gods have gone into seclusion, and I don't have guns or dynamite. I look about for a rock formation, thinking to dislodge a boulder. But the expanse in every direction is smooth as a wintry sea.

I return to the snowbank, an idea from childhood taking shape in my mind. Reaching out with both arms, I embrace the top part of the bank, squeezing as much of the snow as I can against my chest. I do this again and again until I have created a large uneven ball that stands as high as my waist.

I pack the ball down on every side, then add snow again, the mush sticky as glue. Occasionally I turn the ball to make sure it is not too heavy to move, until I've pushed it to the cliff's edge, where it stands higher than my head. I am ready. I put my shoulder into the giant ball, dig my cleats in, and shove with all my strength. For a moment the mass seems immovable. Then, as I continue to strain, the ball trembles, tips, slips to one side, tilts toward the other, and begins sliding down the slope.

But it is moving too slowly and not rolling over. I ease over the edge myself, and though the footing is precarious, I reach as far underneath the ball as I can, attempting to lift it over. I am not having much luck when the pitch of the slope abruptly steepens.

The ball, of its own volition, rolls over, flinging me backward. It goes over twice more and then twice again—with each turnover picking up speed and an additional layer of snow—until suddenly it goes slithering down the mountainside, seeming to eat a path for itself like some mythical white monster, swelling with every inhalation.

I stand up, willing those on the *Seljegeren* to look up. The earth rumbles underfoot. All along the slope patches of snow, loosened by the vibrations, begin dropping in huge sheets, like a frozen sea pounding a coastline.

Those on board ship become aware of the turbulent glacier. Tiny figures crowd the rail. Snow cascades in all directions, as if an awakening giant is throwing off blankets, and the contour of the mountain changes until it resembles nothing so much as an enormous rumpled bed.

I spot the glint of glasses. They have focused on me. I laugh like a madman and wave my arms in all directions, pantomiming credit for the havoc being wreaked on all sides. Far below, that swollen beast goes thundering down onto the ice pan, bursting with a roar like an artillery barrage into a blizzard of white fragments.

The glacier shifts and shudders. A ravine splits open;

a fissure closes as if it has never been. The noise subsides like a fading nightmare. Debris like that from an exploded star drifts quietly to earth.

At long last, silence. Slowly I begin to hear, through the acoustical phenomenon that never fails to surprise me, faint shouts. Someone aboard the *Seljegeren* is issuing commands. Within minutes, a party from the ship starts over the flats in my direction.

I wait to make sure they have my position absolutely fixed, then begin climbing in the direction of the wooded ravine. But I have my eye on a rocky incline that cannot be seen from below, its entrance concealed by boulders that have tumbled down during the avalanche.

I make an elaborate swing left, letting myself be seen above piled-up shards of ice, making sure that Tor—or whoever is leading the crew—has me in view before I drop down once again out of sight.

Crouching to remain hidden then, I retrace my steps, careful to leave no indication of my return passage, and plunge into the rock-strewn incline. It is hard going.

I am only about halfway down when I hear the search party arrive at the trail above, winded and furious that again they have to hunt for me. I slip behind a column of ice and shrink against the frozen earth.

"Any tracks up there?" demands a hoarse voice I recognize as Tor's.

"It's impossible to tell," a surly crewman answers. "There's been another slide—damn near everything's covered!"

"A shame to waste energy on something with no profit in it," I hear Helmut, the chief hunter, saying, sounding so close he seems only a few steps away. Then I realize he's at the top of the funneling incline below which I lie hidden, speaking as if into a megaphone. "Weather like this, cows'll have their young'uns out in the open. We could get our quota of pelts easy. Where can he go, anyway? Sooner or later he'll have to come in to the ship."

"And if he doesn't?" Tor demands.

"Time enough to look for him then," Helmut says.

"The old man wants him found first," Tor snaps. "It won't take long—between the men coming down and us climbing up we'll squeeze him out soon enough."

"If we don't, I'm giving you fair notice," Helmut warns. "I'm goin' after pelts!"

"Alright, let's move on!" Tor shouts to the men above, only a momentary hesitation showing that he has acknowledged the threat. And the search party begins climbing again.

In some agitation, I continue working my way down the incline, careless now of loose rocks or icy crevices. They still plan to fill the ship's holds with fur! I have wrongly supposed that my warning them about Mirabelle's presence would deter them. Their greed has overcome superstition. My father's arrival has negated my offer to compensate them for sailing home empty-handed.

Arriving at the ice pan sweating and winded, I pause only long enough to get my breath. Then keeping close into the glacier's base to remain out of sight, I move as quickly as my fading strength will allow until I draw even with the *Seljegeren's* bow.

If my calculations are correct, only a minimum number of hands will have remained behind: a watch on the bridge, an engineer below, a guard for the radio officer in the brig, and someone to see to the needs of my father and fiancée and the visiting pilot. I see no one on deck. Because of the way its windows reflect the sun, I can't tell if anyone's in the wheelhouse.

But there's no longer any way to remain hidden. Pulling my parka hood over my head, though it's uncomfortably warm, I stride out onto the ice pan, hoping to get to the ship before an alarm can be raised.

I stride purposefully, as if I have reason to be there, shielding my face so that anyone observing might suppose that I am merely hiding from the sun's glare. But when I arrive within hailing distance and still no one has challenged me, I begin to wonder why—surely no ship my father is aboard would be so lax about security? I quicken my pace—and when I mount the ladder to the deck I discover that I'm not the only one who wishes my arrival kept secret.

From behind the wheelhouse glass, my father lowers binoculars from pain-filled eyes red-rimmed from lack of sleep. Eileen is pouring him steaming liquid from a thermos, handing him tablets I assume are painkillers. She turns to acknowledge my presence.

"Hello, Jason," she says calmly. "You're just in time for tea."

Conflicting emotions work my father's face, no doubt reflecting my own. I'm torn between admiration and resentment, love and rivalry. I'm not sure what to say or do—and neither is he. Does the situation call for an embrace or a challenge?

"I'd like to speak to my father alone," I say to Eileen.

"I'd prefer it if she stayed," my father says before she can leave.

We glare at each other fiercely.

"Why have you come?" I finally demand, thinking that he won't be so arrogant when he hears what I have to tell him.

"That's not much of a welcome, darling," Eileen says, reminding my father with a finger tap on his hand to take his pills. While he swallows them grudgingly, never taking his eyes from me, she pours another mug and brings it to where I stand, stiff and unyielding.

As I take the tea from her she offers her lips. I kiss her

cheek. She smiles as if not offended. But her sidelong glance appraises me intently.

"Your father received a garbled message saying you were ill," she says.

"And I suppose Tor has confirmed it," I say.

"He's very concerned about you," Eileen says, placing her hand on my arm. The touch of her fur makes me blanch. "What is it?" she asks, frowning.

"Seals were slaughtered to make you that coat," I tell her.

"I'll give the fur up, if it offends you," Eileen says with a shiver, and she starts to take the coat off.

"Don't be foolish," my father growls, stopping her. "What's done's done."

"You gave Mother that coat," I say, remembering, as he touches it with a certain familiarity.

"Your mother never wore it," he replies. "I thought it would be an appropriate gift for someone betrothed to a seal hunter."

"That's wrong on all counts," I begin, ready to plunge ahead with an explanation about how everything has changed since our arrival here, when he turns away and moves awkwardly toward the ship's controls. "What are you doing?" I demand.

"Signaling the men that you've been found," he replies, and before I can stop him he reaches for the long cord hanging near the wheel. The ship's horn blares twice, momentarily deafening us.

We all look toward the glacier and see, as a result of that ear-splitting blast, another fall of snow thundering down. When the last echoes recede like a diminishing storm, I see the search party pausing, no doubt bewildered, far above the ravine where they last saw me.

Finally those tiny figures turn and, making a wide circle, start climbing back down.

"They're planning to hunt seals!" I burst out, dismayed, as I realize they are taking a direction that will lead them to the sealing grounds.

"That's the purpose of this expedition, isn't it?" my father asks.

"Not anymore," I reply. "Not if I have anything to say about it!"

My father sighs. He glances at Eileen, as if confirming what they've been told about my behavior. "You know this crew's bound to harvest pelts and damn anyone who gets in their way," he says, as if explaining to a stubborn child.

"It's them who'll be damned," I reply, reminding myself to keep calm. "You of all people should know that. Here of all places you know that it's dangerous to hunt seals. Isn't that why you warned me to sail only in charted waters?"

"What I told you was based on a personal experience that has nothing to do with you," he replies heavily.

"It has everything to do with me," I say.

"Jason," Eileen cautions.

"It's guilt that's got him so twisted and bent," I tell her in a fury. "Thirty years ago, on this island, he promised a young woman he would spend his life with her, never mind that he already had a wife pregnant with his child, pregnant with me!"

"I didn't know your mother was pregnant," my father protests in a voice suddenly so thin it is almost without substance.

"You promised to honor her always," I accuse him. "You exchanged sacred vows!"

"Love honors no religion," my father replies even more faintly.

"You're not claiming love is what you had with Mirabelle?" I scoff, now completely out of control. "She's more honest—she says it was passion. You took her under false pretenses, didn't you? And later promised to do the honorable thing, got her to promise to wait for you for as long as it took, for an eternity, if it came to that . . ."

"You can't know anything about that," my father objects. He has difficulty breathing. "No one knew—not Tor, not the priest . . ."

"Mirabelle confided in me," I say.

For a moment it seems as if my father will collapse. His face matches the color of his hair, and Eileen moves quickly to support him.

"Who is Mirabelle?" Eileen asks, looking from him to me.

"An island woman my father wronged," I answer when my father will not.

"Mirabelle died thirty years ago," my father manages to say. "He's hallucinating, the atmosphere here can play tricks with a man's mind . . ."

"It's more than atmosphere," I say. "You can't deny that what she told me no one else could know!"

My father groans, and Eileen, after a puzzled, concerned glance, helps him to the captain's chair.

I reach deep into my parka and pull out the oilskin. "Mirabelle took me to where she lives, up on the glacier," I continue, determined to have it out, no matter what the emotional cost to either of us. "That's where I found this." I toss it to my father. "There was a note enclosed, in your handwriting."

My father studies the wrapping, then reluctantly unfolds it and fingers the dust, which is all that remains of the paper. He stares then into space, his face working with an emotion so nakedly anguished I am almost ashamed to watch.

"Shall I quote it to you?" I ask.

"I remember what it said," my father whispers.

"Why didn't you go back for her?" I demand.

"Tor wouldn't let me," my father replies at last. "It

184

was an early spring, and there were avalanche conditions—"

"But you were captain," I say, bending close to him. "You could have overruled Tor. There must have been some other reason . . ."

"Jason!" Eileen interrupts, pulling me back. "Let him be! What possible benefit can there be for you in stirring up painful memories?"

I pry her fingers from my arm. "I asked Mirabelle to come home with me," I say, as gently as I know how. "She couldn't, because of her promise to my father. Now I want him to release her from that promise!"

"Jason," Eileen says after a silence, looking at me with the same melancholy she'd displayed when examining me after Lebanon. "Don't you realize how crazy that sounds? To become infatuated with a woman twice your age . . ."

"She hasn't aged," I reply, though I know I'm confirming Eileen's diagnosis. "She's still as young and beautiful as she must have been when my father betrayed her!"

"It's impossible," my father mutters, but he's uncertain. "Even if the priest lied . . . ," his voice trails off. His eyes glaze, looking inward at memory.

"What did the priest lie about?" I ask in his ear.

He shudders but does not answer.

"Mirabelle's waiting for you," I continue. "What are you frightened of? If she's not real, but as you say, a trick of the atmosphere, then where's the harm in seeing her? You owe her that much."

My father stirs from his self-induced, near-hypnotic state. His eyes clear like a receding fog, and he nods.

"Look at him, Jason!" Eileen intrudes, her voice sharp with anxiety, confused as to how to cope with a situation beyond her understanding. "He can't climb in his condition."

"He won't need to," I say, "if I can get the chopper to work."

"Then I'm coming too," Eileen says.

"You can't," I say.

"Why not?" Eileen asks. "It's big enough for three."

"I know," I say. "But we'll need room for Mirabelle."

18

I ASK MY father to pipe all hands on deck. He hesitates, glancing at the shaken Eileen, then pushes himself forcefully up from the captain's chair.

With only a trace of a limp from the pain he cannot hide, he picks up the speaking tube. Again he hesitates, fighting back God or the devil knows what nameless fears. Then, with that fatalistic shrug I remember from my sojourn with him in Norway, he casts aside whatever doubts plague him and presses the switch that sounds the simulated bosun's pipe.

"Attention, all hands, attention, all hands on deck," he says, in a voice in which no trace of weakness remains. "On the double!" he roars, with a sardonic glance at me, as if now that the decision has been made he intends to proceed with all engines full ahead.

The ship reverberates with the pounding of feet along the corridors below decks and up the clanging iron ladders. By the time the three of us get to the helicopter those few crewmen aboard are gathering on the fantail—including Per, who uses his crutch with increasing agility.

All seem unhappily surprised to see me—and look from my father to me with frowning curiosity, as if nervously wondering whether they are about to witness another clash of authority, or will themselves stand in the dock accused of collusion in mutiny.

"Where's Smithy?" I ask.

"With the search party," Per responds uneasily when no one else volunteers an answer.

187

"Did he test the blade's torque?" I ask. And again Per is the only one who can, or will, answer.

"He didn't want to risk starting the engine without you present," Per says.

"You're not going up with a suspect propeller?" Eileen asks in an urgent whisper.

"I'll know when we warm it up whether it works properly or not," I reply. My father's face is stoic, revealing nothing.

"Per," I say loudly then for the benefit of the men, "I'm putting you in charge of this crew. Get those cables loosened, throw them off when I give the word."

"Aye, sir," Per says, hesitating only a moment; and gesturing with his crutch, he herds the sullen crewmen toward the huge stanchions to which the cables are bound.

The ladder the smithy has used to remount the propeller blade is still in place. I climb quickly to recheck the attachment—the smithy, meticulous to a fault, has not only tightened the bolt securely but soldered a protective seal around it.

I use my vantage point high above the deck to check the glacier for the hunting party's progress—they are still a considerable distance from the sealing grounds, though they're closing the gap faster than I'd thought likely.

"At least you still take the normal precautions," Eileen observes when I return to the deck. "That's somewhat reassuring."

"Why don't you brew up some more tea for the old man," I say, taking her aside. "And put plenty of rum in—he'll need it when he meets Mirabelle again."

"You must know she can't be the same person he knew!" Eileen bursts out.

"That's certainly the rational explanation," I agree. But I refuse to be drawn into discussion and return to the chopper, hoping that getting it ready for takeoff won't take too long.

I remove the tarpaulin from the engine, disturbed to find that the heater, attached as a precaution against just the kind of winter storms we have encountered, has stopped functioning.

When did its power go off, before or after the warming winds began? I lift the engine shield and put my bare hands against the block, convincing myself that though it's cold, the fact that my skin doesn't stick to the metal is a sign that it hasn't frozen and cracked someplace I cannot see.

Replacing the cover, I jump back down to the deck, and ignoring my father's questioning look and Eileen's increasing dismay, mount the stirrup and slide into the cockpit. I switch on the ignition, make sure the fuel tanks are registering, tell myself that the zero mark on the temperature dial means nothing until the engine is actually running, and offering a silent prayer to whatever gods might be appropriate, press the starter.

There is a thud, followed by silence, followed interminable moments later by a sickeningly slow grind that barely turns the engine over. But I persist. The starter increases its speed, whining with the strain.

There is a sudden hiccough. Then the cold engine starts, fails, and starts again. I do not trust the automatic choke and hand-feed more gas to the gasping carburetors. Within minutes the blessed engine is purring.

But now the cabin is vibrating unpleasantly from an unevenness on the aft end of the circle the straightened propeller makes. I hastily make adjustments in the torque. Finally, by increasing the engine's speed, I overcome enough of the vibration to convince myself that we will be able to fly—as long as I remember to compensate for what are sure to be erratic flight characteristics.

I set the throttles and motion to my father to climb

inside. Eileen has returned. She says something to him that I cannot hear. He shrugs a kind of acceptance, and taking the thermos from her, awkwardly mounts. I pull him inside, making sure he's buckled securely into the copilot's seat.

"I'll be back in half a minute!" I shout in his ear. "I've forgotten my snow goggles."

In fact, I have them around my neck under my parka, but it won't do to tell him what I have in mind. I jump to the deck, and crouching to avoid the blades thrumming erratically overhead, I pantomime that I've forgotten something to the startled Eileen and run below.

But instead of heading for my cabin, I take the ladder amidships, dropping down six rungs at a time until I'm stepping over the chain to the hold marked Off Limits. I hasten to the storage lockers, then swear at my own stupidity—naturally they're padlocked, and the only keys are in the wheelhouse.

In too much of a hurry to go back, I look about. On a nearby bulkhead in a glass-enclosed case is a fire axe. It takes only two quick blows with my elbow to shatter the glass and retrieve the axe. I make short work of the padlock.

Heavily waxed cartons bound with metal straps are stacked inside the red-painted locker. The straps break easily, and I opened the cardboard to find inch-thick, foot-long waxed dynamite sticks.

I arrange a half dozen sticks around my waist, hiding them underneath my parka. Within minutes I am swiftly climbing the ladders that lead back up on deck. As I head for the noisily ratcheting chopper, Eileen stands in my way. She says something I cannot hear. I bend my ear to her mouth.

"Keep your wits about you," she shouts. "Whatever's going on up there, remember that the air's thin and being deprived of oxygen can cause the brain to work in peculiar ways!"

"I don't expect you to take my word for it," I shout in turn. "I intend to bring back proof."

I start for the helicopter again, and again Eileen steps in my way. She throws her arms about me and I half-heartedly return her embrace, at the same time trying to keep our bodies apart. But she presses close enough to feel the hidden sticks, and as we separate she looks up at me, bewildered, her mouth open to speak. I stroke her flushed cheek, and ducking under the rotating blades pull myself up into the cockpit.

"Where's your snow goggles?" my father asks as I buckle in.

I pull them into view. He nods, though there is the trace of a frown. To avoid his penetrating glance I lean out and motion to Per. A crewman with a sledge is at the chocks that are held by slackened cables. As Per signals with his crutch, the chocks are knocked out of the way. I ease the stick back and we rise from the deck.

The chopper immediately demonstrates a tendency to skew left. I hastily compensate with rudder and stick. Just before it seems we must slam into the rebuilt mast, the chopper tilts and veers sideways and we are over the ice pack.

The terrain underneath slides by like film on an unreeling spool. I have difficulty gaining altitude, and we are rapidly approaching the glacier. I feel my father watching me as I pull the stick back until the wheel is pressing my stomach. Then I quickly adjust the pitch of the rotor blades.

Our crabwise forward motion slows. We hover and slowly rise, tilted like a bird with a crippled wing. I keep increasing our lift until we are at five hundred feet, high enough to leapfrog over the first jagged slopes. I adjust my snow goggles against the continuing glare, and as I move us forward again I can make out, in the distance, the hunting party.

They are approaching the trail that will bring them out above the sealing grounds. I veer off in their direction. As the pitch of the rotor blades changes, the sound reverberates between the glistening spires at the top of the lower slopes. Those in the lead spot us and stop, the others bunching up behind, a dark worm curling up on itself, as if shrinking from the melting snow underfoot.

My father begins shouting, his words lost in the noise of the clattering blades. I can guess what his concerns are. But I feign ignorance. I cup my ear and shake my head to imply that speech is useless.

We come in over the men at an angle that allows me to spot Tor. I lean out of the cockpit and motion with my free arm, waving them back toward the *Seljegeren*. Before I can make out any reaction we are past. I bank us into a slow circle. As we pass them again, I motion again toward the ship.

As we bank around yet again, Tor has broken off from the main party, apparently hoping he can lead them back. But the others do not follow. They continue along the path that will bring them out over the icy ledges where the seals congregate.

Though not entirely unexpected, anger suffuses my face with blood. I push the stick forward and jam the throttle full on. We come down at them in a skewed rush, passing so close the men are forced to flatten themselves against the snow.

As we go surging by and lift back up and around I glance at my father. He has fallen silent, rapt in some inner contemplation, unwilling to interrupt the journey to wherever destiny's pilot—a role that something, I don't know what, compels me to fill—will take him.

I am about to pull out one of the dynamite sticks when I spot a new mass of loose snow just below the tree line, above the trail the men are following. Apparently last night's surprising wind has caused it to drift into that misshapen pile.

I bank and slide sideways down toward the men again. They brandish their *hakapiks* defiantly; some have pried loose chunks of ice and fling them at us as we fly by. My father puts his hand on my shoulder. I shrug him off and head for the snow mass.

As we hover overhead I notice the downdraft from the propeller stirring up the covering of snow. I lower us until we are engulfed in a blizzard of white dust.

Though it's difficult to be sure, the mass underneath seems to be moving. It picks up momentum; the entire side of the slope gives way! With the sudden hollowing out of ground beneath us a vacuum is created. We are immediately sucked lower.

I hastily give the chopper full throttle and pull the stick back. The sluggish controls do not respond. Then, like an elevator whose cables suddenly reverse, we spring upward.

I manage to bank us around. As the snow crashes onto the trail below, a great cloud puffs up like residue from a bomb blast.

When the fragments of ice and snow settle I am delighted to see, through the milky haze, that the trail has been blocked. The hunting party, diving for cover at the unforeseen impact, are slowly digging themselves out.

That barrier should dissuade them, I think. Without delaying further, I lift our craft straight up until we reach an altitude that will allow us to clear the ridge, then set a course that will take us over the trees where I have last seen Mirabelle.

We pass over the trail leading up from the village. The priest and Nicole are still a distance from their destination. I touch my father's shoulder and point, banking our craft in a large circle so he can see them. Nicole waves as we go by. I wave back. The old priest stands hunched and unseeing, holding his ears at the noise, and then we have left them behind.

My father shows little emotion, except to tighten his mouth and look away. And then we are on the stand of trees. I circle it, looking for the tracks either of us may have left. But the snow is unmarked. I then slide us in overhead, slowing until we are barely moving just over the pine tops, their grayish green needles, like witches' hair, shaking in great agitation under the propeller's downdraft.

My father looks at me from time to time with increasing skepticism. I ignore him, peering down into the secluded clearing where I last encountered Mirabelle. The once shadowy interior is drenched with light from the glaring sun, now almost directly overhead. There is nothing, no movement whatsoever anywhere in that small forest, not even the sign of a winter-acclimated bird or rodent.

I take us sideways out of there, then lift straight up to give us a broader view. Except for the priest and Nicole, and much farther away, the hunting party trying to regroup, there is nothing.

Beside me, my father stirs. He picks up the thermos, unscrews the cap, and offers me a drink with a steady hand. Those pills he took seem to have helped. I refuse the drink.

He shrugs, takes a swallow himself, then another, and recaps the thermos—his attitude one of resignation. It's obvious he's now convinced I imagined the whole thing.

I slap the throttle ahead full, steering the craft up the slopes toward the jagged crown of the glacier, gleaming in the sun as if studded with broken mirrors. If I can find the hut, I think angrily, that will have to convince him.

My father straightens and begins to examine the terrain flowing by underneath with great care. Is he looking

194

for landmarks? I doubt that he can find them. Too many slides over the years have changed the landscape in ways he would find unrecognizable. And the clearing was so well hidden that even I will have difficulty finding it. It will take something more than luck.

I stop chasing our fleeting shadow over the icy ridges and fly straight up toward the sun. The air becomes thin and cold, making it difficult to breathe. Our craft starts vibrating, hanging precariously, as if suspended by an invisible thread, unable to climb any further. I ignore my father's stare, waiting for a sign, for some sort of guidance, divine or otherwise, that will show me where the hut is.

Far below, near the shores of the shimmering sea, the seal herd is spread out over the ice floes as far as the eye can see. They bask in the warming sun, the milk-furred pups frolicking about the darker-skinned, somnolent mothers, the bulls gathered in dignified conclaves on the ledges nearby. Somewhere below those outcroppings is where I first saw Mirabelle.

I let the craft drop toward a ravine I can just make out far below. I'm almost certain it's the one I climbed during that frightening storm. Beside me my father is gasping for breath. The air thickens and warms appreciably as we approach the ground, and I begin a traversing pattern, moving from side to side in short arcs, looking for anything recognizable . . . and then I see them!

From this skyward angle they look somewhat different, but I recognize those jagged triangles of rock, like a dinosaur's spine imbedded in the ice by an unexpected upheaval. My breath catches. Anxiety rises in me like mercury in a temperature gauge. I fly along the bony ridge at a constantly lowering altitude until we are almost within touching distance of the towering stones.

Then the ground seems to fall away. Underneath us the clearing appears with the hut still there, though not as I have left it. Part of the roof has collapsed. Half the structure lies in ruins. Beside me, even above the clatter of the propeller blades, I hear my father gasp.

Carefully I lower the chopper into the clearing. This slow speed causes the craft to vibrate with so much force I'm afraid it may shake itself apart. But within moments we touch ground.

I switch the engine off before too much damage can be done. I'm also concerned about disturbing the terrain overmuch, still hopeful that I may find tracks to indicate that Mirabelle, physically alive, has recently been here. There is no doubt, watching my father's face, that she was here once with him, long ago.

We sit without moving, in a silence that reverberates with painful memories.

"How did you find this place?" my father asks at last, his voice hoarse with remembered anguish.

"Mirabelle brought me here," I reply, and flinch at the harsh gaze he turns on me then. He does not believe me.

Angrily, I jump down from my seat and reach an impatient hand up to help him. He shrugs me aside, and moving stiffly, eases himself to the ground.

I begin searching the clearing for some sign of her presence. My own tracks, beginning to melt under the sun's rays slanting past the guardian spires, are still visible. But if Mirabelle returned after she ran from me there is no sign of it. Where can she have gone? She can't have disappeared into thin air. I can't prove anything without physical evidence that she was here.

My father hesitantly approaches the wrecked hut, then stands, head bowed before the partially opened, weather-beaten door, as if praying before some desecrated shrine he is unwilling to enter. I push past him, refusing to accept the hut's ruined condition as proving my experience here invalid. I was inside this place, and so was

196

she, and if in my fevered state I fantasized surroundings to match the exalted nature of our lovemaking, that doesn't make what we had any the less real.

Inside, the collapsed roof has made the room a shambles. I pick my way through the debris, hearing my father enter slowly behind. I push a beam aside. Underneath are the worn sealskins that have served as a bed. My father watches, his eyes narrowing as he recognizes what I have uncovered.

"This is where we slept," I say.

"We?" he wonders. I nod. "Slept?" he repeats.

"Made love," I reply defiantly.

"You and the person calling herself Mirabelle," he says, refusing to accept what I am telling him.

"She has a mole just above the nipple on her left breast," I say.

My father loses all color in his face. He attempts to speak and no sound comes.

"Coincidence," he manages finally.

I shrug and move further inside, dismayed to see the interior of the stone fireplace a mass of rubble from the partially collapsed chimney. I reach in and pull out the rusted iron kettle.

"She made me soup in this," I say.

My father takes it from me, studying the cobwebbed ladle.

"This hasn't been used for years," he points out.

"She made it from some kind of greens," I say, ignoring the comment as irrelevant. "It gave me enough strength to get back to the ship." My father does not respond, but I can see he is troubled. "You remember the kind of soup I'm talking about?" I ask.

"The island women cook seaweed," he finally replies. "They dry it in the summer and use it all winter long."

"Well then?" I say.

"That doesn't prove that she—Mirabelle—made it for you," my father says angrily.

"Who else knows about this hut?" I demand, angered in turn. "How would I have known to look for that note if she hadn't told me about it?"

He is momentarily silenced.

"Where did you find it?" he asks then.

I walk to the other room and examine the mess there. The shelves in the corner are buried under pieces of the roof thatch. I step over splintered wood and cracked stone. As I lift pieces of thatch aside dust clogs my nostrils and I sneeze.

"God bless," my father says.

In that same instant I spot the thick old book lying half under a fallen beam. As I reach for it a splinter enters just under my thumbnail. "Damn it to hell!" I cry, and my father blanches, making the sign of the cross.

I remove the painful stick with my teeth and carry the Bible over to him. He takes it from me and examines it as if hypnotized. "That's from me," I explain, wiping a spot of blood off the cover, then showing him my bloody thumb. "Nothing supernatural about that."

"She kept the note in this?" my father asks, still holding the Bible as if it is hot in his hands.

"Yes," I reply. "Shouldn't she have?" I stare at him, puzzled, wondering why he is making an issue over what seems to have been a perfectly normal act on her part—and then I realize that he, a seaman from first breath, brought up to worry over signs, portents, and omens, would of course be concerned—those holy pages give his note promising eternal devotion a divine, supernatural force.

"But this cabin is uninhabitable," he says, arguing as much with himself as with me. "It's impossible for anyone to be living here!"

I look about the demolished rooms, unable to deny the

198

evidence of my own eyes. "This is where she brought me," I reply stubbornly.

"But she didn't stay," my father reminds me. "When you came to your senses she was gone."

"I saw her again in that pine grove we passed over on the way here!" I tell him. "We stood as close as I am to you now! But it may be true that she lives somewhere else," I have to admit, seeing no sign of human habitation in these wrecked rooms. "When I trailed her up the mountainside her footsteps ended at a cliff—I suspect there's a cave there somewhere, one hidden so well I just couldn't find it."

The transformation in my father's face is startling. He has been patiently hearing me out, full of condescension and pity, doubtless reminding himself of my unstable history, when my last words cause him to go rigid as stone, the color draining from his face until he is as gray as the dust we stand in.

"This cliff is near the wooded ravine?" he manages, at last. I nod. "Show it to me," he orders.

Though I'm full of questions I keep silent. Because of something I've said he's no longer denying the possibility that my encounter with Mirabelle actually took place. From his reaction, I have to believe that he's on the verge of telling me what I want to know.

But the moment passes. Taking a deep breath, he casts a last long look around the hut; then, still clutching the Bible, he follows me out.

We buckle ourselves into the helicopter. Neither of us has anything to say. I press the starter. As we slowly lift up, the hellish racket made by the unevenly rotating blade reverberates all around the enclosure, putting an end to any possibility of conversation.

I look over toward the cabin. Its timbers are vibrating. As I watch, the entire structure collapses!

Dust billows outward from the impact. I throw the

throttle full on to get above that spreading, noxious cloud, holding my breath in a kind of primal, unreasoning fear that if we inhale any of the minute particles floating toward us we will be done for, imprisoned in time forever.

Then the whirling blades flatten the cloud underneath us, diffusing it to the corners of the clearing, and we spring upward into the shining clean air.

19

THE LANDSCAPE GLOWS white-hot under the afternoon sun, vapors curling up like steam. Dazzles of light reflect off the shiny crust, bouncing from snowy crest to slippery promontory to the giant icicles dripping down sheer hillsides. Inner fires roar within the silencing ice, flames from an arctic hell frozen inside.

The sound of our blades trails behind us in intermittent bursts as we slide down the mountain, fading echoes absorbed by the melting snow. In the distance a straggle of insects turns out to be, as we come closer, the hunting party, broken into parts. Some are heading back toward the *Seljegeren*. Others have worked their way around the slide and are now near the bluffs overlooking the breeding grounds, a hard-core few determined to gather a few rare pelts no matter what.

I tell myself they will not succeed. I try to coax more speed out of the chopper. The warped blade begins to thrust us from side to side. I ease back on the throttle, afraid we will be shaken apart.

We drift over the wooded ravine, empty and sepulchral even in daylight, and continue down past the place where I last saw Mirabelle—surprisingly nearer the breeding grounds than I have thought.

For an instant I think I see a flash of color on the bluff. On closer look that sheer cliff remains blank as before. My father notices nothing—his attention concentrated on the undulating terrain ahead.

The hunting party is unaware of us until we have flown

by. The noise trailing us throws them into disarray, and they dive for cover on either side of the trail. Before they can recover we are passing over the ledges on which the herd's sentinels keep watch. They look up, observing our passage with the same passive curiosity with which they might consider a noisy but harmless bird.

Where is Mirabelle? Surely she will not allow her beloved seals to be attacked? But she is nowhere to be seen. At the edge of the boundlessly open, glittering sea, I bank our craft around and head back over the ice pan toward the ledges. It's been left up to me then.

There's almost no distance now between the hunting party and the herd—the first men arrive on the promontory above, and there's no time to start an avalanche that will put a barrier between them. For a moment I despair . . . and then remember how I can create a diversion.

I pull a red-papered, impact-sensitive stick from underneath my parka. My father stares, disbelieving. I bring us down until we are flying just above the ledges. I bank to the pilot's side and fling the stick into the nearest crevice.

A geyser of ice and water explodes almost plane high. I bank the other way, and throw another stick directly onto the ice pan. The ice below buckles and the sea underneath fountains upward.

The bulls standing watch are transfixed by the first blast. At the second they're off their pedestals, scrabbling frantically down the ice pan toward the startled herd, mouths yawning open in screamed warnings we cannot hear over the clatter of our own passage.

I bring us around in a tight circle, flying just below the hunting party on the snow-covered bluffs above, so close they can almost touch us. Then they are left behind as I bring us down over the ice again.

Ahead, the herd has reached the water's edge. They're

spilling in head over heels like a troupe of frantic, tumbling acrobats. Surfacing in showers of spray, they leap and slide over one another in a panicky attempt to reach sanctuary on the adjacent finger of ice.

As I wheel around again I see that the hunting party is slipping and sliding down from the bluff. The moment they reach the ice they run all out in an attempt to cut the seals off. Ahead of them a few hundred feet I can see water glistening in the ragged holes created by the dynamite.

Dropping down so low our skids are almost touching the slushy terrain, I race to intercept, reaching for more dynamite. My father suddenly stirs.

Unbuckling his belt he comes across the cockpit at me, grabbing for the dynamite now in my hand. I pull the stick back sharply and we rise in a giant arc.

My father falls back. I put the chopper into a sideways slip so that he remains jammed up against the opposite door. Out of the corner of my eye I see that we are passing over the cove line, too low for safety.

I throw another stick in the same general direction as the other two. The force of the explosion skews us in a half circle. I fight the controls. We are so close to the breaking ice pan I can feel the spray of ice hitting my face under the uneven turbulence of the chattering blades.

My father shrinks from what seems an imminent crash. Under my lifting hands I feel the chopper respond. As we suddenly rise I reach for the last stick and fling it below as hard as I can. The explosion catapults us upward.

As I struggle to control the gyrating craft, I manage a glance out—part of the promontory has broken off from the mainland. Like a gigantic, snow-covered raft, it is slowly drifting toward the open sea, leaving an insurmountable gap between the herd and its pursuers.

Watching the seals clamber aboard the huge ice-floe, nudging one another with seeming delight, as if enjoying having got the best of their tormentors, I find myself laughing aloud. My father stares at me in consternation, no doubt believing he is in the hands of a maniac.

And perhaps he is, I tell myself. There has been no sign, not a trace, of Mirabelle. There has been nothing to prove I have actually seen her except in my imagination. Yet here I am defending her creatures as if my promises to a nonexistent being have the force of Commandment. If I'm being driven by a self-induced vision, converted by self-dialogue, this frantic search is worse than useless.

Feeling suddenly grief-stricken, as if I've just suffered an irretrievable loss, I let go of whatever it is that has been driving me, dismissing it as a hopeless obsession, and at once relieved and sorrowing, I bank our craft around and set a course toward the *Seljegeren*. My father grips my arm.

"What are you doing?" he shouts angrily in my ear. "Show me where this young woman disappeared!"

I am about to refuse, to apologize for my intransigence, to explain to him how I'm now convinced that everything I told him was based on hallucination, when he points, actually pushes my head around so that my eyes follow the line of his stiffened arm. The priest and Nicole, two tiny figures, are coming out of the trees high on the glacier's slope, heading down in our direction, toward the sheer cliff where I lost sight of the visionary Mirabelle.

"It's the priest, Delmain, and his ward," I shout back, thinking to reassure him.

My father stares at me as if he doesn't understand.

"You remember Father Delmain, surely?" I bellow. "Mirabelle's confessor . . ."

My father doesn't wait to hear more. "Make—them—go—back!" he yells.

For a moment I hesitate, puzzled by his vehemence. Then shrugging, seeing no reason not to indulge him, though I believe any further search to be pointless, I kick the port rudder and shift the stick to move us toward them.

And nothing happens! The chopper tilts and sways and the gleaming horizon seems to shift its position through the canopy glass—but though we are turned about we have not moved ahead so much as an inch! The helicopter, for all that the engine never ceases its muttering roar or the propeller blades their unearthly clatter, hangs in space as if we're caught in an invisible net!

"Belay this!" my father shouts. "All ahead full!"

I wiggle the stick. It feels as if it's attached to nothing whatsoever. I kick at the rudder. There is no response. I pound the throttle forward and more. Only if I can get more power will I be able to break whatever implacable force holds us.

The engine whines into maximum speed. The propeller blades whirl at ever-increasing velocity. Our bodies tremble in the vibrating cockpit. We must grit our chattering teeth to keep them from breaking with the bouncing about. Still the chopper does not move!

I experience a sinking sensation. At first I attribute it to a gut-hollowing fear. Then I realize we are slowly dropping. I look over the side. The shrieking propellers are creating so much turbulence that the snow underneath funnels into a miniature tornado.

My mouth drops open in disbelief. My heart stops. Even through the blizzard our craft is creating I recognize that we are over the spot where Mirabelle disappeared! My father too has gone absolutely rigid. He stares below as if transfixed. There is no question but that he also recognizes this place!

We keep dropping slowly, as in a nightmarish dream. And then, only a few feet from the ground, our downward motion stops.

Thick clouds of snow envelop us. The helicopter is shaking so hard I think it must fall apart. Only our seatbelts keep us from being thrown out.

Suddenly, our engine stops. Its high-pitched whine diminishes; winding down, it coughs once, twice, and dies. The blades lose their momentum, continuing to rotate but at a decelerating speed. We hit the ground with a thud.

In the silence, remembering to breathe again, we wait for the whirling snow to subside. We can see nothing outside the plexiglass windshield.

I look at my father. He is staring into space, as if mentally removed from this time and situation, remembering something that disturbs him so much he groans.

I unbuckle my belt, reach over and unbuckle his. He stares at me unseeingly—then a tremor runs through his gaunt frame, as if he comes back to himself from some other less palpable but all too painful place. I slide out first and turn to help him. But whatever he has remembered seems to have pumped so much adrenalin into his system that he moves like a younger man, jumping down as if his rheumatism no longer exists.

I look about at the ledge we are standing on. The suction created by the helicopter blades has removed so much of the snow that the ice from the glacier shines through. Then behind us, in the stillness, we hear an enormous sigh.

Whirling, we see a massive drift slipping down the face of the cliff. Yawning before us is what has been hidden underneath—a gaping hole, an enormous opening that leads directly into the frozen rock!

I catch my breath, trying to make sense of what I see.

Here is where Mirabelle's footsteps ended. Here, then, is how she slipped out of sight into the rock.

But how can she have gotten through the covering of snow without leaving any trace?

I turn to consult my father—and am startled by the transformation that has come over him. He is advancing toward the opening, trancelike, as if walking in his sleep.

I grab his arm. "You can't go in there without a light," I say. He comes to a stop but makes no other response. "I have a light in the chopper," I say. I can't tell if he hears me or not. "Wait here till I get it," I order, hoping he will respond to the tone of command.

His head swivels to face me. The glazed look in his eyes makes me shiver.

"Is this the place where you last saw Mirabelle?" he asks. I nod. "Then she knows," he says, with so much anguish my own heart is torn.

"Knows what?" I ask, shaken. He does not answer. "What does she know?" I ask again, but he shakes his head and prying my hand loose from his arm starts for the cave again.

It's useless to try to stop him. I run to the chopper. It takes me a minute to pry the flashlight loose from its bracket. By the time I get back my father has disappeared inside.

I rush in after, wondering what could possibly lead my father to walk into this Stygian dark without hesitation— as if he has no need of any light to show him what lies inside, as if whatever demons call him will brook no further delay.

The cave, as nearly as I can tell by the glow of the beam I shine from side to rock-strewn side, goes on endlessly into the glacier. There is no sign of my father. I hesitate, listening, unable to hear him over the sound of my own echoing footsteps.

I finally make out the hoarse inhalations of someone

breathing quick and fast. Moving hastily forward, I shine the beam directly ahead. There is a bend in the cave.

When I hasten round it the light picks out my father, standing still in the silence. He's staring straight ahead, brushing at the light in his face as if at a bothersome moth.

I turn the flash in the direction of his fixed gaze. All I see are glints of ice. Stalactites have formed from the melting snow of a thousand springs, dripping down through the cavern's ceiling, then freezing into spiraling, eccentric shapes, as if some ancient sculptor has gone berserk.

I move forward to stand beside my father. Something else is the object of his rapt attention.

I lower the light in the direction of his gaze to the cavern's floor. The only irrelevancy on what is otherwise relatively flat terrain is a jumble of frozen rock. I move the light past it—then come back to hold it on the pile, staring with growing dismay at what is shimmering in the mote-flecked beam.

What I have assumed to be rocks are in fact something else.

They are bones of some sort.

My eyes grow accustomed to the light reflecting off the chalk white pile. Those skinny limbs glow as if radioactive. They are human!

Are they Mirabelle's? Is this mouldering heap all that is left of that warm, wonderful creature who took me in her loving arms to heal me? Or have I been so deranged that when clasped in a bony embrace I hallucinated flesh and hot blood?

I take a few stricken, tentative steps closer. I make out a few rags, all that is left of the clothing that once covered this skeleton now lying in so disorderly a pile, as if its former possessor collapsed for a desperately needed few moments of rest, only to have it prolonged for an eternity.

Appalled, I kneel beside those pathetic, dreadful bones. I hesitantly pick up a frozen shred of cloth, examining it to find whatever trace of color may identify it as once being part of Mirabelle's scarf.

I don't know how long I contemplate these macabre remains, pushing away the dreadful thought of how long it must have taken for once-vibrant flesh to fall away from these awkwardly sprawled bones, not wanting to accept the fact that my feverish search has come to so depressing an end—when I am suddenly horrified to see, under the clutch of a bony hand grabbing at its skull, as if at the pain of a headache that is nearly unendurable, the steel beak of a *hakapik,* imbedded eye-socket deep.

20

I AM IN SHOCK. I fight the sense of what I am seeing, unwilling to accept the evidence of what lies under my horrified gaze. Surely this victim of mindless violence could not be Mirabelle; she was—*is*—too elusive a being to be caught unaware by someone in a murderous rage.

I turn to my father. His hoarse breath is coming fast. In the glare of the flash I see that in spite of the dank, skin-congealing air, beads of sweat to match my own are forming on his lined brow.

"Is this Mirabelle?" I ask, not sure that I will be able to endure the answer.

He stumbles forward and falls to his knees beside the skeleton, a sinner begging forgiveness. A horrible groan sounds in his chest, as if something deep inside him is struggling to escape.

"What happened here?" I ask. He does not answer. "This was no accident," I persist. He remains silent. "Who is this?" I demand, determined to have the truth from him.

"Macafee," he whispers finally, and we both recoil, as if afraid the dead man, hearing his name, will rise.

"Macafee?" I repeat, and on closer look I spot, reflecting in the light, a tiny pearl nestled in what would have been the lobe of an ear. A new concern surfaces in me. If this disintegrating heap is all that is left of Macafee, where—or *what*—is Mirabelle? "Was it you who murdered him?" I ask, the terrible question out at last.

"It wasn't murder," he protests, denying what lies

before us. That protective arm had been thrown up to ward off a deliberate blow, the *hakapik* coming down with so much force it has not only penetrated the hand but gone brain-deep into the skull.

I turn the flash reluctantly back on that pathetic sprawl, outlining Macafee's bony shape in a search for any weapon he might have been carrying.

"He was defenseless," I point out, turning the light back on my father. "What else would you call it?"

My father stares as if unable to believe this pitiless interrogator can be his own son. Then his mouth begins working. A howl bursts from his lungs. The grief damned up for so many years ricochets off the cavernous walls like the lament of a soul in hell.

In a rush of sympathy I turn the flashlight off, unable to bear the sight of his ravaged face, giving him whatever privacy the nightmare-laden dark will allow.

At long last he falls silent, an occasional hiccough the only remnant of the emotion that has wracked him. Keeping the flashlight aimed at the ground, I switch it back on—palming the beam to keep that reflected light from shaming him further.

But seeing the bones in my own hand through my suddenly transparent skin reminds me of the kinship I have with Macafee, and I harden my will against this near stranger who may have committed the unforgivable crime.

"Did you kill him, Father?" I ask again.

"He forced me to it," my father replies, after so long a silence I imagine strange rustlings in the surrounding dark, as if an unseen other also waits for his answer. But my nervously probing light reveals no one.

"When Mirabelle and Macafee disrupted the hunt I was angered beyond reason," my father is saying, his face disembodied in the glowing dark. "Macafee got away. But we captured her. I ordered the men, who had worse than murder in their hearts, back to the *Seljegeren,* and escorted her back to her hut myself.

"Macafee was not there." My father lowers his voice, as if he too worries about who may be listening. "She asked me to leave. I refused. She came at me then like a shark after blood, and it was all I could do to keep her from clamping her teeth in my throat. When I finally wrestled her down she looked as deep into my eyes as I into hers and asked why didn't I take what I wanted? I said I wasn't that kind of man. But I told her I was mad for her, and if she gave herself to me, I'd do anything she asked, including seeing to it that no one would ever again hunt her damned seals. Then she surrendered to me! And it was as if we'd been meant for each other from creation's beginning. After, though I pledged my undying love, she said she had sinned against Macafee and could not remain with me until he had forgiven her."

My father hesitates, swallowing hard. I am as upset as he is. I can picture him as a young man, young as me, his head turned by that fiery creature's indescribable beauty, while she, believing she can convert the handsome young captain to her way of thinking, rewards him . . . and I shrink from the thought of them making love, as we had, as if they had invented passion.

"I was in a terrible state," I hear him saying, as if from a great distance, as if echoing from someplace remote in time. "I couldn't imagine my life without her. Come hell or high water I was determined to have her. I decided to tell Macafee what had taken place before she could. I would persuade him to give her up. So while she was asleep I slipped away.

"But when I found him here, hiding in this cave," my father continues hoarsely, as emotional as if it had happened yesterday, "a place so out of the way I found it only because Delmain, after I gave him a note for Mirabelle, directed me to it—the priest hoping, I know now,

212

that I would resolve what burdened his own conscience and that of the villagers—when I found Macafee here, cowering in the dark, I thought a simple explanation would cause him to release Mirabelle from her commitment. Instead he commiserated with me.

"He commiserated with me," my father repeats, glaring at the bones of Macafee, the remembered anger still burning in him now. "He said he knew that when he had run, humiliated, from the foreign hunters, he had lost her love. He was not surprised that she had found herself attracted to someone stronger than himself."

Jealousy makes me giddy. But no impressionable young woman could have resisted my father as a young man, tall and golden-haired as a Viking god, especially since he had promised to help her create a sanctuary for her beloved seals.

"He told me he understood my falling madly in love with her," my father continues. "Mirabelle was irresistible, he said. But he had the gift of second sight, he told me, and loved her too much to let her go off with a man like me, who would someday betray her.

"I told him he was wrong," my father goes on, clenching and unclenching his fists with the frustration he'd felt then. "I begged him to reconsider, promised him transport to a more hospitable place, money enough to write his poems without interference—and he rejected every proposal as if it was of no consequence whatsoever!

"He said their relationship was more sacred because of where they had exchanged their vows than any ceremony held in any church," my father continues, and as I listen to his hoarse and emotional voice I can imagine that young poet, haggard with a winter spent in isolation, weakened by the sparse diet, standing up to the arrogant, demanding young sea captain. "And he asked what I had promised Mirabelle.

"At first I denied I had promised her anything," my

father says, taking deep, shuddering breaths before he is able to go on. "Then I admitted I had told her that this would be my last hunt, and I would see to it that the seals would be safe here forever after. 'And she believed you?' Macafee asked, treating me with so much pity and contempt I felt the bile rising in me like phlegm in a whale's spout.

" 'Maybe you even believe it yourself,' he said to me. 'Because you're infatuated with her, and your holds are almost full, you can delude yourself that you need never hunt again.'

" 'You would cause her so much unhappiness just to keep her from being with me?' I asked him, not quite believing him still.

" 'But she won't be unhappy!' " My father raised his voice as the poet's voice must have been raised against him. "He said she needed to be protected from her own trusting nature. He said he would kill her love for me without any more thought than I gave to killing seals! 'And how are you going to do that?' I asked him, thinking the hardships he had experienced had made the fellow crazed.

" 'I'll tell her you've got a wife who's pregnant,' he said," my father goes on, the remembered outrage still thick in his voice. " 'What are you talking about?' I asked. 'My wife is barren as this glacier—she can't have children, the doctors told her so. She offered once to give me a divorce, she will have no reason to refuse me now!'

"And Macafee laughed," my father goes on. "It wasn't at all mean, it was worse—it was pitying. 'Ask the priest,' he said. 'He was aboard your ship when the wireless brought the message in, from Boston, from your wife, giving the happy news.' 'You're lying,' I said. But I remembered hearing the *Seljegeren*'s foghorn, signaling me to return. 'Your wife is pregnant,' Macafee repeated. 'And it's my guess that she's carrying a son.'

"I underwent an emotional upheaval," my father continues, beginning to breathe more rapidly. "I became confused as to my true feelings. I wanted a son—a person created in my own image—who would carry on in my place. But how could I give up a love that very few are lucky enough to experience in a lifetime? I fell into a mood so black it clouded my thinking. I asked myself why I couldn't have both. In this dark cave, in which it seemed anything could be hidden, even from God's sight, I tried desperately to think of how both would be possible . . ."

"And so you killed him?" I demand, trying to swallow my revulsion, in the muffled silence hearing his heart's thudding even over my own.

"Not in cold blood," my father replies, shakily denying that atrocity. "My brain was spinning, my emotions pulled by so many different currents I didn't know what course to take. Macafee could see how confused I was, he had a poet's eye for looking into someone's innermost nature, and he pressed me, insisting I couldn't have the son and Mirabelle too. 'Make up your mind which it is to be,' he said, and when I couldn't answer he became as sorrowful as if what he was about to say was being forced on him by my own indecisiveness. He'd have to make my choice for me then, he said; he'd inform Mirabelle himself that my wife was carrying my son!"

"I was in a fury," my father goes on, his voice strained with the rage he'd felt. "I told him I would tell Mirabelle, but after I took her off this accursed island, by force if necessary, that I was not about to leave her to waste the rest of her life with someone as cowardly as him . . ."

"And?" I urge, as my father's voice trails off.

"And he said in that case he'd tell the priest," my

father goes on, barely able to say aloud what he recalls so vividly. "And the priest would bring the villagers to prevent me from doing anything of the kind. He started out of the cave. I pulled him back. He struck out at me to get free.

"And without thinking I struck him back," my father groans, remembering. "I'd forgotten all about the *hakapik*. I didn't realize I held the *hakapik* in my hand!"

We stare at each other in that darkened cave, lit only by the blood-reddened glow of the light I grip in my transparent hand. But my father does not see me, of that I am certain. He is swimming in memory, reliving the horror of discovering that he has taken the life of another human being.

"Father?" I murmur, to bring him back, worried about him lost too long in the dreadful past.

"I couldn't believe it had happened," he answers, with a start. "I yelled at him like a madman, blaming the poor damn fool for provoking his own death. Then I wept bitter tears, grieving as much for myself as for him, nearly frantic wondering how I was going to explain this to Mirabelle. When—or if—she found out, she would never forgive me. The very thought of giving her up drove me to the edge of madness, and beyond.

"I covered him with rocks," my father goes on, swallowing, his throat dry with too many tears shed, "and ran back out into the fading daylight. And I heard Mirabelle, somewhere high on the glacier, calling for Macafee! I ducked out of sight, hoping she had not seen me, and put as much distance between the cave and myself as I could. I stopped only once to wipe the blood off my hands, became sickened to my soul over the stain on the virgin snow, and in a near-deranged state hurried down to the village to look for the priest.

"Delmain was horrified," my father continues, cross-

216

ing himself. "He accused me of having contrived his silence by confessing. He believed my remorse was makeshift, a connivance to keep Mirabelle from the truth. I denied it, of course. But ever since I have been tormented by the possibility."

We stand without speaking, the only sounds my father's harsh breathing and the faint rustling I cannot identify in the darkness that sends a chill down my spine.

"And did the priest help you?" I ask finally, pushing away any thought about who, or *what,* might be waiting in the surrounding dark.

"Yes, to my everlasting sorrow!" interrupts a voice behind us before my father can answer.

Both of us whirl, nearly startled out of our wits. I shine the light on the intruder: Delmain's sightless eyes glitter like clouded ice.

"Where is Nicole?" I demand, recovering, stepping in front of Macafee's bones while I explore the darkness back of the priest. "She mustn't see this . . ."

"I told her to wait outside," Delmain replies. "I don't need her here—every detail of this accursed place is fixed in my brain." He walks forward unhesitatingly.

We stand aside, watching him stop just short of the bones. He kneels by what is left of Macafee.

"Are you praying for his immortal soul?" my father asks bitingly, but his attempt at bravado is weak.

"No, for yours and mine," the priest replies. He crosses himself and rises slowly to his feet. "I should never have tried to keep this from Mirabelle," he says.

"I knew it! You told her Macafee was dead!" my father says.

"I told her nothing," Delmain replies grimly. "When I brought her your note I gave her my Bible, left her reading an appropriate passage, and hastened here to perform last rites over this poor wandering soul. I wanted to see to it that he was buried properly. She came in just as I got him uncovered . . ."

"You told her that it was me who did it," my father moans, agonized.

"I had no chance to tell her anything," the priest replies. "She became hysterical when she saw the *haka-pik*. I begged her to come with me. She refused, saying she intended to stay and keep vigil. There was no reasoning with her. I left, intending to return with some villagers—but no sooner had I gone outside than the glacier trembled. A fall of rock carried me halfway down the mountain. When I managed to get back I found the cavern sealed!"

"She was trapped in this cave?" I ask, now certain that the whisper from the surrounding dark is a signal from someone, or some*thing,* I have known.

"The last I saw of her—or of anyone—she was here," the priest replies. "I lost my goggles in the slide. That day the sun burned like the eye of God, reflecting light off the ice that cut like daggers at my eyes. By the time I got to the village I couldn't see. I tried to give directions to the cave, but the slide had so changed the shape of the glacier that no one was able to find it."

"And what about you?" I demand in a fury of my father. "Why didn't you bring your crew to help out?"

"I tried," my father replies defensively, remembering those awful moments. "When I heard there'd been an avalanche I tried to get back. But Tor thought I'd gone out of my mind. He had me bound hand and foot, and set sail for Boston! By the time we arrived I had let myself be convinced that it was all for the best . . ."

The priest nods in reluctant agreement. In the lengthening silence I think about what I have been told. And I experience a feeling of dread so strong it makes me nauseous.

"There must be another entrance to this cave!" I burst out. "Otherwise how could I have seen her?"

The priest does not answer, but makes the sign of the cross at the echoing darkness that lies just beyond the glowing circle of light.

21

I REMOVE MY shielding hand from the light, letting the beam inch past Macafee's bones along the floor and sides of the cavern, all my senses recoiling from what might step forward out of the dark. If Mirabelle is a pile of bones like Macafee, then *what* did I make love to in the glacier hut? I shudder but persist. We can't stand here forever. But neither can we leave without discovering the truth, however horrifying.

Slowly I move forward, careful to avoid what is left of Macafee. The others follow. I shine the beam ahead. The frozen rock seems to absorb whatever feeble illumination the beam throws off, the darkness receding very little, as if it is as reluctant to reveal its dreadful secrets as I am to discover them.

I stop so abruptly the other two bump into me. In the sudden hush I hear something stir deep within the curtain of black.

"Do you hear that?" I murmur with a shiver.

My father leans forward, cupping his ear. Judging by Delmain's frown, the priest hears it too. Then there it is again, a rustle in the darkness we have been advancing upon.

My blood runs cold. Is that a cautious footstep, and then another?

"No one can be alive in here after all these years," my father mutters, but there is a shudder in his voice.

I shine the flash directly into the heart of the cavern. The darkness is like a black ocean, diffusing the light in little wavelets to either side. But nothing blocks the beam in front except its own weakness. Though I continue to probe the dark I wonder whether we are not victims of our own imaginations.

Then I hear it again, soft, like a careful footfall. My skin prickles. I look at my companions. The priest cautions for silence. With held breaths, we strain to hear it again. Then we do—a slither over rock.

"It's melting snow," Delmain suddenly says. We stare at him. Because of his blindness his other senses are more acute than ours. "The spring thaw has finally come," he explains. "Water's dripping somewhere."

I shine the beam along the cavern's roof—and there, further back, stalactites like crystal chandeliers gleam in the light. They are indeed wet. At once relieved and disappointed, I hold the light steady on a shining spire, watching as a tear forms, swells, elongates, and finally slips off its slender tip.

I turn the beam on another spire, see that it too is slick with water, then focus on another and yet another. One spiraled as a unicorn's horn suddenly falls and shatters, as if the light beam has been just the pressure needed to break it off. The sound reverberates throughout the cavern.

I lead the way forward again, a few slow steps at a time, until we are stopped by a forest of gleaming stalagmites. Over the years the slopes above have leaked melting snow down through the strata of rock until the slow drips, freezing, have created this frozen jungle of nightmarish shapes—in the unsteady light shadows jump like ghostly monkeys from branch to slippery branch. Beyond this maze the cavern stops abruptly, a sheer wall of ice barring further passage.

I am about to turn and go back when I hear a high-pitched snap and ring, like fine glass breaking. My light falls on a stalagmite that is darker than the others—much

221

larger too. Off to one side, partially hidden by the other shapes, the oblong column reaches from ground to ceiling, a newly formed jagged crack down its side marring its otherwise smooth expanse. I might have not seen that frozen cylinder at all if it had not suddenly cracked—most likely from the rising temperature.

My father and the priest have apparently heard or seen nothing; they are turning to head back. I tell myself it would be better if I went back too. But something draws me irresistibly to the half-hidden column.

I find myself standing before that block of ice, cloudy as frosted glass, uneasily wondering what that indistinct shape within it can be.

My neck hairs stiffen. That gleam of color is familiar! As I bend closer, the remembrance of where I have seen it before comes back in a rush—it's the color that guided me through the storm, the fading rainbow weave of Mirabelle's scarf!

I'm nearly overwhelmed by conflicting emotions of anguish, gratitude, and dread. I rub away the spot where my excited breath has further clouded the surface of the huge stalagmite, then shine my flash directly against it. Gradually, as the light pierces the gloom, I become aware that encased within the column of ice, her sea-green eyes looking deep, deep into mine, is Mirabelle!

My blood congeals. I scream. I can't help myself—the shock of coming upon her in this way is so terrifying I have to release my feelings or explode.

"What is it?" my father shouts from behind. He stumbles through the darkness to join me. "Jason, are you alright?"

I am struck dumb. When he arrives out of the gloom, blinking, he doesn't seem to notice what holds me transfixed. Is this, too, hallucination? I ask myself.

And then my father looks into the blue-cold ice, brilliant under the light.

"Mirabelle!" he mouths, awestruck, and steps closer to the column. "Mirabelle," he whispers, and puts his hands to the stalagmite, as if he might feel her lovely presence through the transparent sheath.

Putting his forehead directly up against the ice, his overheated skin seemingly unaffected by the cold, he meets her terrible gaze with an imploring stare.

Though I know it is impossible, I think I see her lips beginning to form an infinitesimal smile.

"Mirabelle!" he roars, and wrapping his arms about the column he attempts to wrestle the stalagmite free, as if intending to carry her off.

"Father!" I shout, grabbing to pull him away, and he puts an elbow into my side so hard I hear a rib crack. I go sprawling backward, the rock-hard ground bruising my spine. But the pain that causes me to cry out seems to belong to another, and when the priest calls out of his darkness to ask what is wrong I yell at him to stay where he is.

I get up and throw myself at my father, wrapping both arms about his waist, and yanking hard, I fall backward, taking him with me, twisting just before I hit the ground so that his weight does not take all of my breath. He grunts with rage and frustration and manages to get up on one knee before I'm at him again, forcing him down in spite of the slashing pain in my side, trying to keep him away from the stalagmite.

But he thrashes out from under me like someone berserk. I grab his beard with both hands, pulling his head down until his straining neck and shoulders give way and he sprawls face first over my shoulder into the dirt.

Though he groans like a wounded bull, I keep my hold. Struggling to my feet I start dragging him back toward the cave's opening. Something, I don't know what, causes me to look back.

The fallen flashlight has wedged into a rock, tilted so that its beam floods the stalagmite. Mirabelle is in full view. Though trapped in her cold, transparent sarcophagus, her eyes have followed us. And her expression has changed—she is regarding me with something akin to horror!

Distracted, I loosen my grip. Immediately my father grabs each of my arms and with a jerk of his head tears his beard free. Then whirling me about as if I am the hammer in a competitive throw, he flings me with all his force against the wall of the cave.

The breath whooshes out of my lungs. Everything goes black.

When I come to, I don't know how many moments later, I am lying on the ground. The priest is standing nearby, barely visible in the reflecting light, hands raised in supplication, head cocked, waiting for answers to his repeated questions: "Captain? Jason? Melman? Where are you?"

My father again has his arms around the slippery, glasslike coffin imprisoning Mirabelle. He is straining mightily to break the column away from the ice binding it to the cavern's roof and floor.

I struggle to my feet, swaying as my head dizzies, sucking in a breath to clear it. The priest wheels to face me.

"Jason?" he demands.

I am about to answer when I hear an electrifying shriek. I whip around to see my father slowly turning the stalagmite. The ice binding it to the cavern's roof is producing that anguished protest. As I watch, transfixed, wondering from what source my father has managed to draw such reserves of power, there sounds a sudden series of reports like pistol shots. The sheathing of ice enclosing Mirabelle instantly webs, lines radiating from top to bottom in every direction.

224

"Father, be careful!" I shout, all feelings of jealousy and anger disappearing in that heart-stopping, anxious moment; forgiving him all I want him to forgive me.

Though I'm not sure he's heard me, he does drop his arms, taking a hesitant step back. He stares wonderingly at Mirabelle—has she moved?—and she stares, fixedly, at him.

Both the priest and I are as frozen in place as Mirabelle, too stunned to step forward. Then, as we watch, the column shatters. Shards of ice fly every which way, crashing, fragile as the crystal they resemble, into bits. When the frightening noise, reverberating throughout the cavern, subsides, Mirabelle stands free.

All of us wait—spellbound, unwilling or unable to blink or breathe—to see what Mirabelle can or will do now that she is free of her icy prison.

My father is the first to move. With a gentleness that somehow does not surprise me he reaches his hand up, brushes ice out of her flamelike hair, and carefully breaks off pieces clinging to her face and neck. Will she collapse now that her protective shield no longer exists?

I watch, dumbstruck.

It seems to me that she stirs under my father's loving ministrations. Does a swelling vein in her throat pulse, her full breast rise with an intake of breath?

It's difficult to be sure. The beam from the flashlight is growing dim. In the uncertain light it begins to seem as if she moistens her lips and swallows.

I am faint from lack of oxygen and will myself to breathe. Are the faint lines in her face deepening? I can't be sure, but it seems as if the youthful flesh is beginning to sag, the erect frame to stoop, the flame of her hair burn to ash. Her lips, those wonderfully full lips, thin to reveal nearly perfect teeth. Her widening smile, in the fading light, is becoming a skull's grimace . . .

"No!" I shout, praying my cry will be loud enough to

prevent the earth from turning, to stop time from advancing, to release my father long enough for us to be reconciled—in that instant pebbles, disturbed by the wrenching free of the stalagmite's tip from the cavern's roof, begin trickling down, along with a rain of slush.

Even as I become aware of it the fall goes at a quickening speed from shower to downpour. In the blur I can barely make out Mirabelle, whose shrinking, clawlike hand is pulling my father, my brave, smiling, love-starved father, into a final embrace—

"Watch out!" I yell, near-frenzied, as larger rocks begin thudding down. "Get out of there!"

I start for them—too late.

With a roar like a dam bursting, the ceiling collapses. My father, picking up the inexorably aging creature who was once Mirabelle, tries to make a run for it. But as I watch, horrified, the two of them are buried under tons of rock and ice and snow pouring into the cavern from the slopes above. Before I can avoid it my legs are taken out from under me by the mounting flood of slush, and I'm carried helplessly back toward the mouth of the cave.

"Run!" I scream at the priest, who stands as if hypnotized in the path of the torrent.

But he's also picked up by the rising tide, and within moments the two of us, tossed about by this raging wave, flailing like drowning swimmers against the current, are carried into the open air.

Eventually, the slush comes thundering to a stop like breakers on an unprotected shore, depositing us atop a ridge as if we have no more significance than debris from a receding storm.

22

SOBBING FOR BREATH, nearly petrified with terror and grief, I finally manage to begin crawling back over the snow—which still shifts and heaves like a tumultuous white ocean—trying desperately to get back inside to rescue my father from Mirabelle's eternal embrace.

But there is no entrance. The opening has disappeared! I claw at the icy debris over the spot where I think it might be, throwing aside rocks, lifting boulders twice my body's weight, until I collapse in a paroxysm of anguish and exhaustion, calling hoarsely for someone to come help.

Nicole is the first to arrive. She has somehow avoided the onslaught of snow and ice and picks her way over the shifting, unstable terrain to kneel at my side.

"Hush," she tells me. "Help is coming. Are you hurt anywhere? Where is *Pere* Delmain?"

"Over here," a feeble voice speaks, and there, lying partially under a small boulder, is Father Delmain, his face bloodied and his arm, twisted at an awkward angle, apparently broken.

Nicole offers me a handful of snow. I suck the cool crystals greedily through parched lips and then go kneel beside the priest. Beyond him, where the glacier slopes downward, I see a party from the *Seljegeren* climbing toward us, Tor in the lead and Eileen, carrying her medical bag, a step behind.

I struggle to my feet. Making a megaphone of my hands, hardly recognizing that croaking voice, hoarse as a bird of death, as my own, I shout at them to hurry. When I'm sure they see me, I motion frantically for them to increase their pace and turn again to the never-ending task of uncovering the cavern's mouth.

"What are you doing?" Tor asks when he arrives, almost out of breath himself, looking about in awe. It's as if the glacier has split open and disgorged its entrails out on the slopes, the subterranean earth and rock coiled in steaming heaps on the melting snow, the priest and I little more than indigestible lumps.

"They're buried somewhere under here!" I reply, gasping with frustration and anxiety, pointing indecisively to the place where I think they may be. "Get the crew started—we've got to dig them out before they smother!"

"They?" Tor asks wonderingly.

"My father and Mirabelle!" I cry, almost weeping over my inability to make anyone understand. "She's there with him! Don't waste any more time—you there!" I shout at a knot of men standing entranced. "Get up here and help!"

They do not stir, staring up the slope apprehensively.

"Get them up here," I yell at Tor in a fury. I start at the steaming pile again myself, flinging rocks aside, putting my shoulder up against one of the larger boulders, my feet slipping as I try to get purchase on the unstable mass underneath.

The pile suddenly shudders.

Tor grabs my arm. "We've got to get out of here," he shouts. "The whole thing could slide and bury us all!"

Infuriated, I try to push him aside. He holds on and kicks my legs out from under me, wrestling me to the ground.

"Lars," he yells, as I struggle to get free. "Get up here, quick!"

The second mate arrives before I can wriggle out of

228

Tor's grasp. Tor holds my arms, Lars my legs. Eileen, who has been setting the priest's arm, hastens over, taking a syringe out of her bag.

"No!" I scream, jerking about like someone possessed. "My father's under here somewhere with Mirabelle! We've got to get them out!"

"Nothing could be alive under there," Eileen says, in what she means to be a comforting voice, which only enrages me more.

Two deckhands kneel on my arms and legs to stop my frenzied bucking. Eileen, losing her calm, is having a difficult, nervous time inserting the needle into a small plastic bottle, but she finally manages to fill the syringe with a colorless fluid.

I plead with her not to do it. But she avoids my eyes and jabs the needle into the fold of skin where my neck joins my shoulder. I shudder as she depresses the plunger. Though I continue to resist, as she withdraws the needle I feel the substance entering my bloodstream.

Within seconds, no matter how I struggle against it, a lassitude begins to overcome me.

Tor and Lars, feeling my muscles go slack, motion the deckhands off. Lifting me up, they start walking me carefully off the still-undulating pile toward the safety of the ravine.

I protest, but those plaintive cries I hear in my mind never reach my tongue. Though I do not quite lose consciousness, everything has the elongated, interminably slow, terrifying quality of a nightmarish dream.

The men below have gone to the stand of pines. By the time we arrive they have already constructed a stretcher out of green branches. Using their own belts they strap me on.

They work hurriedly, casting uneasy glances at the unstable slope, speaking in whispers, afraid the least sound will cause the hill to give way.

"Please don't do this," I beg, making a superhuman effort to speak aloud as four unshaven, sunburnt men with scabbing faces lift me and start down through the ravine toward the ice pack below. "Please let me stay! I have to talk to my father! I have to ask him to forgive me!"

But my words come out in a slurring monotone, hardly distinguishable from a moan. I am overwhelmed with sorrow, my heart swollen, my head swimming with the pain of this unendurable loss. Eileen walks alongside, putting a hand out from time to time to feel my heated forehead.

I shrink from her touch.

Discouraged, she leaves to walk by those carrying the priest. It is cold as we enter the stand of trees. I look up through the pines, my welling tears making the pale sky shimmer.

Someone else is walking beside my stretcher. I try to make out who it is—but the sun's rays, slanting through the woods, put an aura about her head that keeps her features in shadow.

Even through the sedating influence of the drug my flesh shivers with dread. I squint to make out the features, and I see a blaze of color—it can't be possible, yet she's wearing Mirabelle's scarf!

"Mirabelle!" I cry.

"Hush," replies my companion. As we emerge from the woods into the warmth of the afternoon sun, the healing light floods her lovely young features. I recognize Nicole.

"Where . . . did you . . . get that?" I manage, able to point only with my chin, my arms bound under the straps.

She does not understand. I try using my eyes, looking from her sympathetic ones to the scarf, back and forth until at last, catching on, she touches the faded wool.

"This?" she asks. I nod, grateful that she finally understands, exhausted by the effort. "It was buried in the snow near *Pere* Delmain," she says.

My outcry brings Tor and Eileen on the run.

"What is it?" Eileen demands of Nicole.

"He wanted to know about this scarf I found," Nicole explains, bewildered.

"Mirabelle's scarf," I groan, repeating it until comprehension comes to them.

The small procession hesitates. Tor holds out his hand and Nicole places the scarf in it. Everyone stops while he and Eileen examine that faded wool.

"We've got to go back for them!" I cry feebly. "She and my father may still be alive! Or at least my father might," I continue, remembering with a shudder the creature he held in his arms.

Tor hesitates, trying to decide. Then behind us there is a sound like a thunderclap. Everyone freezes. We hear a distant rumbling, like a train pounding over rails—the avalanche, temporarily stopped, is underway again. Only the ridge stands between us and its tumultuous rush down the mountain!

The earth under us quakes. The glacier is reshaping itself once again! Where there have been gentle slopes sheer cliffs heave into view, where gullies have lain hillocks rise, where fissures have gaped the ice is now seamless. The terrain slowly stabilizes into something unrecognizable, a landscape never before seen by any mortal eye.

Finally all is still, and there is a silence profound as what must have been before creation. I begin to weep inconsolably, lamenting the loss of my father and a love that once seemed more real than anything I have known in my life. Now both are gone forever; no one can ever find the cavern's entrance.

"Hush," a soft voice murmurs, and a warm hand

strokes my brow. I look up through streaming eyes. It's Nicole. She smiles. I am strangely comforted.

At a motioned command from Tor the procession starts up again. As my weeping subsides, someone begins to hum. The melody is familiar. Mirabelle has sung this. But who sings it now?

I strain against the straps. Nicole bends to me, breaking off the song.

"Where . . . did you . . . learn that?" I whisper.

She seems surprised. "I don't know," she replies, thinking hard. "It just came into my head. From nowhere—from everywhere." She moves her arms to encompass the new landscape.

I fall back on my makeshift stretcher, overwhelmed. No, I tell myself, what I'm thinking isn't possible.

Exhausted by trying to absorb this knowledge that comes unbidden from someplace beyond reason, I go limp on the bouncing stretcher. The encroaching darkness overcomes me.

I come to as we are boarding the ship. Ropes have been lowered from the deck and are attached to the makeshift stretchers. With heart-stopping halts and lurches, the priest and I are winched aboard.

The first person I see is Per, whose pale eyes regard me sympathetically.

"I think she's here, Per," I say, after making sure no one is close enough to overhear.

"Who is, sir?" Per asks, startled, looking about with some concern.

His eyes fall on Nicole, who's watching Eileen put the priest's broken arm in a sling. Nicole is standing with her head tilted in a pose at once proud and yet attentive, poised as if for flight. Per looks back to me, his brows raised questioningly.

"Mirabelle," I murmur, and his eyes widen with apprehension. "It's alright," I continue hastily. "Say nothing to anyone. Least of all the doctor."

"I understand, sir," Per says at last, swallowing hard.

Eileen finishes with the priest and comes over to us. "Is he still awake?" she asks Per. "What's he saying? Do you have anything to tell me?" she asks, seeing my eyes open.

I am momentarily tempted. I want to explain how this mysterious place has opened a channel between mind and feeling that has brought me an understanding deeper than thought. I want to tell her what I have learned. I want to say that I am both less, and more, than my father. Though his blood runs in my veins, his genes in the marrow of my bones, my father's lust for the hunt was a primal urge stretching back into the mists of time; mine has become submerged by a long-overdue recognition that we are kin to every creature.

Then I remember Eileen's profession. I shake my head no. "There is nothing to tell," I say. Disappointed, she turns away.

"Tell the priest I want to take him and Nicole to Boston with us," I say to Per, making a strenuous effort to fight off the effects of the drug. "There's nothing on this island for either of them. I'll see to the girl's education . . ."

"I can't leave the seals," someone murmurs in the sweet voice I remember. Nicole. "Who would guard them?"

"I'll burn the chart so that no one will find this place again!" I say, aware that I'm repeating my father's words but determined to fulfill the promises he's made. "I'll take the villagers too. The seals will be safe. Tell her, Father," I beg of the priest.

"The villagers are old," he says. "They'll want to live out their days here. As I do."

233

Under my pallet I feel the *Seljegeren*'s deck stretch as the ice pack loosens its grip.

"The anchor's floating free!" the aft lookout calls.

"*Allons-y, ma chère,*" Delmain says.

"*Adieu,*" Nicole says to me, touching my brow, and taking the priest's good arm she leads him toward the rail.

I gather all the strength I have left. "I'm coming back!" I try to call. "Wait for me!"

Does she hear? I'm not sure. At the rail she turns and favors me with a farewell smile. I sink back, exhausted and forlorn, and begin sliding into the unwelcome darkness.

"Up anchor!" I hear Tor command from the bridge. "Prepare to sail!"

I hear what remains of the crew rushing to their stations. The anchor grinds its way up from the once-frozen, impenetrable depths. I feel the deck plates throb as the engines go into Reverse Slow. The *Seljegeren* slowly slips away from the melting ice, screws churning as we back into the widening channel toward the open sea.

From somewhere on the ice pack I hear the bark of a seal, at once plaintive and triumphant.

I will come back, I vow to myself. After Nicole grows up, after she has reached a certain maturity, when she is old enough to consider whether any chaotic feelings she possesses may be those of a troubled spirit, I will show her this log.

Then she can tell me whether, like my father, I may be forgiven.

I have to come back. She is the only one who will know whether I am truly mad, or have been privileged to witness a miracle.

Fore And Aft

An Afterword by
RAY BRADBURY

PREFACES SHOULD BE in the back of books.

And they should be short.

Why short and in the back? Because an author should stand on his own, be brave, display his wares, and poise ready for praise or criticism. Then, when the reader has had his read, he can take a long look at a short foreword.

Does the reader agree with the words put down by such as myself up front, or lagging behind? Anyway, here I am, wondering: What would I do if I were the editor of Sid Stebel's magical and mysterious novel?

I would, first off, hire the ghost of Gustave Dore, that magnificent artist-illustrator of a century ago, hand him this novel, and say: "How's that?" Then I'd stand aside as Dore ran up some sketches or engravings much like those polar exhalations he caught on paper for *The Rime of the Ancient Mariner*.

Stebel's book offers a dozen or so opportunities for such as Dore to perform—the frozen territories themselves, plus the phantom shadow-shapes gliding under the icefields, plus the innumerable adventures through this good ice pack, an avalanche caught and held long enough by Mr. Stebel to allow you to enjoy the downfall before it takes you the rest of the thrilling way down the slope to *THE END*.

In a marketplace already crowded with semi-fantasy or fantasy works, Stebel performs on skis, while *they* slog it out in snowshoes.

See how he came downhill! Did anyone time him? Who had the watch?

If you have enjoyed this book and would like to receive details of other Walker Adventure titles, please write to:

Adventure Editor
Walker and Company
720 Fifth Avenue
New York, NY 10019